THE ONLY ONE LAUGHING

REBECKA RATCLIFFE

I

ISBN-13: 978-1-7322635-5-0
ISBN-10: 1-7322635-5-0

Cover design by: Steve Ogden Art

Printed in the United States of America

Find more about the author at www.storymcstoryface.com
and www.littlevoicespublishing.com.

This book is dedicated to Portland, Oregon

Stay weird

CHAPTER 1

"That's weird," the woman said.

"What?" asked the man.

"I swear I packed the book I was reading, but I can't find it anywhere." She rifled through her large hiking backpack again, frowning.

"I don't know why you pack books for a trip like this. It's so much extra weight," the man grumbled, fumbling with the complicated system of tent poles to erect two blue nylon cocoons in a flat spot.

"You can complain about it when I make you carry it." She paused, her brown ponytail tensing with repressed rage as a new thought occurred to her. "Did you take it out of my pack?"

"Jesus, Alice, no, I did not take it out of your pack. If you want to pack that shit all over Mt. Adams, I'm not going to sneak around hiding it to save you from yourself."

Alice narrowed her eyes. She did not put it past Nathan to do just that. She looked for her copy of *The Great Gatsby* one last time, stalling so she wouldn't have to help with the tents. It looked like she was going to be alone with her thoughts this trip. And Nathan. Alone with Nathan and her thoughts. She sighed.

In the trees and a little further up the mountain, her copy of *The Great Gatsby* was living its best liberated life. Thick fingers with hard, yellowed nails turned the pages slowly and carefully, anxious to avoid damaging the thin pages of the paperback. The language and story were a little confusing. It seemed to be about a bird and a flower, except they were people who lived in two eggs. Elko was going to have to study this later.

He rose, brushing dust and grass out of the light brown and cinnamon hair that sparsely covered most of his body. His nose was flat and broad, and his full lips were drowned in a sea of russet beard. His eyes were the deep, dark brown of coffee beans with a high caffeine content, under a thick foam of brows. He tucked the book into a carry pouch he'd stolen from a camper on a previous excursion.

Alice and Nathan had moved on to sniping at each other over camp set-up work shares and who should be obligated to make dinner as a result. Elko found this fascinating. Who was in charge? "Alice should just tell Nathan to cook dinner," he thought. She had the clan leader energy, but she was wasting all this time defending her choices. Clan leaders didn't do that. Clan leaders did not give a shit whether you liked their choices or not. Humans complicated simple things.

Then again, Elko wasn't the foremost expert on

clan leadership. As the second son of Maura, the harthoth clan leader, he was the "spare." He wasn't going to lead anything, as he was so often reminded by the others, including his older brother, Manura. That was okay with him. He had better things to do with his time than study herd movements and weather portents, and had been doing them for three decades without once fulfilling an obligation more official than sitting in the third seat at meals.

Elko's most singular pursuit was the study of humans. It was singular in several ways, including being completely off-limits and forbidden, so he had to do it alone. He also did it alone because no one else was interested. The only time he'd tried to confide in his closest friend, Fliggo, they both left the conversation frustrated and annoyed. Fliggo was not very bright, and he just couldn't grasp most of what Elko was saying. It was better to talk to Fliggo about delicious berries or nice climbing trees. Something he could relate to.

Elko was growing bored with Alice and Nathan and their run-of-the-mill bickering. If he wanted to learn how to be disagreeable, he could just sit with his mother and brother for a few hours. Thinking about the many disagreeable hours he'd spent in their company, he realized he needed to get back to the clan before the late meal. There was supposed to be some big ceremonial thing to kick off summer involving Manura and the fire spirit, a deity Elko didn't believe in after seeing humans casually flip fire out of some thing in their pockets, and Elko was

3

supposed to say something complimentary about Manura. Something "more appropriate than last time," he'd been warned.

It wasn't his fault none of the clan had a sense of humor. Literally. They had no word for "joke." So, when he tried to work the firepit a little, his roast was met with uncomfortable shifting and murmuring, turning into a stern admonition to sit down from his mother. Tonight, he was going to say what was expected of him. Probably. His brother was a bully, and barely smarter than a marmot, but he was the next clan leader, and Elko didn't have to push his luck all the time. Maybe.

He headed back up the mountain to the secluded home grounds of the harthoths. He traveled fast, they all did, thanks to living at altitude their entire lives and some exceptionally strong glute muscles. The closer he got to home, the less excited he was to mumble his mealy-mouthed praise about Manura.

He jumped on a broad, flat stump, tossing his bag of human contraband aside. He brushed his beard and hair down with his hands, clearing his throat.

"Family and clan, it's great to see so many of you here tonight for Manura. He's been on fire recently, but thankfully we were able to put him out in time for the party." In Elko's mind, a swell of laughter forced him to pause. "In fact, when we told him this party was about fire, he nearly lit himself up again. Fire…now there's a weird idea, right? Who but a deity would decide to make the most important thing ever that hard to start? Shouldn't we have a harder time putting—"

"ELKO!" called a harthoth voice from up the mountain.

Elko jumped down from the stump and moved far enough away from his bag of stuff for plausible deniability.

"ELKO!" the voice called again, closer.

"Here!" he replied, moving toward the searcher. He was close enough to the boundary of their lands to claim he'd been there all along.

"Elko. There you are," said Yongo, the first advisor to his mother. "You must come now. Something terrible has happened to Manura."

CHAPTER 2

Elko was forced to leave the intriguing puzzle of Jay Gatsby behind and run after Yongo all the way back to the secluded clan grounds. Mt. Adams was a popular hiking and camping destination for humans, but it was also enormous and inaccessible in parts year-round. The harthoth had secret ways behind and over and under natural obstacles that made their isolation possible. Hundreds of acres were protected from human incursion, creating enough space to support several dozen clan members. Strictly speaking, they weren't supposed to leave that area, but Elko regularly did, his mother knew he did, and they didn't talk about it. It kept her disaffected second son out of her prodigious hair.

"Yongo! Wait up!" Elko called as they approached the stone and hide dwellings of the clan. "What happened?" He knew Yongo didn't think he was worth bothering with normally, so he needed to know more about what he was walking into.

Yongo slowed, slightly out of breath thanks to his advanced age. "Your brother had an accident during the preparations for the ceremony tonight. He was working to light the rehearsal tinder for the practice fire for tonight's ceremonial flame, and he reached over just as it lit. His hair caught aflame, and the scented oils he uses spread it too quickly for him to put it out. He's been badly burnt."

Elko had the grace to feel chagrined at his earlier jokes at the expense of his brother. He couldn't have known, of course, but guilt rejects the rational. Then again, it wasn't the first time Manura's stinking oils had caught him on fire. Before, he'd been able to quickly pat it out and pretend his singed hair was a special favor of the fire god. "See how I tame fire!" Guess fire wasn't his to rule after all.

He rushed past Yongo to Manura's dwelling, where a crowd was gathering. Moaning howls came from inside, along with soft, urgent voices. Shouldering through the crowd, he entered the dark interior. His brother was on his bed, crying out in pain. He did not look good. The fire had burned through his hair to his skin in places, and it was red and raw where it showed. The healer was there, trying to put some kind of mushy green paste on the wounds, but Manura was flailing too much for it to hit the target. Green globs of goo slid down the walls, the healer's face, the sides of the bed. A few splotches were on the wounds. It looked like Manura had exploded from the gut of a day-old elk carcass.

Maura, clan leader and mother of the injured, stood just outside the range of the green gunk, concern creasing her face above her silver beard.

Elko moved to her and saw her hands were blackened, the silver hair on her forearms curled into charcoal at the tips. "Are you alright?" he asked, and she nodded absently, all attention on Manura. "What can I do?" he asked.

His mother seemed not to hear. He touched her arm lightly, and she winced and pulled away. "Not now, Elko. Your brother is hurt," she hissed.

Elko felt his insides shrivel up. He'd rushed here to help, to be there for his family, and he was still just an annoying pest. He looked around the room. No one was looking at him. Invisible, he slipped back out the door, head down.

"How is he?" demanded someone in the crowd.

"He's hurt," Elko mumbled, quick-walking away before they could ask him any more questions. The gathered harthoth murmured but let him go. They expected him to be useless, and he was. No need to waste their breath.

Elko's dwelling was on the edge of the clan grounds, the small size an unpaired but eligible harthoth was allocated. He sat on a stool at his small table, his chin propped on a forearm, and thought about how nothing ever changed, nothing was going to change, and nothing was what he should learn to expect when he did make an effort. He was genuinely worried about Manura, the burns were much worse than he'd expected. There was nothing he could do but wait, though.

He dug his carved wooden box out from under his bed and took out his most valuable and least

8

acceptable possession. He'd stolen this wind-up radio from some hikers many years ago, attracted by the constant flow of speech in the human's language. At first, he hadn't understood any of it, but with the help of pilfered books and many hours of spying, he was able to follow most of it. There were some incomprehensible things, still, like endless broadcasts of some boring ritual called "baseball," but he had a few favorite stations.

He wound the radio for a while, slowly, trying not to make too much noise with it. He usually waited until the end of the day, when no one would interrupt him, but they were all absorbed in the Manura crisis right now. He could get away with it. He clicked it on, volume low, and his favorite station came to life.

"I went to rehab in wine country, just to keep my options open," squawked the tinny little speaker. This station was an AM broadcast maintained by one person, a woman with a soft, deadpan voice who played comedians doing stand-up routines for several hours every evening. Sometimes the recordings had an audience. Elko liked those best. If the jokes fell into silence, it was harder for him to know what the funny parts were supposed to be. This world, where people so readily laughed at the absurdity of their lives—it was as exotic in its own way as magazine pictures of endless water and giant feather shaped trees, but it was everywhere. It was inside people, somehow, and an undiscovered land inside the harthoth. It was his oasis, but a deserted, lonely one.

He let the station play for a few minutes, smiling at the familiar rhythm. He didn't know what the parts were called, but he knew there was an explanation, and then the joke, and then the pause for laughter. He didn't dare let it go for long, though, he couldn't risk exposing his collection of artifacts. He reluctantly switched off the radio and hid the box under his bed.

It was none too soon, either, as he heard someone outside as he straightened.

"Elko." The voice did not ask if he was there, or available. It commanded him to appear. His mother.

Elko scurried out, his stomach sick. Why would she come to talk to him directly rather than summoning him to her?

His mother looked at him critically in the fading light. Elko hastily scrubbed a hand over his hair and beard, standing as straight as he could. He could not read her expression, but he could smell her fear and worry.

"We need to talk about Manura," she said, "and how this affects you."

CHAPTER 3

"Is he dead?" Elko blurted.

Maura looked as if she'd been slapped. "No, he's not dead. He may not survive, but he continues to fight for his life. We should all be assuming the best."

Of course, he'd said the wrong thing, as always. "Of course, I mean, I just wasn't expecting you to come talk to me yourself."

"You are my son, and there are things you need to understand."

"Do you want to come in and sit down?"

Maura pushed past Elko and sat on the stool he'd vacated. His room was tidy, almost spare, because all of his favorite things were hidden. She surveyed it, looking at the small bed, the bags hanging from pegs on the wall that held food and tools, the dust and pine needles in the corners.

"Are you happy living like this?" she asked.

"Sure, I guess. I'm not unhappy." It was the most answer he could give her. Being the family afterthought and hiding his human studies were not the options he would have picked, given choices, but it wasn't terrible.

"I'm afraid it's not going to stay this way, Elko. Your brother is very gravely injured. The future may well change everything for you, and for all of us as a result."

His mother talked in riddles a lot, and Elko was confused as usual. "Manura is strong. If something happened to him, I would miss him, of course, but I would be all right."

"You would be the heir."

Now it was Elko's turn to feel a phantom slap. Even though he should have realized this, he hadn't realized this. His mother stared at him, waiting for his reaction.

"Uh...that's a bad idea." He saw the disappointment in her face and knew he should have thought more carefully about what he said, but it really was a bad idea. "I don't want to lead the clan. The clan doesn't want me to lead the clan."

"If your brother dies, you will lead the clan after me. That is how it is, Elko, and you always knew this was a responsibility that might befall you someday, no matter how hard you have tried to shirk it."

That stung. How could he shirk a responsibility that was a "maybe"? Was he supposed to stand behind Manura like some pathetic shadow? The realization that she'd expected exactly that was a punch in the gut.

"What about Elder Ulbro?" His mother's brother was younger than her, and already had a child. He could assume the Clan Leader mantle. In fact, it was no secret he wanted the role desperately. He was constantly offering to step in so Maura could "take a break," a transparent attempt at a bloodless coup. If they declared Elko the new heir, the annoying undercurrent might turn into something more overt.

"Ulbro does not have support for his claims." Maura paused, seeming unsure whether she should go on. Elko waited her out. "Ulbro lost the support of the clan when he was a young harthoth. There was an incident. Even if he were to declare himself, and we supported him, the clan would not follow him."

This was much too juicy to allow her to stop there. Elko narrowed his eyes and made a "go on" gesture with one thick finger.

Maura sighed. "Ulbro always thought he should be the next leader just because he was a male. Our father told him hundreds of times that it was the first-born, period, but Ulbro wouldn't be deterred. He spent most of our early years tormenting me for being born before him. One night, he decided to humiliate me in front of the rest of the harthoth. He climbed into a high tree and made as if he was stuck and needed rescue. All his squalling and yelling attracted everyone. When one of the older males started up to get him, he screamed. 'I want Maura! Only Maura!' When I moved to the front of the crowd to climb up and get him, he put his plan in motion. He yelled some nonsense about the old ways, and let go with a stream of pee, intending to soak me and make some archaic claim about dominance. No one believes in the old ways, but he thought he'd found a way to jump in front of me.

"There was some gusty wind that day, and Ulbro hadn't figured that into his aim. He'd also seemingly drank the entire creek and had no ability to stop what he'd started. The entire assembled clan was damp before it was over." She sighed again. "That was probably bad enough, but Grandmother Bonmo was disturbed by the commotion and came out of her resting dwelling to see what was going on. Ulbro peed on her as well, then when he was flailing around trying not to, he fell out of the tree on top of her and broke her arm. She beat him badly with her good arm, then announced to everyone present that he would never, under any circumstance, be leader of anything."

Elko was shocked and frankly, a little awed by this story. His great-grandmother had been a fabled clan leader, subject of many reverent fireside stories, a figure almost mythical to him. He knew his uncle was socially outcast, but this...this was special. The more he visualized Uncle Ulbro falling out of tree, a stream of urine still flying, the harder it was to suppress a giggle.

His mother frowned. "Are you feeling well? You look as if you have a frog jumping in your mouth."

Elko bolted out the door before he lost it. Around the back of his dwelling, he did his best to smother his laughter in the sound of retching. His mother would be disgusted, but being overcome by his stomach was preferable to being overcome by hilarity. That, she would never understand. When he could finally control himself, he loudly spit a few times to make it more convincing and returned.

His mother was gone. He shouldn't have been surprised, but he was. It seemed like there was more to that conversation, but she thought everything was resolved. Had to get back to the first-choice son, after all, and ensure he had every chance of recovering so Elko never ascended.

Elko's thoughts were a confusing swirl of terror and resentment. He didn't want to be clan leader. He didn't want to be ignored. He wanted, somehow, to be respected for who he was, not for his position, but that was never going to happen when he was the second son of the clan leader. He couldn't NOT be the second son. He sat on the edge of his bed, his face in his hands.

"You in there?" The voice was a welcome interruption. Fliggo's friendly, dopey face appeared in the doorway. Elko relaxed. A conversation with his best friend since childhood might help calm him down.

CHAPTER 4

"Sad about Manura," Fliggo said, plopping down onto the floor. Fliggo was large for a harthoth, a little over six feet, and hairier. His dark hair left little skin showing. Even his fingers had a tuft of bristly hair at each knuckle.

"Yeah, it's pretty awful," Elko agreed. In a lot of ways, he mentally added.

"He might die."

"I've heard. He looked bad when I went to see him."

Fliggo found a small twig on the floor under the table and fidgeted with it. Long pauses were a normal part of his conversation. It made him seem even slower than he actually was, and most of the clan thought Fliggo was hopelessly dumb, but Elko knew from experience to wait patiently.

The thought that eventually occurred to Fliggo was surprisingly perceptive. "Are you going to be clan leader, Elko?"

"I hope not," he answered ruefully.

"Me too." Fliggo broke his twig in half.

"Wait," Elko blurted. "Why do you say that?" He was annoyed by the immediate agreement.

"If I asked any harthoth who they wanted as new leader, I don't think they would pick you first. You play too much."

"Oh, well, I guess you have someone else all picked out? You?" Elko was getting heated.

If Fliggo had had any sense of humor, he would have laughed, but what he did was much worse. "No, that's stupid. No one would pick me first. Just before you."

If Elko had ever hit his friend before, this would have been the second time. Fliggo shrugged him off like a biting fly and frowned.

"No."

Elko closed his eyes and took a deep breath. "Sorry. I'm upset about Manura."

"I think I will go." Fliggo got up and threw his stick pieces on the floor, a sign he was really upset.

"I said I'm sorry," Elko said to his friend's back. Fliggo ducked out the door and went into the night without another word.

Elko stewed. He was supposed to step into his brother's footprints, but it was clear no one had any confidence in his ability to do the job, not even his best friend. He couldn't even argue the point with any credibility, because he didn't think he was up to the job either.

He sat on his bed and stared into the darkness. His harthoth eyesight allowed him to see reasonably well in the dark, with a sepia wash. He felt like everything in his life had been drained of color. There would be no hiding anything as clan leader. There would be no spying on humans. There would be Yongo up his butt all day and all night with official business.

He brought his radio out again and stretched out on his bed, the quiet patter of jokes and laughter soothing him. He wished for the millionth time that he could just live in that world, the one where everyone smiled and laughed and wasn't so uptight about everything all the time. He didn't want to be clan leader. He didn't even want to live with the clan, where everyone expected him to be something he wasn't. No, that wasn't right. They expected him to *fail* at being something he wasn't.

"This is KLOL AM, coming at you from Portland's tax haven to the north, and I'm Penny Coyne, your one and only DJ, Station Manager, and Weather Girl. I look out my window here in Vancouver and see light rain, so if you're headed to the city, expect to get damp. I'm about to sign off for the night, but I'll leave you with an oldie but goody, a recording of The Smothers Brothers I found in my parent's basement last week. There's a fine line between comedy and tragedy, don't stop until you find it."

Elko switched off his radio, stunned by a sudden epiphany. He didn't have to become the next clan leader. He knew from the magazines he'd stolen that he didn't look that much different than some of the humans. Most of the difference was hair. He knew their language. He knew about laughing.

He could head into the damp city. He could live among people. No one would expect him to be in charge. No one would know Elko, the clan's disappointing second son. A fresh start was one journey away.

He jumped off the bed and grabbed one of the bags hanging on the wall. He hurriedly emptied it of tools and instead put his radio and other precious contraband in it, including several books. He imagined Nathan having a few things to say about that, but he cared as little as Alice about Nathan's opinion. He grabbed a sack of dried fruit and meat strips. He took one last, long look around.

His dwelling looked deserted already. His heart had never been here. "So long," he said to the emptiness. The room did not reply.

Elko's departure, like most of his existence, went unnoticed.

He moved easily down Mt. Adams, retracing familiar routes to get to the campground where Alice and Nathan were undoubtedly in uncomfortable, uncompanionable sleep in their separate pods. He retrieved his bag near the stump with *The Great Gatsby*, a pair of similarly filched binoculars, and a hat with a large footprint and "Bigfoot Brewing" on the front. He didn't understand the design on the hat, but he thought it might work if he needed a disguise.

The Takhlakh Lake Campground was quiet, the fires out or just a few embers glowing in banked fire pits. Even in summer, this high elevation was cold at night. The thin air at nearly a mile up sent people off to their beds early, exhausted by wandering around looking at things they hadn't seen before. Elko settled in to catch a few hours of sleep. Even if the clan noticed he was gone before morning, which he doubted, they'd waste a lot of time searching for him inside the boundaries of their grounds. Once they discovered he was in forbidden territory, he'd be so deep they'd never find him.

CHAPTER 5

Alice and Nathan were up early in the morning. Elko spied on them for a few minutes to see if they'd get along better, which they did not. Alice grimaced at the coffee, Nathan stomped off to the lake, Alice sat in a chair and glared at a tree. Elko idly wondered if pushing Nathan in the lake would help her mood. No time this morning for pranks, sadly. They were camping in tents anyway, not what Elko needed.

He snuck over to the bigger campsites where people had trailers and watched the morning's activity. Most of the campers were having breakfast or preparing for the day's outdoor activities. A couple of the trailers were silent, either because the occupants were asleep or very early risers. In site 42, he saw what he was looking for.

"Did you empty the ice chest?" yelled a woman, older than Alice and wearing a yellow hat with a gray ponytail hanging out the back.

"Yes, Lynn, I emptied the ice chest," said another older woman wearing an identical hat over short blond hair. The hats were like Elko's but didn't have anything on them. "I dumped it on the fire to make sure it was completely out. Did you secure the awning? We don't need another attempt to take flight."

Their trailer was about the same size as Elko's dwelling, and they already had a small pickup truck attached to the front of it. The truck and trailer were matching color schemes, white and dark blue with chrome trim. It was what Elko imagined when he read about a spaceship in one of his stolen books, modern technology advanced so far it returned to the realm of mystery.

Lynn and Gerry, as he found out the other woman was called, finished packing up and securing their belongings. After a last scout around the campsite and trailer for trash or forgotten items, Gerry started the truck to warm up. The smell was awful, burning chemicals, but it soon faded into the background smells.

"Well, I'd better hit the head before we hit the road," Gerry said, leaving the truck running with the driver's door open.

"Me, too," Lynn replied, and they hiked off toward the toilets, holding hands.

Elko's muscles tensed. He could easily make it to the driver's door and take off before they returned. The campsites were not right on top of each other, so no one would see him until it was too late. He was ready to do it, and he almost did. Only one thing stopped him.

Stealing a truck required you to have some

earthly idea how to drive. Realizing his most likely destination as driver was the nearest tree, Elko forced his muscles to relax. Hearing about people driving was not the same as knowing how to do it yourself. The comedians never explained *how* to drive, and they especially never talked about driving best practices. They mostly talked about how bad "other people" were at driving. Elko would end up being the "other person" they were talking about.

Quietly, he went to the door of the trailer and tried it. It was unlocked. He slipped inside and closed the door behind himself. His search for someplace to hide was alarmingly discouraging. The trailer was somehow much smaller on the inside than the outside. He opened cupboards and cabinets, finding them tiny and stuffed with Lynn and Gerry's belongings. He had to settle for lying down in the crevice between the bed and the trailer wall and hope it wasn't too long before they got going. He fiddled with a panel in the middle of the space that had to be the door until he got it most of the way shut and crammed himself into hiding.

The sensation of movement was both freeing and nauseating. On the one hand, he'd successfully stowed away in a moving vehicle. His clan would never find him. He doubted they even understood what a vehicle could do. On the other hand, his body did not understand how it was moving through space without moving. His stomach was confused about whether it should keep or eject its contents. He felt like he'd been spinning in circles for an extended time, but he didn't have the choice of falling over because he was already prone.

He grabbed the side of the bed and sat up, which made things slightly less bad. Holding on, he rose and sat on the edge of the bed where he could see out the window. He clapped his hands over his eyes. The forest along the road off of Mt. Adams was blurring by at a speed he was not prepared for. He peeked through his fingers. The trees were still trees. The trailer was riding on wheels, on the ground. He wasn't in space, a concept that flat-out terrified him. He was still on the mountain. Besides, watching out the window helped his stomach calm down.

After a few minutes, he opened the other eye. He was already beyond where he'd ever been, even with his sneaking down the mountain to spy. Signs told of the exotic locations they could choose to travel to. Trout Lake and White Salmon. Cook. He was suddenly very hungry. He nibbled on some of his provisions and it settled his stomach the rest of the way.

He alternated looking out each window, seeing the small towns they passed through and a few people. He was surprised to see people wore clothes ALL THE TIME. He'd hoped it was just a thing they did for pictures, or on special occasions, but no. He had a hat, and he was pretty hairy, but that was not going to be enough.

One of the women in the truck was a similar size, so Elko reasoned she would have something he could wear. He searched through more of the stuffed cupboards and found some clothes hanging on triangular hangers. He pulled a t-shirt with the word "PRIDE" in a rainbow over his head, and with a little trial and error, made it look like he was wearing it. Loose pants that fell to mid-calf were next. Both items were light purple and smelled of something like flowers but worse. He took his hat out of his bag and put it on his head. Studying his reflection in the mirror, he didn't think the hat was quite right. He bunched up the long, gingery hair on his head and threaded it through the back of the baseball cap like he'd seen Lynn do. Better. It helped with the claustrophobic feeling of his hair being plastered down the sides of his face, too.

The Columbia River was to his left as the truck and trailer continued traveling. The Columbia was wider than he'd ever imagined. Boats of all sizes sailed the waters, and individuals standing on ovals skimmed the water with sails and kites. He thought about what it would be like, riding on the water like that, and felt his stomach roll again. Maybe not.

Crossing over the Columbia at the Bridge of the Gods was terrifying again. The trailer vibrated as if it would shake apart, and then Lynn and Gerry stopped to exchange something with the person in the little house at the end. Elko had to duck down again until they resumed moving. The Gods required some sacrifice, it seemed.

When they were at speed again, Elko watched the signs. They were approaching a place called "Portland," which seemed to be mentioned on every sign. It must be a pretty important place, if everyone needed to know how to get there every few minutes. Maybe even the most important place. Maybe a lone harthoth could blend in there until he could call it home.

CHAPTER 6

There was a lot more road. Elko was hypnotized by view from the window, too many things all at once to make real sense. After another hour, the road widened into multiple lanes and the buildings were closer together and taller. A giant rose painted on the side of a building promised he was entering the "City of Roses." All he could smell was the car exhaust and an artificial not-roses scent from his borrowed clothes.

It was the middle of the day, and it was getting hot in the trailer. When the women stopped next, he would make his exit and begin his life as a Portlander. Not knowing when that would be was creating some real anxiety, though. He was going to need to pee soon, and while he had some notion of how to use the toilet from his reading and one comedian in particular who could not stop talking about it, it sounded fraught with possible issues. He thought he should try it for the first time when he wasn't also hurtling down the road at speeds he couldn't comprehend.

As the city loomed into view, Elko felt small in a way he never had, even living in the grand shadow of Mt. Adams. Trying to imagine how many people would live and work in such a place was mind-boggling. His need to pee rapidly declined as his insides rolled over and his testicles tried to crawl back into his body. He looked at the city, searching for green places and trees, and his panic subsided as he found them. It was a big city, and full of unfamiliar things, but it had havens he understood.

The other cars were close on this highway, shifting and speeding around in a seemingly random series of impulses. Elko thought it was a miracle they didn't all crash into each other constantly. Several seemed to *want* to crash into other people who barely escaped. He understood so little about driving. He shook his head and shrugged. He'd worry about that if one of them finally bashed into the trailer.

The women were good at driving and navigated the branching arteries smoothly. A brief period of slowed traffic gave Elko a chance to study the river and bridges that spanned it. The bridges were all very different. He wondered why they didn't just pick one style that worked. They crossed over the least ornate one, just a deck of concrete with another deck of concrete over the top of it. If he'd already crossed the Bridge of the Gods, this must be the Bridge of the Underservants of the Third Advisor's Least Favorite Cousin.

They rolled into a section of road in the shadow of

a mountain covered with houses. Leaving the multi-lane highway, they exited onto a road called "Barbur Boulevard," which was carved into the mountain. Elko wondered how often one of the houses fell on this road. He hoped it didn't happen while they were traveling on it.

Now that his terror at the scale and strangeness of the city had subsided, his need to pee made a nuisance of itself. He opened the door to the tiny bathroom, jostled by the uneven road surface, and considered his options. A vision of Uncle Ulbro peeing uncontrollably on everyone and everything surfaced, and Elko snickered. He was already creating enough of an issue for these women by stowing away and stealing their clothes. He'd give it another few minutes.

As it turned out, a few minutes was enough. The truck slowed and pulled into a gas station. Elko wasn't going to get a better chance. He was still close to the river, likely close to some forested area, and he needed to make his exit. Grabbing his bags, he opened the door just a crack and peered out. The station attendant was inserting the fueling nozzle in the truck and looked over. She raised one eyebrow but didn't say anything. Elko smiled at her in what he hoped was a winning way and opened the door as if he owned the place. She shook her head, hot pink hair swinging, and wandered back into the station.

This was easier than he'd expected. His disguise was even better than he'd thought. He'd left his old life behind. The hardest part was over. He climbed out of the trailer, carefully closing the door, and strolled confidently into urbanity.

His confidence waned after four or five steps, but the panic kept his legs moving. He had to force himself not to run. The city outside the trailer stank like burning fuel, concrete, and other things he couldn't even begin to identify. Cars whizzed by on the road in front of him in both directions. His lizard brain told him to run up the hill as fast as he could to get away from them, but that was the opposite direction from the river. His instincts told him the river was where he needed to be. To get to the river, he was going to have to cross Barbur Boulevard.

Elko forced himself to stand still and observe what was happening around him. There were a few other people on the sidewalk, moving toward whatever it was they wanted to get to. There was a small group standing together and silently staring down the road. One man sat on a low wall and smoked a cigarette, a stench Elko knew he would never get used to. He walked away from it.

At the corner, a woman with a baby in a stroller blocked most of the sidewalk. Elko stopped to figure out how to get by her, but she solved the problem by stepping out into the street. The cars were lined up at a standstill for her, as if she'd commanded them to give her passage. She pushed the baby out first, which seemed bold, but Elko knew a seizable moment when he saw it.

A couple of quick steps put him a few inches away from the woman. She glanced over nervously, saw

Elko in his lavender outfit and jaunty ball cap, and quickened her pace. They crossed the entire street a few inches apart, at a light jog by the end as she tried unsuccessfully to put some space between them.

The dragon was slain. Elko was across the street, thanks to this woman and her child. Emboldened by his second major success, Elko turned to the woman and yelled Penny Coyne's inspirational sign-off. "DON'T STOP UNTIL YOU FIND IT!" She turned, startled, and gave him a little finger wave. Elko smiled. Things were going just great.

CHAPTER 7

Walking through the city was different than riding in the trailer. The smells were overwhelming. The houses had different smells coming from them, and the restaurants made him very aware of his hunger. His hunger did not eclipse his very urgent need to pee. Harthoth customs required some privacy, even if Uncle Ulbro thought differently. Humans seemed to be even less cool about bodily functions. He went behind one of the restaurants to find some cover. It was deserted, with several large garbage containers. He ducked in behind the largest dumpster and let fly.

Relieved, he turned his attention to the dumpsters, which smelled both awful and delicious. The cooked food smells were exotic and enticing, even if there were layers of rot underneath. He opened one of the lids and took in a large, exploratory sniff. His better-than-human olfactories separated the scents and put them on three conveyors—delicious, unlikely to kill you, and probably deadly. He followed his nose to a thin plastic bag and tore it open. Half-eaten curry and rice on a foam container called to him, and he grabbed a chunk of chicken and stuffed it in his mouth. His face exploded.

The harthoth used plants to make their food taste better, but they didn't do *this*. It was a spicy curry, and he'd never even conceived of something that might taste like this. He grabbed a handful of white rice and chucked into the fiery inferno. It helped, but it didn't solve the problem. He'd heard the word "spicy," of course, but the intellectual concept hadn't tried to murder him.

There wasn't anything to drink in the dumpster. He leaned his head against the metal and panted. After a long minute, the heat resolved into flavors. Flavors that were completely new. Flavors he wanted to try again. He grabbed another piece of chicken and gingerly put it in his mouth. This time, the heat was muted, and he could almost enjoy the taste. By the time he finished the leftovers on the plate, he was sweating and wiping his streaming nose above a big grin. The *flavor*.

In another bag, he found some stale naan. The bread was tough and chewy, like the jerky he'd brought. He grabbed the whole bag.

"Hey, you!" A small, dark woman in an apron was peering at him from the open door to the left of the dumpsters. She had a plastic bag in her hand.

"Mfffphm!" Elko replied. He waved a handful of hard naans at her.

"You need to get out of here," she said evenly.

"Yokay," Elko said, and still chewing, walked away. The woman waited until he was half a block away, then she threw her bag into the dumpster and shut the lid with a clang. Startled, Elko turned in time to see her wrinkle her nose at the urine smell and shake her head. He felt bad. Clearly, peeing where he ate was an error.

He made turns that kept him descending toward the river. While there were houses crammed in together on most of the blocks, there were small respites of green that grew larger as he went. The signs eventually told him he was in the River View Natural Area. He could smell the water. The exhaust smell was still in the background, but the green things and the water made it one note instead of a whole chord.

His stomach was unsettled. He could tolerate some dodgy comestibles, but he needed something to drink. The ball of dry bread and hot spices was becoming increasingly insecure the more he walked. Signs in the natural area were just numbers. They told him nothing about where he was or where he was going. The river smell grew stronger as he hiked. A few people were on the paths, wearing shorts and sandals, carrying big sticks. They moved to the side of the trail to let Elko by. Several gave him a small head nod in greeting. He tried nodding back to the fourth person and was encouraged when they smiled at him. He was blending in better than he'd hoped.

The trail dumped him out onto another busy

road. He looked for a walking man light like Barbur Boulevard. He was disappointed. He could see the river now and was thirstier than he could remember ever being before in his life. He watched the cars hurtle by both ways until he felt like he had the timing down. If he could see a car, it was in the space he intended to briefly occupy before he could possibly get out of the space. He needed to see no cars.

He stood there swiveling his head back and forth for several minutes before the coast was clear. He took off across the street at a run, vaulting into the underbrush on the other side, cushioning his fall with his bag of garbage bread. Peering back, he saw a person staring at him from the trail, alarm on her face.

"You alright?" she yelled.

Elko considered this. His first real opportunity for conversation, and he didn't want to screw it up. "Yes, I am fine! There were no cars to hit me!" He stood and spread his arms, showing he wasn't injured.

The woman smiled and chuckled softly. "That was pretty dramatic!" She had black hair that fell to her shoulders and seemed young, not yet a full adult in harthoth years for sure, but close to a human adult age. Her smile was nice. Elko liked it. He struck a ceremonial pose, arms crossed in front of himself and head cocked to the left. He crossed his right leg over the left and lowered himself into a brief, shallow squat.

The woman laughed and clapped her hands

several times before turning back into the forest. Elko's body glowed with a sensation that tingled and left him breathless. He stood stock still for a moment, listening to his racing heart. He could hear imaginary echoes of her laughter and applause in his mind. As the sound diminished into a memory, he wanted to scream for it to come back. He wanted that warm feeling to never leave him. He wanted to run back across the road without looking and make her do it again.

Elko had gotten his first laugh, and it was intoxicating.

CHAPTER 8

After his scalp stopped tingling with the pleasure of his ovation, Elko realized he was still very, very thirsty. There was more green space on this side of the road and a slope down to the water. He picked up his bags and trotted down the bank.

There was a scrim of brownish-green foam at the water's edge, marking where the small lapping waves reached. He knelt and stuck a finger in the water, swishing it around. The water was ice cold a few inches from the shore. He left his bags and waded in until the current pushed against his knees. His pants were wet. This was a completely new revelation. The stretchy material sagged with the weight of the water and clung to his legs unpleasantly. He put his thumbs in the waistband to take them off, but realized lowering them while in the river would make it worse.

Stuck in his clingy situation, he cupped his hands, raising the off-color elixir of the Willamette to his thirsty mouth.

"Whoa, there, man, I wouldn't do that!"

Elko's half-wet pants became less of an issue when he fell into the river. He spluttered back up in a few seconds, but the damage was done. His lightweight clothes clung to his skin, translucently revealing his abundantly hairy body.

The man standing on the bank next to all of Elko's worldly possessions was average height and dressed in jeans and a dark green hoody. He had dark skin and long black hair in a loose ponytail. His face showed concern, but Elko was only in danger of dying of embarrassment, not drowning.

"HI!" Elko yelled, too loud. "I mean, hello." He waded out of the river, dripping and pulling at his soggy, ineffective clothes. "What would you not do?" He didn't know how to stand casually in this situation and settled for one hand on hip and his head cocked.

"I wouldn't drink that water, man. That is some nasty shit in there, didn't you see the brown scum?"

Elko sniffed his wet fingers. This man had a point. The water smelled a little rough. Nothing he wouldn't take his chances with, but it seemed like it would offend this man if he drank it now.

"I am very thirsty," he said instead.

"You must be, to want to drink that. Come up here." The man rummaged in his own backpack and brought out a small plastic bottle of water. He offered it to Elko.

Elko took the bottle, and gripping the top and bottom, twisted the entire thing until it sprang a huge leak. Most of water sprayed on the ground and the helpful stranger, but there was some left in the bottom. The campers at Lake Takhlakh had made that look a lot easier.

"Okay, wow," the man said mildly. Elko drank what was left from the tear in the thin plastic, finding it a little weird tasting but probably better than the river.

"Thank you." He handed the bottle back to the man, who put the trash in his pack.

"Do you have some dry clothes? Need to get home?"

That was a thunderclap moment. Elko didn't have other clothes. He didn't have a home. For the first time, he understood the depth of his unpreparedness.

His benefactor saw it, too. "Hey, it's okay. I know a place. Get your stuff and come on."

Elko scrambled after him with his bags over his shoulder. After another slightly less terrifying crossing of the road, they hiked around the edge of the natural area.

"I'm Rami, by the way. What's your name?"

Elko had considered this, but not hard enough. He knew humans usually had two names, and he didn't. He knew that he'd never heard of a human with his name and suspected it would be unusual. He didn't want to be unusual. He wanted to be like everyone else. He hadn't expected to be asked so soon.

Desperately, he searched the signs around him. A truck drove by with "Franz Bakery" on the side. "Franz" was good, but "Bakery" seemed like a weird name. "Widmer Brothers" was hard to say. He glanced at Rami's face, realizing he was taking much too long to answer the question. He leaned to the side and peered at a sign behind the man.

"Lewis," he said confidently. He remembered the two names thing. He leaned again. "Lewis *and* Clark."

Rami grinned. He glanced behind him and chuckled. "Alright, that works for me if it works for you, Lewis. Let's go."

Lewis. He liked that so much. He decided to think of himself as Lewis from now on. He was momentarily stunned he could become someone else so easily. He came to the city as Elko, second son of the harthoth. He fell in the river, and he came out as Lewis Clark—a new being with a completely unblemished past. He could define himself however he wanted. It was like a field of fresh snow, with infinite possible paths waiting to be manifested. It was paralyzing. What if his first step in this human guise was a misstep? He stood staring at the ground in front of him, petrified.

Rami was a few steps away watching him. He didn't say anything, allowing Lewis some room to process whatever it was he was processing. He put his hands in his pockets, relaxed and patient. Lewis was hit with a wave of gratitude for this moment of grace. He scrubbed an arm across his damp eyes and sniffed loudly.

"Allergies, am I right? So much pollen," Rami said. Allergies were something else the harthoth didn't have, but Lewis had an idea they made you sneeze until everything was ruined.

"No, I'm not sneezing."

"Yeah, I know. I would have heard it. You okay?"

"I'm afraid to take the next step." The truth of that statement made Lewis self-conscious. "I mean, I don't know what to do so I know I'm doing the right thing."

"Welcome to humanity, my friend, and the condition of us all."

Lewis studied Rami. Was the man saying he knew about the ruse? Nothing in his posture or expression said he meant anything more than a few kind words of empathy.

Lewis straightened. If humans doubted themselves, then a harthoth doubting himself as a human was even more convincing. Maybe. He took a step.

Rami led him through the neighborhood and up the hill. They stopped at a small glass shelter. Some of its glass was intact, but most was spidered into crazed safety glass patterns or broken in glittering piles on the ground. The logo read "TRI ME," punctuated by a thick layer of stickers. "We'll catch the bus, it'll be quicker. It's getting late and the mission closes at seven."

CHAPTER 9

Lewis nodded and focused on the part he did understand. He was now on a mission.

When the blue TriMet bus pulled up, Rami held a small card up to a reader, and then did it again with another card. Lewis followed him onto the bus, damply sitting on an unoccupied vinyl seat. Rami handed him the second card.

"I usually have a spare or two in case I meet someone who needs one."

Lewis held the card carefully and cluelessly.

"It's a bus pass. It'll last until the end of the month."

Lewis nodded and put it in one of his bags. That was going to be important though he was finding he preferred walking to the jolting, jouncing progress of the bus. He looked around. It was about half full. Every other person took pains to avoid meeting his eyes, staring at their phones, tablets, and one anachronistic physical book. He leaned over to peer at the cover.

"I've read that!" he exclaimed, pointing at the

book, a paperback thriller. "I read it!" He turned to Rami and raised his eyebrows. "I read that book!"

Rami smiled. "Yeah, was it any good?"

"No, the ending is terrible! I thought the whole way through it was going to be the husband, and then BOOM, it's the nephew!"

The elderly woman reading the now spoiled thriller glared at him, mouth open, and slammed her book shut. Rami put two fingers to his forehead and winced.

"Was I not supposed to say that?" Lewis whispered loudly.

"No, dude, people like to find out things for themselves."

Lewis nodded. He wished he weren't finding everything out for himself. He tried to catch the eye of the reader to make some gesture of apology, but she wouldn't look at him and got off at the next stop. Maybe it was harder to escape your essential nature than just changing your name.

He watched the city flow by, feeling squeezed by the narrow car lanes and tall buildings on either side. Rami sat next to him, swaying with the movements of the bus. Lewis was surprised to see large trees and grassy areas in the middle of the city. In his mind, cities were just buildings and parking lots. Here, there were trees too big to climb. He caught a glimpse of a massive sculpture of an elk right in the middle of the street. He breathed a little more easily.

The people were an amazing assortment. He

didn't get the time he wanted to study any of them as the bus trundled past, so each person was one thing. Purple hair. Business suit. Piercings. Enormous backpack. Two hurrying people collided and sprayed their drinks across the sidewalk. A man shuffled along pushing a stroller full of garbage bags. There was a lot of hair on the heads and faces of the people he saw. That gave Lewis a small shot of confidence.

"People are pretty hairy," he said to Rami pleasantly. That got him a surprised chuckle.

"Yeah, we are, I guess. You haven't been in the city long, have you?"

"No, I just came today. It's less concrete than I expected."

"That is very true, Lewis. Portland is pretty fluid, as cities go. Where did you come from?"

Lewis panicked again. He really should have concocted some backstory during the trailer ride. "North," he said, choosing a partial truth. He pointed up at the roof of the bus, then swooped his finger downward. "I came down."

Rami shook his head. "You are one different dude, Lewis. I bet you're Canadian."

"Errr...Canada, that's right. I am Canadian. Hockey!" He mimed hitting a baseball. Maybe if people thought he was from another country, they'd excuse some of his missteps. He knew Canadians were polite, really into a sport called "hockey," which had to be their version of baseball, and liked maples.

"You are a long way from home, then, but you

are welcome. Our stop is next," Rami said as he rose to get off the bus. Lewis followed him onto the sidewalk.

"There's two!" Lewis exclaimed, pointing at a bus going the other direction. "Catching the bus" made it sound like there was only one bus, but now he could see there were two.

"There are a lot more than two. Is there only one in your part of Canada?" Rami walked toward the corner as he talked.

"Oh, yeah. My part of Canada is really, really small." Nonexistent, actually. Lewis decided to be quieter until he knew what he was talking about. Being Canadian seemed to excuse a lot of ignorance, but he felt like he was close to blowing it.

They walked a few blocks north, and over a couple. People didn't stare and point at the harthoth. People barely glanced at him. His abundance of untidy russet hair was a life choice. His purple PRIDE outfit didn't stand out at all. There was a woman dressed as an actual rainbow on one corner, singing a cappella. "The sun'll come out tomorrow..."

"Here we are," Rami said.

"What's the mission?" Lewis whispered. "Is it top secret?"

Rami laughed. "Given the large sign, I don't think so," he said, pointing over his head. The sign read "Stumptown Ethical Atheists Mission." He knocked on the large, red door three times, waited for a buzz, and pulled the handle toward him. It opened onto a narrow wooden staircase leading down, dimly lit by bare red bulbs hanging from the sloped ceiling.

Lewis did not want to go down there. It was unnatural, going underground. If he went into the Stumptown Ethical Atheists Mission, he'd be going to hell. That was true in the harthoth mythology, and he guessed a few others. You wouldn't catch a harthoth dead underground.

"I think I'll stay up here," he said, backing away a step.

Rami gave him an encouraging smile. "If it's not your scene, we'll take off, I promise. They have a mean baba ghanoush, though, and you need another outfit and some shoes. They have showers and beds, too, if you want to stay tonight."

Baba Ghanoush was a funny name for a mean person. Lewis said it to himself and chuckled. He said it again, pushing his lips out in an exaggerated "noosh." He looked at the staircase. He looked at Rami, who seemed fine with this descent into the hidden depths.

The shadows of the buildings around him threw the city into premature twilight. Lewis was already inside the city, under the looming skyscrapers. Maybe he could think of this as going into a building with a very sloped floor. He took a deep breath and faced the doorway, catching the faint scent of exotic cooking.

"Does Baba Ghanoush know we're coming?"

CHAPTER 10

The bottom of the stairwell opened into a dark, low-ceilinged room. Lewis felt the earth pressing down on him. The room smelled very strongly of cooked vegetables and spices, with an undercurrent of unwashed body and very old mortar. It was large, broken up by supporting posts at regular intervals. A dozen more ceiling fixtures would have moved the lighting from cavernous to dim, but half a dozen people were managing to eat dinner.

"Rami!" A small silver-haired woman in blue flannel and jeans came through the lines of tables and squeezed Rami in a fierce hug, her long ponytail swinging as she energetically waggled the much larger man back and forth.

"Eve, I'd like you to meet Lewis Clark." Rami gestured for Lewis to step forward.

"Lewis Clark?" Eve said, raising one eyebrow.

"I'm Canadian," Lewis volunteered, swinging at his imaginary hockey ball again.

"Okay," she replied with a smile. "We don't care if you're Bigfoot, you're welcome to a meal and shopping trip in our boutique. I see you can use some shoes for your own big feet. How about you pick out some things, grab a shower, and then we'll get a hot meal into you. Do you like baba ghanoush?"

"I've never met him," Lewis answered.

"Well, we will get you introduced," Eve said, lightly patting him on the arm.

The clothes room had a bewildering number of choices. Lewis elected to keep his hat, and with Rami's assistance, picked out two full outfits, a flannel shirt and a hoody, with two pairs of jeans and several sets of underwear. Covering his feet with socks felt really strange, but the worst thing in the process were the *shoes*. Imprisoning his feet was as unnatural as going underground.

He clomped to the showers feeling every pressure point and poking seam inside the sturdy brown loafers. Rami showed him how the showers worked and where the soap and towels were and left him to it. He was happy to find out the toilet was not as difficult to manage when the room wasn't flying down the highway.

If the warm water was a revelation, the soap was a waking nightmare. He'd squirted a large amount of the shampoo on his head before realizing it smelled like nothing he could imagine in nature or beyond. As he gagged at the pine-ish scent, he realized he should have used a lot less. Maybe none. The suds just kept sudsing, making his eyes sting and sinuses burn. By the time he got all of it out of all of his hair, the small shower stall was full of warm steam and the water was starting to cool.

He was not especially happy when he managed to meet Rami back in the main room. He smelled weird, his feet hurt, and the underwear was already bunched up in his butt crack. Dreadful things were happening underground, as he'd expected. He craved the open sky and free feet.

"Hey, how's it going so far?" Rami asked.

"I don't like the smell of the soap."

"Yeah, most of the stuff here is donated, so it's kind of up to luck what you get."

Lewis sensed another social misstep, which he tried to recover from with gratitude. "Thanks for the clothes, though, I like this hoody." It was true, he did like the soft sweatshirt. It was dark blue with a loose fit, like wearing a blanket around on your body.

"Maybe you want to turn it around so the hood is in the back?" Rami pulled his own hood up to show how it was supposed to work. "I don't know about Canada, but here the tags are usually in the back."

Lewis pulled his hood up experimentally, covering his face. That explained the underwear, too. He turned the hoody and decided to fix his underwear later.

Eve came over to appraise his progress. "Looks good, Lewis. How do you feel?"

"I feel hungry," he said. "Also warm. Thanks for the shower and evil-smelling soap."

Eve chuckled. "I think we'll all be glad when we get through that particular scent. Come eat."

Rami grabbed two trays and sat across from

Lewis. The plate had a medium bowl of finely ground brown paste surrounded by cut vegetables and flatbread. Lewis put his nose close to the bowl and inhaled deeply. It didn't smell spicy this time, so he followed Rami's lead and used a carrot to shovel a big glob into his mouth. It had a few of the same flavors as his garbage curry, but it was delicious without the fiery inferno. He quickly cleaned his plate.

Lewis had a million questions about the mission, but he didn't know where to start. He looked around at the other people. They were wearing new clothes, like he was, and focused on eating. Most sat alone. A few looked like they'd had a rough time lately. One woman spoke quietly to her plate of food between bites.

"So, which one is Baba Ghanoush?" he asked Rami, who was only halfway through his food.

"You just ate baba ghanoush. It's the dip."

Lewis stood up too fast and his folding chair clattered over behind him.

"The dip is people?" he stammered, backing away.

"Whoa...no, man, the dip is not people. They're atheists, not cannibals. It's eggplant." Rami was holding one hand out toward him, the universal calm yourself down.

Everyone was staring at Lewis now. "But—you said—and Eve—" He fumbled to a stop.

"Eve did what?" Eve said from behind him.

Lewis knew he'd made mistake after mistake today, but this time he felt tricked, and stupid, and discouraged. He straightened. Drawing on decades of pretending he had a decorum appropriate his Clan standing, he turned to Eve.

"Thank you very much for your generosity, Eve. I will be going now."

Rami stood. "You can stay the night here, Lewis. Clean bed and a quiet night's sleep. We can talk this out in the morning."

Every scary harthoth story about being underground surfaced all at once, and Lewis felt his hair stand on end all over his body. This did not calm him down.

"No, I don't think I will," he squeaked a couple of octaves higher than normal. He grabbed his bags from the cubby against the wall and headed for the stairs, thudding in his heavy shoes.

"Lewis, wait!" Rami said, but he didn't chase after him. Lewis didn't look back.

"Come back anytime, and I mean it! The door is always open!" Eve called. Lewis believed her. He might even take her up on it someday. Right now, he needed the sky and time to sort through the overwhelming crush of things he'd seen and done.

He also desperately needed to ditch these bullshit "shoes."

CHAPTER 11

As Lewis burst through the outer door, the smells of the city surrounded him again. He clomped heavily for two blocks, breathing in great gulps of the evening air. People on the sidewalk moved aside like a river current.

The night was cooling as the sun went down, but he felt hot in his new clothes as he ran. Slowing, catching his breath, he saw a small park with trees and a bench. Sitting on the bench with his bags, he removed the terrible shoes. While he was tempted to chuck them into traffic, it seemed like he might need them for something. They didn't fit in his bags, so he slid them in under the bench, all the way into a dark recess created by the concrete back and legs.

"To the pit with you, torments from hell," he said, carefully backing out from under the bench to avoid bonking his head. He rubbed his feet, sitting on the bench with his eyes closed. The city noise had been jarring and foreign at the beginning of his long day, but now it was calmer, more background. He rested his head on his bags and fell into a deep sleep.

His dreams were chaotic. His brain tried to bring the city sounds into places they didn't belong—sirens were the screams of his brother, Manura, as the fire burned him, or the sound of a plane overhead was a giant mosquito, chasing him into the underground tunnels of a dark, fetid underworld. There were people laughing, and people laughing at him, which bothered him for some reason he didn't understand. He was trapped inside a giant shoe while it constricted around him until he couldn't breathe. He woke with a gasp into pale sunlight.

It was early morning, and the streets were quiet except for the dog walkers and runners. The dogs were extremely interested in him, but their leashes kept them from giving him an up-close olfactory review. He'd seen a lot of dogs at the campground, but at a distance. They seemed nicer than bears. He watched a large black dog lift a leg and pee endlessly on a lamppost. Dogs had special privileges in that respect, it seemed. Lewis was going to have to find somewhere more private.

He spent a few minutes sorting his thoughts. He'd survived his first day in the city. He knew two people and one place he could go if he needed food or shelter. He had a bus pass. He didn't have any way to measure that, but it seemed like a pretty successful start. He hadn't perfectly impersonated people, but none of his mistakes were devastating. More embarrassing, he supposed, and he didn't really embarrass that easily.

It was time for the next adventure. He grabbed his things and walked up the street, following his nose to a small blue hut he could do his morning business in. It was unpleasant. Spicy turned out to be a forever thing.

On the corner of Burnside and 10th Avenue, Lewis stopped in his tracks and stared. The building across the street was low in the front, with two taller wings in the back. Painted in cream and red, it stood out against the darker high-rise buildings behind it. A large marquee dominated the entrance.

"Powell's Books," he breathed. He felt chills up and down his spine as if the name had been an invocation of magic. Here was an entire building full of books. After stealing books from campers for several decades, he'd been able to keep a few dozen. There were that many *in one window*. This must be a *library*.

Lewis walked up the short set of stairs to the door and reverently pushed. It didn't budge. There were people inside walking briskly with piles of things. He waved at one, maybe they had to open the door. The woman raised her arm and tapped something, then pointed at the lower half of the door.

"Closed." Lewis understood. He sat down in front of the door and waited with his hands pressed to the glass and his face three inches from it.

When the door opened an hour later, he was first in line. He couldn't contain his wonder at the vast room full of books. Tall shelves and wide tables covered with them.

"Would you like a map?" A short woman in a brown cardigan and funky glasses offered him a fold-out paper map. "You're in the Green Room, here. Is there something you're looking for?"

The map showed nine color-coded rooms on three levels, organized by categories like "Humor" or "Self-help."

"Can I just walk around?" he asked, not believing that he could or that this place was real.

"Sure!" The woman leaned toward him and cupped a hand over her mouth. "Just make sure you don't advertise the sock feet, okay?" The rule-bending, rogue librarian winked conspiratorially and went back to straightening books.

Lewis hardly noticed. He floated through the next two hours in a daze, working up the courage to touch the books, then read a few pages, then sit with one for a few minutes. He eventually found the humor section and the comics. Sitting on the floor cross-legged, he read.

"Hey, mister, I need that." A small boy pointed at the bookshelf behind him, and Lewis scooted over.

"Look at this," he said, showing the boy a cartoon cat hating a Monday. "He really hates Mondays!" He chuckled. The boy grabbed the book he wanted and ran back to his dad. Lewis put Garfield back and pulled out a book with a black man on the cover. It said "A Standup Guy" on the cover, and he realized he knew the name of the author. This was one of the comedians he listened to on his radio.

After reading the first few pages, Lewis became aware of the increasing crowd in the store. Most people were absorbed in their own book explorations, but he felt eyes on him more often than not. Looks at his dirty socks, his bags, made him uncomfortable.

He slung his bags over his shoulder, and still reading, made his way back to the green room. As he walked toward the door, a piercing noise suddenly surrounded him. Lights flashed on either side of him. He froze.

"Excuse me, sir, you need to pay for that," a very tall man said, putting himself between Lewis and the door. This was not a library, after all.

Lewis knew about money in theory. He didn't have any, obviously. He closed the book and clutched it to his chest. "I don't have any money," he confessed.

"Please give me the book," the man said, holding out a hand.

"I don't think I can," Lewis said. He really didn't feel like he could. These were the words of a personal hero, something like a holy book. Thinking of it sitting on the shelf, unread, was impossible.

"Sir, I don't want to have a problem." The man seemed resigned to having a problem but didn't want to start one.

"I'll pay for it." The voice was young, and female. When Lewis turned to see who it came from, he was surprised to find a person he recognized.

CHAPTER 12

"Hello, again," said the young, black-haired woman who'd applauded his tumbling at the River View Natural Area. "My name is Chloe." She took the paperback out of his hand and gave it the tall man, who ducked back behind the counter and rang it up. Chloe used her debit card to pay and accepted the book back with the receipt. She offered it to Lewis, who took it sheepishly.

"I thought this was a library," he said in explanation. "Thank you."

"Honest mistake." Chloe was wearing a red t-shirt with a large fist on the front and ripped jeans tucked into her brown boots. She had glacier blue eyes and a small gold ring in one nostril. "You wanna stand and stare at me for a little longer, or should we go get a cup of coffee and you can share your name too?"

"Lewis," he blurted. "Lewis Clark."

Chloe snorted. "Well, let's go explore the coffee shop, Lewis."

The smell of the coffee shop was overwhelming once he stepped inside. There were more books, piles of them, but small tables were crammed in the space with mismatched chairs. This coffee aroma was thousands of times stronger than he'd smelled while spying on campers. It smelled bitter and rich. He hadn't wanted to try something so badly in his entire life.

"You want a cup of coffee?" Chloe asked, slinging her own bag onto a chair at a free table.

Lewis had to assume nothing here was free after the fiasco at the door. "I don't have money."

"Oh, I got you. Black? Cream? Sugar? Want a latte?"

"Does it come just plain?"

Chloe nodded and went to the counter while Lewis sat down. She bantered easily with the barista, ordering a vanilla latte and a black coffee. The young man laughed at something she said and turned to make the drinks.

Setting a ceramic mug in front of Lewis, she took her seat across from him. Steam rose from the coffee, bringing him the scent of a land even further than this one. He cupped his hands around the mug, feeling the heat and wondering if he was supposed to go ahead and burn his mouth or wait until it had cooled. Chloe didn't drink hers immediately, so he waited. A rainbow skimmed across the surface of the black coffee, oils reflecting the sunlight coming in the window.

"So, what's your story?" Chloe asked. She was openly studying him, and Lewis wondered what she was seeing.

"I'm Canadian," he said. When she didn't immediately respond, he clarified. "You know, Canada? Hockey?" He waved his arms.

"Yeah, I've heard of it. Is that why you're so hairy? Part bear?"

Lewis felt a cold wash of fear. "No, I'm a human," he blurted.

Chloe's face transformed when she giggled. One of her canine teeth was slightly crooked, making her look younger. She took a sip of her coffee, smiling.

Lewis picked up his mug and sucked in a big mouthful of single-origin fair trade Ethiopian brew. He immediately spit it back into the cup, sloshing onto the table and his lap.

"That's coffee??" he yelped, setting the mug at arm's length on the table.

"Have you never had coffee before?" Chloe asked, one eyebrow raised and head tilted. She handed him a few napkins.

"No, they don't have that where I'm from."

"Canada? They don't have coffee in Canada?" She sounded more skeptical than she looked.

"It was very remote." A little truth probably wouldn't hurt at this point. "That's terrible. How do you drink that?"

"I don't. Black coffee is for people who hate themselves or hate everyone else, or both."

Lewis nodded. He could see how this liquid could be a potent weapon against your enemies. He saw Chloe shifting in her seat, ready to leave now that she wasn't sure he was telling the truth.

"I mean," he said, "of course they have coffee in Canada. I just haven't tried it before. It smells a lot better than it tastes."

"Uh huh."

He was losing her. "Where are you from? Have you tried everything from there?" he tried.

"I admit, I have not. And I can also admit, I don't like everything I've tried. Fair point." She relaxed, no longer poised at the edge of flight. After a moment of silence, she asked, "Why that book? What was it that made you want it so badly?"

Lewis perked up. "The guy who wrote it, I used to listen to him at night on my radio. He's funny, but I think he also says important things. I learned a lot from him about humans."

"Yeah, I can see that. I study humans, too. Comedy is a way to say a lot of things that aren't socially acceptable but still true."

"You study humans?" Lewis was confused. Chloe looked human, but maybe she wasn't? Maybe the harthoth weren't the only hidden clan.

"I'm an anthropology student. We try to figure out what makes humans...human. What differentiates us from a potted plant. How we relate to the world and each other. Don't they have anthropologists where you're from?"

He could see she was teasing a little with the last remark. "I was the only one. The plants had to stand in so I could have an argument."

That magical laugh. Lewis wished he could pluck it from the air and keep it in his pocket.

"You wanna come meet some more anthropologists, Lewis Clark?" she asked.

CHAPTER 13

Chloe was surprised he had a bus pass. Lewis sent a silent thanks to Rami for making him look slightly less weird and helpless. He was going to have to find Rami and see if he could repair any damage he'd done bolting from the mission. He was embarrassed by all his mistakes and overreactions so far. Every minor victory was marred by a bigger blunder, and he had no idea what he *should* be doing. He'd run off to the city with no plan other than running.

It was almost lunchtime, so the bus had an assortment of people on it. Young mothers, students, seniors, and a few dressed-up professionals. One woman sat near the door with a collection of trash bags and a small dog shivering in her lap. She crooned to the dog, not noticing any of the comings and goings around her.

It was too loud to talk without shouting, so Lewis and Chloe sat next to each other in silence, looking out the window. When they changed buses across the river, there were fewer suits and more hoodies.

He was desperately hungry. To take his mind off

it, he tried a mental riff on his trip so far. "This guy, he doesn't know how to cross a street, so he waits for a baby to show him." That didn't make him feel better. His thoughts wandered to his family next, and how Manura must be doing. Maybe dead. That was worse than his inner comedian insulting him.

To get his mind off his failed attempt at getting his mind off his stomach, he asked Chloe where they were headed.

"Reed."

Why hadn't he thought of that? He took out his book.

When they got off the bus, he saw the Reed College signs. The campus sprawled across acres of lawn and ancient oaks. The buildings didn't have a cohesive, planned look. An enormous, old building with an elaborately crenelated facade dominated the central space, but to the left stood ugly industrial buildings made of stained concrete and glass. A series of small, oddly painted houses proclaimed different languages. As they walked deeper into campus, he could see more large, red brick buildings further back that followed a more planned aesthetic.

They arrived during lunch, and a large number of college students were congregated near the cafeteria. Lewis could smell the food as soon as they got off the bus, but closer to the cafeteria, it was overwhelming. His stomach growled again.

"Let's get you something to eat," Chloe said with a significant glance at his stomach.

"Is it free?" He wasn't going to assume anything.

"Sure, if you don't mind scrounging." She opened the door and gestured for Lewis to enter. The space was a crowd of tables and young adults wearing every shade of the rainbow in their hair and every shade of black on their bodies. Off to one side was a table with trays and plates of food that looked half-eaten. Chloe pointed at it. "Help yourself. It's all fine, the scrounge has rules about what you can leave."

Lewis saw sandwiches, salads, and noodles with vegetables and white cubes of something. He grabbed a tray and loaded it up while Chloe used her student ID to get a fresh tray of food, including the noodle dish and two waters. She handed one water to Lewis and led him to a table with two other students. She didn't introduce them, but they nodded at her.

"I'm Lewis," Lewis offered.

"Cool," the boy said, continuing to read the very thick book on the table.

The other diner rolled her eyes. "I'm Maureen, and the guy with no manners is Phillipe. He has a paper due. He thinks if he reads every book in the library, the paper will magically fall out of his ass in two days."

"I don't think it works like that," Lewis said mildly, surveying his feast of other people's leftovers.

"Fuck off, Maureen," Phillipe mumbled.

Chloe smirked at both of them and forked up some of her lunch. Lewis did the same. The noodles were good, but he couldn't figure out the white cubes.

"What are these?" he asked. "They don't taste like anything."

"That's tofu," Chloe answered. "Don't they have that in Canada, either?"

"Nope." Lewis was going to act as if the harthoth clan grounds on Mt. Adams *were* Canada. Easier to keep the lies straight if he told the bald truth, no matter how preposterous it sounded. They also didn't have noodles and sandwiches, but he didn't need to volunteer that. Philippe looked up and frowned at him for a second before going back to his tiny print.

After he'd eaten most of his food, Lewis sighed and patted his stomach. "Good," he said.

"I thought you might eat me, how loud your stomach was growling." Chloe wiped her mouth and fingers carefully and threw her wadded napkin on her empty plate. Lewis did the same and put his tray and dishes in the bus tubs with her. Maureen and Philippe were absorbed in an argument about authoritarian regimes and didn't look up. "Let's go meet my friend, Tom. He can do some things for you while I go to class."

Lewis wasn't sure what he needed done, but his calendar was open.

Tom was in one of the ugly dormitory buildings close to the main road. His room on the second floor had crisscrossing "Caution" tape on the door. A strand of multi-colored blinking lights spelled out

"TOM." When the door opened, Lewis was nearly overwhelmed by the skunky odor of marijuana smoke, something he'd experienced from a distance at the campground.

"CHLOE!" squealed the guy at the door. He was very thin, with raging acne and bloodshot eyes peeking through a mess of shaggy black hair. His dark clothes hung off his scarecrow frame. He hugged Chloe loosely and then stood back to look at Lewis.

"I have to go to class. This is Lewis, I met him at Powell's today. He's from *Ca-na-da*," she said, winking. "I have a feeling you can do a few things to make him less *Canadian*?"

Tom stood back, appraising. "Oh, yes. I see several things that are very *Canadian*." He walked around Lewis. "Yes, yes, yes."

"Also, he needs one of your specials. I'll front him."

"Oh, Chloe, nobody is gonna believe he's an undergrad."

"I know, but you're the magician. Make him a grad student. Sometimes they're older."

Lewis was lost. "I *am* older than you," he volunteered, "but I'm not that old for Canada."

Chloe and Tom looked at each other and burst into giggles.

"Okay, I see why you brought the stray home," Tom said. "Go to class. I have work to do."

CHAPTER 14

Tom hustled Lewis into the room and shut the door with a shooing wave at Chloe. Despite the smell, there was no active cannabis smoke in the air. Tom opened the window with a mumbled apology about the "weedsmosphere." The room was small, with one narrow bed and a desk. Three walls were plastered with pictures and posters of young men in black leather. A giant rainbow flag covered the fourth wall. The desk held a very sophisticated computer and a rack of related equipment.

"So, let's see your Canadian ID, that'll help me with the paper trail." Tom held out a hand to accept Lewis' nonexistent identification card.

Lewis thought fast. It would have to be truth, again. "I don't have that," he said, shrugging sheepishly.

Tom's eyes widened. "REALLY?" he squeaked.

"Yeah. I came here in someone's camp trailer."

Tom snorted. "Chloe is gonna owe me BIG TIME. Is Lewis even your real name?" Lewis waited a beat too long to answer. "Never mind, it is now. Let's get you ready for your close up."

Getting Lewis ready for his close up involved a lot of things Lewis did not expect or enjoy. Tom made him brush every tangle out of his hair and beard, then twisted his copper mane into a loose braid. Lewis found out about razors and tweezers and beard trimming, unnatural activities that scraped and pulled and stung. When Tom was done, he turned Lewis to look in the mirror on the back of his door.

"From someplace in '*Canada*' to Portland, may I present Mr. Lewis Clark."

Lewis gaped. He didn't recognize himself. The man gaping back at him looked like...a man. He still had plenty of hair, bushy eyebrows, and a full beard, but with his hair braided and tamed, he looked like other men he'd seen around Portland. Shedding the excess hair had shed the visible evidence of his harthoth identity. Elko was truly gone.

Tom was smiling at him, but there was curiosity in his eyes. "You really didn't expect that, did you?"

"I don't think I've ever looked like this." More honesty.

"Do you like it? Or hate it?"

"It's...great. I just didn't think about it before I saw it. I'm human." He regretted being quite that honest immediately.

"You were human all along. You were just hiding it under all that fur. Now let's do your papers." Tom had taken his odd comment in stride. Maybe humans spent more time questioning their own humanity than Lewis realized.

Tom had several printers, a laminator, a laser cutting machine, a large camera, and a backdrop he assured Lewis was lifted from an actual DMV.

After an hour of focused computer work, he handed Lewis an array of cards with his picture and name on them. There was a Reed College student ID, an Oregon driver's license, and a Nova Scotia driver's license. A couple of unlaminated cards completed the suite of forgeries. Lewis had questions, but they all betrayed his ignorance.

"Thank you?" he offered. He suspected he wasn't appreciating fully how much these were worth.

"No problem. Those are okay for a lot of things, but they won't be enough if an actual police officer tries to check them, so don't drive crazy or rob any liquor stores, and don't tell *anyone* where you got them."

"I don't know how to drive or rob," Lewis offered to reassure him.

"Okay, good. Big relief vibes. Also, I don't have a lanyard for the student ID, but Chloe can deal with that. Speaking of which, she should be back any minute."

As if summoned by Tom's words, she knocked softly on the door and opened it.

"Yoo hoo...oh boy," she said, smiling at them. Her black hair was windblown, and Lewis could see blond roots peeking through the disheveled strands. Her glacier eyes with blond hair would make her look like a magazine model. He wondered why she hid it.

"Yeah, he cleaned up pretty good," Tom said. "I did an Oregon and a Nova Scotia, because I figured the further away, the better. Also a Reed, but you need to get him a lanyard."

"I can do that. Put it on my tab."

"Your 'tab' is enough to pay for my tuition at this point, Chlo. I have to get to practice. Lock the door on your way out." Tom grabbed a backpack by the door and a padded stick as he rushed out the door.

"Let me see." Chloe held her hand out for the cards. "Oh, these are great," she mused, checking front and back of each before handing them back. "Let's go see your new school, Lewis Clark."

Lewis followed Chloe on a tour of the campus. They didn't go into any of the buildings, and he was glad when she described the underground connecting tunnels. Clearly, humans did not have the same horror of being under the earth as the harthoth.

Reed Canyon was the most interesting part of the tour. Bisecting the campus, the canyon was acres of forest and natural watershed. Reed Lake fed a lively stream flowing through the bottom. Lewis stopped on the pedestrian bridge to look south into the wild area. The city was utterly foreign, but he could find a way to live here as long as he found refuge in places like this.

As Chloe showed him the rugby pitch and more bus stops, it began to rain. This late in spring, it was just as likely to be a pouring hailstorm as a light shower. Chloe had no umbrella or raincoat. She lifted her face to the sky and let the rain run down her cheeks like tears. She looked very young in that moment, and Lewis wondered at a world where these barely adults navigated so many complex things alone. At her age, he'd been spending all his time sneaking around the woods to avoid his mother, mostly because he still lived with her.

"I have to get back for my study group," Chloe said. "I mean, we call it a study group, but we mostly screw around with the lab chemicals and see who can make the worst smell. You can eat from the scrounge table whenever you want now. Have your student ID ready in case someone asks, but don't let them scan it."

"Thank you," Lewis replied. He was indebted to Chloe, but didn't know what to do about it, or even the extent of what she'd done for him. In his clan, he would have pledged a future favor, but he didn't know what he could offer. "Why did you do all this for me?" he asked instead.

Chloe grinned. "I like to add variables to the system, Lewis, and see what happens. You're the most interesting x in the equation in a long time." Her smile showed the crooked canine and mischief. "Where do you think you'll end up tonight? My house has rules about no overnight guests because most of us don't like people very much."

"The canyon looks pretty interesting." Lewis couldn't wait to explore it further, if he was being honest.

"See you tomorrow, then. Don't let anyone see you go down there. Most people are chill, but the less attention the better."

Lewis nodded. Chloe said goodbye and left for her study group. He wished he'd had her confidence at that age. Maybe he could have made a place for himself in the clan that didn't make him want to run away.

CHAPTER 15

Thinking of the clan made him unexpectedly homesick. Slipping down into the canyon when he didn't see anyone looking, he hiked to the lake and sat in a small thicket, hidden from view. He was soaked, which normally wouldn't bother him, but his wet clothes made it significantly more unpleasant. The unfamiliar feel of the rain hitting bare skin on his face was startling at first, almost painful. Tom's grooming had left him more human. He felt exposed.

He spotted a hollow under a large rhododendron where the moss was drier and crawled in with his bags. The rain slackened to a gentle patter on the broad waterproof leaves, and he dozed off.

It was dark when he woke up disoriented and cold. He'd been dreaming he was giving a speech to the clan, and it was going worse than normal. His relatives were seated together in the ceremonial space, glowering at him. In an attempt to lighten the mood, he threw in a joke. "If bears are made of berries, what are bobcats made of? Bobs?" Torches appeared and flared in the hands of his clan. Not content to let him die a comic's stage death, they were going to light him on fire.

Lewis shook his head, clearing the disturbing images. He wasn't homesick anymore. He remembered vividly what it was like to be an outsider in his own family, written off as a weird harthoth disappointment. It wasn't his fault they didn't get it. He never found a way to loosen them up, never connected, never transcended Elko.

He didn't feel like he was doing much better with his human friends. He made them laugh when he didn't mean to but hadn't been quick with deliberate jokes. Being laughed at, unintentionally funny, was okay, but it wasn't anything like his idols. He wanted to *make* people laugh, like he'd made Chloe laugh at the nature preserve, which seemed much harder than he realized.

It was dark, but not that late. He wasn't going to be able to go back to sleep without getting something to eat. He hiked out of the canyon and swung by the cafeteria, but he wasn't quite brave enough to go inside by himself. Across campus, he could see the bus stop glowing in the night like a magical portal.

Getting on the bus was simple, and there were plenty of seats. It was going back toward Portland. All good. He decided to go back to the mission and see if he could find Rami.

Riding the bus in the dark was disorienting. Lewis

couldn't see the landmarks he'd ridden past just that afternoon, and stretches of darker road made it hard to determine how far he'd gone. He had no idea how to judge distance from the lurching progress of the bus. He felt panic rising inside. The flashing reader boards and voice announcements didn't help him. He started to sweat.

He'd changed buses with Chloe at some point, but he hadn't paid any attention to the stop or the bus numbers. Crossing over the river, he decided this was about where he'd changed buses before and got off. Once he was out on the sidewalk, though, he had no idea where he was or what bus to catch. He knew the river was at his back, so he could go north or south. Trotting at a good clip, he made turns until he was hopelessly lost in downtown Portland.

The buildings didn't all look the same, they looked alien. Late diners strolled and people spilled out of a theater at the close of a show, crowding the sidewalk. Lewis shouldered through them.

HOOONNK! A car ascending from an underground parking garage stopped a few inches away from him, a monster rising to prowl the night. Lewis skipped aside and ran, his bare feet slapping the pavement. A man half-heartedly called out, "You okay, buddy?"

Lewis kept running, dodging people lined up in front of a garishly painted donut shop, running past small trailers with food cooking inside, barely managing to avoid knocking anyone over. He couldn't run at his top speed without barreling into people, so he ran at about three-quarter speed. There were so many people, everywhere, and they weren't paying attention to anything outside their own bubble of food or friends or more-than-friends. He dashed across another street in front of a bicyclist. Angry, tinny clanging chastised him. He ran into a shopping cart, bruising his hip, and skidded on his hands and knees on the sidewalk. The small, bent man attached to the shopping cart pulled a broken umbrella from the pile of bags in the cart and shook it at Lewis. "GET AWAY!" he yelled, spraying spit.

Lewis felt his adrenaline spiking, and leaped back to his feet, scrambling several yards in a flailing stumble. He still had his own bags, by some miracle. He zigzagged down the street, limping on his bruised hip. At the next street, he took half a second to look for cars.

One car arrested his attention. Swooping in front of him, blocking the crosswalk, the black and white Portland Police cruiser was a festival of too-bright lights as the officers flipped on the red and blue flashers on the roof. Lewis covered his eyes, cowering in the artificial glare. The driver opened his door and stepped out, casually putting his stocky body to Lewis' right side. His partner, a tall woman, came around to Lewis' left.

"Hey, buddy, everything okay?" the cop to his right asked. "Some people saw you running, and they thought you might need help. Do you need help?"

Lewis did need help, but the help he needed

would remove him from this situation entirely, not further embroil him with the police. Tom had told him about driving carefully and the peril of robberies. Tom had not mentioned he should avoid getting lost, being scared, or panicking, which Lewis realized now was self-evident.

He made a few stalling noises, straightening up and trying to control his breathing. Flop sweat mingled with fear sweat and exertion sweat, for a brew of stench he was sure the cops could smell.

The woman tried to reach out. "Can you tell me your name? I'm Officer Ramirez, and this is Officer Sweeley."

"My name is Lewis Clark," Lewis said. He saw the officers exchange a glance. Why did everyone do that when they heard his name?

"We heard you were in danger of getting hurt, maybe running into the street," Officer Sweeley added. "So, we wanted to check on you, see if you need help. Are you running from someone, Lewis?"

"No! No, I just got off the bus in the wrong place, and I got scared when I realized I was lost. Then a car came out of the ground, and I didn't know they could do that, so I ran."

"Okay, Lewis, being lost can be scary, I get that. Where were you headed?"

"I was trying to get to the mission. I went there yesterday, but it's underground, too, and I left." The cops' faces hadn't softened. Something he was saying wasn't right. "Being underground is unnatural." That didn't do it either.

"Lewis, did you take anything tonight? Have a few drinks?"

"No, of course not. Tom *did* tell me not to do any robberies," he scoffed. These police were not going to trick him like that.

The officers exchanged a long look that was clearly some kind of telepathic communication. Officer Ramirez shrugged, and Officer Sweeley sighed. "Do you have any ID on you, Lewis?" he asked without much hope.

"Yes, I do," Lewis said proudly. He was, in fact, so proud to have the correct answer to one question that he'd forgotten Tom's other advice about not letting the police check his ID.

CHAPTER 16

Lewis dug out his new Oregon driver's license and handed it to Officer Ramirez. She used her flashlight to examine it, looking carefully at both sides. She shrugged again and handed it to Officer Sweeley, who examined it for himself. He leaned to his shoulder mic and said a few things in staccato code. He handed the license back to his partner. Lewis remembered Tom's warning about his ID and cops, and felt like he was going to throw up.

"Hey, Mark, what's the story?" another voice, a *familiar* voice interjected. Lewis snapped his head to the left and saw Rami strolling into the vortex of lights. He had a wildly disproportionate feeling of relief to see someone who knew him. "Hey, Lewis."

"Rami! You prowling the streets again tonight? Unsaving some souls?" Officer Sweeley joked, and the tension inside the red and blue bubble evaporated.

"Yeah, I was hoping to run across Lewis, here, actually. It's almost like some supernatural force made me walk three blocks out of my way so you could deliver him to me, if you want to believe in such things."

Officer Sweeley made the sign of the cross. Rami and the officers burst out laughing. Lewis didn't get the joke, so he smiled and nodded.

"This guy one of yours, then?" Officer Ramirez asked, holding Lewis' ID out.

"You could say we're working on that," Rami answered, accepting the ID and glancing at it. "How about I take him the rest of the way and you two get back to saving the city?"

"Yeah, if you got him. He was running into traffic, and we wanted to make sure he wasn't gonna hurt himself, mostly. He says he got lost."

"I did," Lewis interjected, not wanting to be talked about without engaging the narrative a little.

"Alright, Lewis, let's get out of here. Thanks, Mark, Camila," Rami said, waving at the officers as they flipped the light bar off and pulled slowly away. He walked north and Lewis tagged after him.

"I need that back," Lewis said after waiting what he thought was an extraordinarily patient amount of time.

"I'm not gonna ask where you got it, but it was quick and high-quality for a guy who I found wearing clothes he most likely stole from a middle-aged lady. Here." Rami handed him the license without breaking stride. "If they'd run that through the computers, what do you think would have come up?"

"Probably nothing good," Lewis admitted. "I

wasn't supposed to show it to them."

"That's both correct and very wrong, dude." Rami stopped and faced him. "What were you running from?" he demanded.

Lewis sighed. "Everything, I think. I got off the bus in the wrong place, then I got turned around. There were so many people, and then a car jumped out at me from underground—I panicked. Then I was running, and everything made me want to run more."

"Dude, you *do not* make sense to me. Maybe someday you'll tell me what your deal is. As long as you weren't running from somebody, I guess it's your business. You hungry? We have black bean sliders tonight."

"Okay. Thanks."

Rami nodded and resumed walking toward the mission. Lewis followed, wondering if he would ever be able to tell anyone what his deal was.

Lewis braved the underground cavern of the Stumptown Ethical Atheists Mission for the black bean burgers. When the room felt too small, he closed his eyes and imagined he was in a tree in the park. He wiggled his toes. He lied to himself and said it was the first floor. He absolutely didn't think about cars leaping out of the darkness to squash him into a smear of slimy guts.

Rami ate with him, but he didn't ask questions until Lewis was done eating. When the questions came, they weren't what Lewis was expecting.

REBECKARATCLIFFE

"Where'd your shoes end up?" Rami asked.

Lewis didn't want more shoes. "I am saving them for special occasions," he said lightly.

"That right? They're not in your bags, though? Did you leave them where you're staying?"

"In a manner of speaking, yes." Lewis gave Rami his best neutral face.

Rami smiled and shook his head. "Alright, keep your shoe secrets. What are you in Portland for, Lewis? There are obviously depths here I didn't see when I pulled you from the waters."

"I don't know," Lewis admitted. "It was more about coming *from* something than *to* something."

"Do you need a job? Or do you have a job?"

"I'm more of a student. I know some people at Reed College."

"OH." That meant more to Rami than Lewis had intended.

"What did he mean, 'unsaving souls'?" Putting Rami on the hot seat effectively changed the subject.

"This is an atheist mission, like the sign says, which is kind of a contradiction. Eve doesn't believe in God. She believes in humanity, even though it's probably harder to keep the faith lately."

"I didn't really believe in the gods at home," Lewis agreed. "They spent a lot of time praying to a fire god. People can carry fire around in their pockets."

"Eve thinks people spend a lot of time praying for things they should do themselves."

"If that's Eve's opinion, what's yours?" Lewis asked.

"I think people might want to do both and see how that works out. People assume I'm an atheist, too, just because I work with Eve a lot, but it's more complicated than that."

Lewis waited, but this seemed to be the end of the conversation. He thanked Rami and Eve for the meal and headed back into the night as quickly as he could without looking like he was fleeing the scene.

Eve had given him a map of the bus routes, but he didn't trust himself to read it correctly. He walked toward the water, knowing Reed was that direction. The city around him was cool, almost chilly, bathed in yellow-orange light and neon. Open doors spilled music, conversation, and food smells onto the sidewalk. He crossed Naito Parkway to Tom McCall Waterfront Park. The river sparkled, reflecting the lights on bridges and boats. A large cruiser glided downstream, a party in full swing aboard.

Lewis turned upstream and strolled along the sidewalk. The river was wide and fast-moving, a force of nature masquerading as scenery. The traffic flowed alongside the park in its own multilane river of asphalt. Lewis was getting used to the smell of traffic, and the not-quite-fresh smell of the Willamette. The occasional smoker standing outdoors was another story. Why people would do that mystified him.

Up ahead, a building on the river side of Naito glowed with exterior bulbs around the roofline. Every window spilled colored light like a great cathedral, creating pools of red, blue, and purple on the surroundings. There were tables outside under large burgundy umbrellas, every seat taken. As Lewis came closer, he smelled food and yeasty fermentation.

He heard someone talking inside the restaurant over a sound system but couldn't make out the words. Suddenly, laughter erupted from the crowd in a roar. People clapped and cheered. Lewis felt electricity roll up and down his spine.

Moving faster, he rounded the front of the restaurant. The sign above the front door showed an anchor and twisted rope, with letters in a circle reading "Numbknots Yachtery & Brewpub." A sandwich board at his feet proudly proclaimed it to be "Numbskulls at Numbknots—Open Mic Comedy Night!" in large bold font. Lewis slipped in the front door.

"Yeah, kids, man. If someone had told me I wouldn't be able to transfer out of the job after five or six years, I don't know if I would have had them." More laughter. "And a 'promotion' just means you get more of them. Imagine a boss trying to tell you 100% more work without a raise is a 'promotion.'" Pause. "Never mind, none of the women in the audience have to use their imaginations." With this crowd, at this performance, the woman on stage was killing.

"It's a ten dollar cover tonight, man!" yelled a large, brown-haired man in sunglasses and a vest that said "Security." He held out his hand for the money.

"I don't have any money," Lewis admitted.

"Are you going on? No cover if you're going on." The security guy gestured toward the stage where the woman was finishing her routine and waving herself off stage.

Lewis was dumbstruck in the doorway of Numbknots. He mumbled something about only performing on stumps and backed out the door. He didn't go far, though. He sat on the lawn, listening to what he could hear of Numbskulls at Numbknots. New possibilities unfurled before him like enormous maple leaves in spring, and he finally knew what he'd been running toward.

CHAPTER 17

The open mic ended at midnight, but Lewis sat on the grass until closing time, listening to the music and people inside. They left in pairs, or groups, but no one left alone until the lights flashed and the music stopped. The people leaving in pairs were extra friendly with each other, stumbling together and laughing at private jokes. The men leaving alone (all the singles were men), strode away as if they had someplace to get to very purposefully and slightly carefully.

Lewis got up when the lights winked out on the patio and made his way to the bus stop for Bus 19, the route the map said would take him back across the river to Reed. No one else was waiting, so he sat on the bench in the shelter, thinking about Numbknots and the possibility of going on stage in front of an audience himself. Anytime he'd tried his material at home, the harthoth just stared at him, or yelled at him, or made him sit through a long speech about "being serious" and "saying less weird things."

He got out his book. He didn't need the light from

the bus shelter to read, but it felt cozy. He read.

"The first time I got on stage, I thought I owned the world. It's not like that for most people. Most comics are neurotic introverts who have to say these odd things or they will die. I walked on with swagger, ladies and gentlemen, and started my first set by insulting every single person in the room.

"This went about how you would expect, but I somehow did not expect it. As the silence in the room thickened into a slurry of hatred, I felt my stomach shrivel in on itself, threatening to liquefy and run out my bowels. That feeling, my friends, was the feeling of *learning*."

The bus didn't come, because the buses don't run in the middle of the night. Lewis fell asleep thinking about that feeling of *learning*, one he was all too familiar with.

Dawn brought the city back to life, and Lewis startled awake to the sound of traffic and light rail. The bus finally started its day with a crowded ride back over the river. Each person around Lewis had their own distinctive scent, some overwhelmingly artificial, some natural and still overwhelming. He edged away from the blond woman in a pantsuit clicking away at her phone. She smelled like an entire field of flowers had rotted in her pockets. The man on the other side of the pole edged away from Lewis.

At Reed, he made his way to the cafeteria and went inside with only a small hesitation.

"LEWIS!" Tom called from across the room. Chloe was bent over a plate of eggs and looked up with open curiosity.

Lewis grabbed some likely looking items from the scrounge and sat down.

"How was last night?" Chloe asked as Tom swung back into his seat.

Lewis carefully considered what would make him sound like he had things under control.

"I caught an open mic night downtown." This was the most urbane thing he could come up with, and it wouldn't raise questions about his adventures bolting through downtown and meeting the nice police officers.

"Really? Where?" Tom asked through a mouthful of toast.

"Numbknots? It's by the river."

"Anyone good?"

"There was one woman who really killed. She had a lot of material about her kids."

"Oh, old people stuff," Chloe dismissed. Lewis winced, but she didn't see. "You found somewhere to stay?"

"Sure," Lewis half-lied, thinking the canyon was fine for now. He ate his half-eaten croissant sandwich and a pile of scrambled eggs.

"I have to get to class in a minute, you want to come?" Chloe said. "I'm sure Dr. Perkins would be chill if you say you're just sitting in for the day and show your ID."

The class was in the Anthropology department, a

comprehensive seminar on how societies normalize desirable behaviors to enhance group survival. Dr. Perkins just nodded and watched as the students spent most of class arguing about whether a patriarchal society normalized behaviors that were beneficial for everyone, or just the males. Lewis was fascinated.

"Do you have an opinion, Mr. Clark?" Dr. Perkins asked at a lull when the students stopped to breathe and stare fiercely at each other.

Lewis didn't realize she meant him until Chloe elbowed him. "Oh. Uhhh…" He struggled to put his thoughts into words. "I think whoever is in charge will encourage behavior that benefits them, so you have to be careful who you put in charge. Don't pick your crazy uncle, to start with." Dr. Perkins frowned slightly, but didn't say anything. Chloe looked out the window.

"That's right!" One of the young men in the class took off in an unwarranted and antagonistic direction only tangentially related to what Lewis had said.

After class, Dr. Perkins stood at the door, giving many of the students a personal word or reminder. She moved in front of the exit when Lewis and Chloe approached.

"Thanks for sitting in, Mr. Clark. I'm curious—where did you do your undergrad? I usually know everyone in the department by this late in the year."

"In Canada," Lewis said. He did not fill the expectant silence.

She did not seem satisfied. "And what are you taking here?"

"Oh, Lewis is in a kind of special program with Dr. Miller, so he'd been slaving away in the basement all term," Chloe interjected. "I doubt you'll see him in the sunlight again."

"I don't like basements," Lewis gloomed, "but I guess I'm going to be in them a lot."

His resigned tone made Dr. Perkins chuckle. "Grad student reality, I'm afraid. Tell Jack I said hello next time you talk to him. We miss his kombucha."

Chloe smiled and steered Lewis out of the building with a hand on the small of his back, as if the little missus needed to be presented to the next business associate. When she judged they were far enough away from the building, she put her backpack down on the grass, laid down next to it, and burst into loud, uncontrolled laughter.

Lewis sat next to her. "What's so funny?" he asked.

"Oh...oh," she struggled to catch her breath. "That was amazing. I did not expect her to ask you to join in."

"I guess I sounded pretty dumb," Lewis said, embarrassed by Chloe's laughter.

"No, no, it's not that. I mean...that wasn't the most insightful thing I've ever heard, but you triggered about five people with it, and the conversation got more interesting afterwards. You weren't wrong. People just don't want to talk about common sense stuff in there. They want to seem like they're the smartest person in the room."

"My crazy uncle might end up in charge, back home." Lewis suddenly felt guilty about opening the door for that possibility. "He'll probably be better than me, though."

Chloe sat up and frowned at him. "Than you? Were you in charge of something?"

CHAPTER 18

Chloe didn't miss anything. Lewis hadn't been careful enough.

Now he needed to make a decision. Tell the truth, all of it, tell part of the truth, or make up something about a family farm in Canada and try to keep track of more lies. He was doing such a spectacular job with that so far.

After a long minute of silence, he chose none of those options. "I was stopped by the police last night." The diversion worked.

"You were WHAT?"

"They seemed nice."

"I guess they were, since you're here talking to me. Were you shoplifting again?" Chloe stood and brushed off her clothes. She was wearing a lime green shirt with a leaf logo on the front, two short, black braids, and ripped jean shorts.

"No, I was running through downtown Portland." Lewis was learning not to elaborate beyond the facts.

"That explains the special aroma. You can shower

at Tom's. This was before you caught a comedy show?" Chloe walked toward Tom's dorm. Lewis fell into step with her.

"Yeah. I had to sit outside because I didn't have money, but you can still hear everything."

Chloe stopped and looked thoughtfully at him. "You're going to have to get some money somehow, Lewis. I could give you a little bit, but my parents would notice any big changes in my account. Better if you figure it out for yourself as part of your journey to self-actualization."

Lewis nodded. He was going to have to look up "self-actualization," because her tone left it up in the air whether this was desirable or not. She was right about the money part, though. Even his magical bus pass would run out at some point. Spring would turn into summer would turn into fall, and sleeping outdoors would be a lot less attractive.

Tom's shampoo and body wash turned out to be slightly less offensive than the mission's donated scrub. Lewis used the smallest amounts he could. Humans used a lot of soap. The biggest drawback of clothes was how they captured stink. They both made you sweat and collected the moisture, aging and amplifying something that should evaporate into the air. He was going to have to figure out *why* clothes were such a necessity.

"You did what with the police?" screeched Tom when Lewis poked his head back into the room. The undercurrent of marijuana smoke was overshadowed by something sweet and fruit-like.

"I just talked to them. They saw my ID, but my friend Rami got it back before it was a problem."

Tom's mouth hung open. He had bright red lipstick on, and the effect was extremely dramatic. "You had it for less than a day! How did you manage...you know what, I don't want to know. Just don't tell them where you got it, okay? Never. Tell. Them."

Lewis nodded very solemnly. Tom closed his eyes and took several very deep breaths. Chloe watched all this from the bed, where she sat cross-legged eating something.

She held the bag out to Lewis. "Gummy worm?"

He did not want to make another ignorant baba ghanoush assumption, but worms were not generally something the harthoth ate unless they were very desperate. He gingerly fished one out of the bag, wincing at the unfamiliar feel, and smelled it. It was the source of the strange odor in the room. He put the entire thing in his mouth and bit down. He immediately spit it back into his hand.

"That's awful!" he said. "How do worms taste like that?" He studied the glistening, fruitish corpse.

"Another thing they don't have in Canada, eh?" Tom said skeptically. Chloe shushed him and he rolled his eyes.

"Not where I'm from," Lewis said, dumping the wet worm back in the bag. Chloe looked down into the bag, frowning, and set it aside.

"Lewis needs a job," she said.

Tom shook his head. "NO WAY," he said

emphatically. "He had the ID I did for literal hours, Chlo, and handed it to the police. I am not compounding this with federal papers, even if I could, which I can't."

"I bet you could."

"As far as you know, I can't, and that's where it's going to stay."

"Can someone explain what you are arguing about?" Lewis said, tired of being the non-participating subject of every conversation.

Chloe frowned at Tom. "Tom is drawing his ethical line between forging ID to get you into a bar and ID that actually helps you survive."

"That's not fair!" Tom protested. "There's a big difference. One is a little harmless fraud, the other is identity theft if it's going to work like you want it to. There is a very clear line there, whether you like it or not."

Identity theft. Lewis didn't want to steal an identity. He liked the one he'd created from thin air perfectly well.

Tom and Chloe were sniping at each other, and he didn't want that, either. "I don't want another identity. Something will work out. I won't stop until I find it."

Chloe narrowed her eyes in the charged silence.

"See, Chlo? Have a little faith. Lewis thinks it will work out."

Chloe bounced off the bed and left the room without another word.

"What happened?" Lewis asked, surprised and

worried by her sudden exit.

"Welcome to Chloeland, Lewis, you get used to it. She has to process not getting her own way. She'll get over it. I have to run. See you later, dude, thanks for sticking up for me there." Tom grabbed a blue nylon backpack and hurried out, leaving Lewis in his room alone.

Uncomfortable being in Tom's private space without him, Lewis wandered out to the canyon, back to his spot in the rhododendrons. He read in his book about the period when his idol went from obscurity to slightly less obscurity. He imagined himself on stage at Numbknots Yachtery and Brewpub, not just on open mic night. Headlining as "Lewis Clark." Even the possibility was magnetic, pulling him back across the river.

The bus was easier to navigate in daylight. He got off on Naito Parkway and walked down the riverfront to Numbknots. They were open for lunch, but not as crowded as they had been the previous night. Gentle classic rock rolled from the speakers. He went around the building to the dumpsters to forage.

He was standing on a crate with his butt in the air trying to reach a half-eaten hamburger when the door behind him opened.

"Dude, that is not cool. Not cool at all."

Lewis nearly fell the rest of the way in. He managed to right himself and turn to look sheepishly at the man in chef's whites holding a glistening black trash bag. "I didn't pee anywhere, I promise," he said. It was not a brilliant opener, but the man laughed.

"I appreciate that, I guess, but you can't dumpster dive, dude. It's not sanitary." The cook's head was bald, gleaming in the sun, and his face was open and friendly despite the situation.

"There's a lot of food in there, though. Don't you have some way to give it to people who can't pay?"

"No, we can't do that, but I feel you. I wish we could, but it would violate all kinds of codes. What's your name?"

"Lewis."

"Alright. My name is Bill Ben, which is a long story for another time. Do you know how to wash dishes, Lewis? I'm fucking desperate, and there's an unmauled cheeseburger and fries in it for you."

Lewis realized he was being invited inside the building and lied his ass off to cross that magical threshold. "Sure, I can wash dishes. I did it all the time in Canada."

CHAPTER 19

The inside of the Numbknots kitchen had a smell that was three parts food, one part fermentation, one part grease, and one part steamed disinfectant. It was overwhelming unless Lewis focused on one part at a time. The food, a slightly elevated version of bar fare, smelled the best.

"Watch your step in here," Bill Ben said without noticing Lewis had bare feet. The reason became very obvious as Lewis followed him across the kitchen to the dish room. The floor was slick with spattered grease from the fryers and grill, and someone had spilled a swath of red sauce very recently. There were rubber mats with round holes in front of some of the workstations that were safer, but weird on his naked soles.

Tiptoeing to an open doorway, Lewis caught a blast of super-heated steam and sanitizing detergent that made him cough violently. He tried to stifle it before it became obvious he'd never seen a dishwasher in his life. The thing was belching poisonous clouds like a medieval reptile.

Bill Ben looked at him with concern. "You're not sick or something? Because if you are..." He trailed off into an implied rescission.

"No, no, I'm fine. Just been a while since I've seen the dragon in person."

Bill Ben chuckled. "This one won't eat you unless you feed yourself to it. Come over here." Bill Ben efficiently showed him how to stack rinsed dishes in the rack and send it through the conveyor, pushing one button to start them disappearing into the tunnel. The roaring water and mechanical noises from inside the tunnel sounded aggressive. When the rack emerged, Bill Ben grabbed three of the steaming plates with one hand, clattering them loudly together. Grabbing another three with the other hand, he stacked them on racks just outside the dish room at the beginning of the cook line. He pointed out the proper locations.

"Just put the glassware in these racks and the bartender will come back and get it from you." He pointed at a mountain of stacked tubs on the counter, in the sink, and on the floor. "That, my friend, is the result of Jaxopher the Unreliable not showing up for his lunch shift and Vinnie the Perpetually Stoned forgetting his dinner shift. Dinner's starting in a few minutes. See what you can do."

Lewis nodded solemnly. This was his chance to be the hero of this story. Jaxopher was the disappointment, not him. Vinnie was the screw-up, not him. He could truly transcend his old self, right here and now, because he was where he was needed. He bucked one of the full tubs out of the sink to give himself room to work. He grabbed an empty rack, a dirty plate, and the overhead sprayer.

The result of spraying a flat surface full blast with high-pressure hot water would have been more comical had anyone else seen it. He shook water off his face, waiting for the shock and pain of extremely hot water to recede. He had a brief flash of what Manura must have felt, burning alive, and squelched it down as quickly as it surfaced. Taking a deep breath, he changed the angle of the plate and tried again. The scrim of saucy remains sloughed off into the sink and he racked the plate.

By the time the rack was full, Lewis was soaked. He pushed the rack onto the conveyor and mashed the button. Watching the dishwasher swallow the rack, he decided he didn't so much care for tunnels either. They were a sneakier version of underground. On the other side, he grabbed three plates like Bill Ben had, yelped, and dropped them back into the rack. They were scalding hot. He retreated to the sink, shoving another rack into the machine before unloading the first.

He lost track of time. The restaurant kitchen was busy, all the kitchen staff moving in and out of each other's space in practiced chaos. "Behind you!" "Coming through!" As Lewis made progress on the dishes, more were added to his pile.

The bartender collected glasses and brought tubs of dirties. She was the only one in no kind of uniform at all, just jeans and a black tank top that showed off her intricate tattoo sleeves. She looked at Lewis curiously, and at his feet with a raised eyebrow, but said nothing to him all night.

As the pace started to slow, Lewis let out a deep sigh. He was tired and sweaty, and his scrounged breakfast was long behind him. A low whistle from the doorway startled him and he turned to find Bill Ben shaking his head.

"What happened, man?" The chef was looking at the two tubs of dishes waiting to be cleaned, his arms crossed.

"They kept bringing more!" Lewis said, amping up an aggrieved tone.

Bill Ben tried to frown at Lewis. Lewis frowned back, not sure he was reading the situation correctly and desperately hoping he was.

To his relief, Bill Ben's face broke into a delighted grin, and the two men laughed together at their shared joke. Lewis glowed.

"You are a dishwashing machine, my friend. I was hoping you'd put a dent in it so I could get home before tomorrow morning, but you not only kept up, you caught up. Come on and eat. It'll be slow from here on out.

In the kitchen, Bill Ben plated him a double cheeseburger and a mound of fries. Sitting on an overturned pickle bucket, Lewis discovered the sublimity of the combination of fats and starches.

He finished the night floating on a high of cholesterol and a job well done. When the last dishes were cleaned and put away, he found Bill Ben wiping down the grill with an oiled rag. Junior line cooks were removing the mats and mopping the floors. The mop sloshed over Lewis' right foot, giving him a disgusting lesson about the benefit of shoes.

"Well, Lewis, it was an interesting night," Bill Ben mused. "I am wondering some things. Come with me for a second." He walked to the little office and unlocked the door, motioning for Lewis to sit in a chair in front of the small desk. He closed the door and sat in the only other chair behind the desk. "You don't have shoes."

"Oh, I have shoes, I just hid them under a bench. I guess I should get them."

"Okay, that's one thing on my list. Number two, you said you're from Canada? Are you just visiting, or passing through, or what?"

Lewis hadn't considered that at length but blurted out an answer. "I guess I live here now."

"You can't live at Numbknots."

Lewis thought it was a joke. He decided to play straight with Bill Ben and see where it got him. "I have some friends, and I have a place I can sleep. I don't have any money, though."

"Can you work? Legally?"

"I don't think so? I just have a driver's license and a bus pass."

Bill Ben let out a heavy sigh. He reached into his front pocket and pulled out his wallet. Removing two twenties, he held them out to Lewis. "Here. And I should tell you never to come back, but I have a feeling about you. You're one of those cosmic hitchhikers who show up when a person least expects them, and I have a policy about that."

Lewis waited for him to elaborate. He did not. Lewis finally asked what his policy was.

"That is between me and the universe. Speaking of secrets, however, you working here is a secret, and one I could get in a lot of trouble over, including OSHA violations for your unprotected tootsies. Wear your shoes tomorrow. If anyone asks, you wandered into the kitchen by accident and did all those dishes trying to find a way out."

Lewis put the money in his pants pocket and left before Bill Ben could change his mind. In the wee hours of the morning, he found his shoes under the bench where he'd secreted them. Working his way up from the bottom apparently started with his feet.

CHAPTER 20

"What's the special occasion?"

"Huh?" Lewis was sitting across from Tom eating half a scrounged veggie burger when Chloe flopped down in the chair next to him. She was wearing a glittery top that said "Cute and Full of Rage" across the front. Her black hair was in two short pigtails

"You have shoes on. You invited to a party or something?" She watched his reaction while she took a big drink of water.

Lewis sat up straight. "I have a job, thank you very much." Tom smirked and concentrated on his fries.

Chloe's eyes widened. She hadn't been in the commons for two days. That the world had moved on this far without her involvement was clearly a shock. She narrowed her eyes, recalculating.

"How'd you do that? Did Tom cave?"

"No, Tom did not *cave*," Tom interjected. "Tom is a man of principle. Tom was not involved."

"I don't think I'm supposed to talk about it, but I think I can say that I have a natural talent for dishwashing."

Chloe shook her head, but there was the hint of a smile on her face. She launched into a recap of her latest seminar and the futility of making Philippe understand the subtext behind somebody's something if Philippe was going to continue to insist on being a rhetoric-addicted asshole. Lewis got himself seconds and his own glass of water.

He had a tidy little pile of twenties growing in his pocket thanks to his talent with the Hobart. His things were stashed in the rhododendrons in the canyon under a small pile of branches. He carried one bag to keep his shoes and socks in when he didn't have to wear them. He wasn't sure what he was going to do with the money, but it made him feel better to have some.

Chloe finished her tirade as Lewis finished his food. She grabbed one of his hands and held it too firmly for him to snatch it away.

"Your nails are trashed," she said, pressing on the end of one and making him flinch. They looked fine to him. They were thick and jagged, deep yellow —normal for a harthoth. If anything, they looked a little whiter from all the water and detergent at Numbknots. He took his hand back and frowned at them.

Chloe dug in her bag and brought out two small bottles. One was dark blue, the other was black. "Pick one, or I'll pick for you."

"Do the blue, it matches his shirt," Tom said.

Chloe grabbed his hand and placed it flat on the table in front of her, unscrewing the bottle cap. The smell from the liquid inside burned his nose and made his eyes water. Chloe had it on his thumb before he realized what was happening. Tiny bits of silver glitter sparkled in the wet polish.

"Hold still," she murmured, focused on covering all his nails. Lewis kept his hands still until she'd done all of them. "That'll dry fast, maybe five minutes. Gotta run." She stuffed the bottle back in her bag and left.

"That's a good color," Tom mused. His nails were the same bright red as his lips.

"Do I need to color my lips blue, too?" Lewis asked.

Tom shrugged. "You can if you want, but it's not required. That's all the apology you'll get, by the way." Tom left to go back to his room and study, and Lewis was left to wander campus alone.

The feeling of the nail polish on his nails was heavy, not physically, really, but emotionally. The intimacy of someone touching his hands that way was unsettling. A harthoth would never have done that. He couldn't fathom what it meant, and Tom's comment wasn't much help. He held his hands out in sunlight and turned them from side to side, catching glints of metallic glitter like fireworks. He was relieved Chloe was no longer mad at him, but this was confusing. She was confusing.

He went back across the river for his shift, waving at Bill Ben as he headed to the dish room. Jaxopher was making one of his unpredictable appearances, so the dish room was slightly more caught up than the first time Lewis took over. He let the skinny, nervous kid out before he claimed his territory.

After a few minutes, the bartender came back with a tub of dirty pint glasses. "Nice nails."

Lewis was startled to be spoken to, finally, after three days. He stood up, sprayer in hand, and drenched the wall with high-pressure steaming water that splashed directly back on him.

"Ooooooh!" he yelped. He let go of the sprayer handle and wiped his face.

"I'm Titania, and I already took a shower, thanks anyway," she said as she set the dishes down.

"I'm Lewis, from Canada," he said. "My friend put this on my nails."

"It's a good color. Suits your whole rugged bear thing. Grab those for me," she said, pointing to a rack of clean glasses while she grabbed another "Now that you have a name and shoes, you can bring those up front."

Lewis lifted the rack and followed Titania through the kitchen. Her hair was in long coils, like a harthoth elder might wear, and he couldn't shake the feeling she was his superior because of it. Her tank top was bright red, glowing in the dim lighting of the bar. She motioned for him to set the glasses on the counter and thanked him. He headed back toward the kitchen

"Lewis Clark?"

He froze. The voice was familiar, but it was not one of his friends. He considered pretending he hadn't heard, but if he hadn't heard anything, why was he frozen to the spot? He turned.

"It is you! I thought I recognized that copper hair. What are you doing here?"

Dr. Perkins was sitting at the bar with a pint glass in front of her, half-full of amber liquid.

"Oh, hi," Lewis mumbled.

"It's Hilda Perkins, we met a few days ago at Reed? Didn't you say you were working with Dr. Miller?"

"Yes, Dr. Perkins, hello. That's what we said for sure." Lewis regretted letting Chloe tell lies to this woman, because he was having trouble recalling exactly what she'd said now. He'd assumed he would never see Dr. Perkins anywhere again, especially outside of the school.

"Are you working here, too? I'm surprised you have time for that."

"I'm surprised, too." That was true, but what he was surprised about and what Dr. Perkins was surprised about were miles apart.

Dr. Perkins narrowed her eyes. "Does Jack know you're working here during your program?"

"Sure, it was his idea," Lewis blurted. "Gotta get back at it!" He walked as quickly as he safely could through the kitchen and out the back door, breathing hard.

No one was supposed to know he was working here. No one was supposed to connect his completely fraudulent presence at Reed with his real life, which he'd just this moment realized was here, in the dish room at Numbknots.

How was Portland so enormous and so small at the same time?

CHAPTER 21

Titania found Lewis out by the dumpster when she came outside for a smoke. "You know the fancy professor, huh?" She shook a filtered Camel out of the pack and offered it to him.

The mechanics of smoking weren't entirely clear to Lewis, but the attraction was a complete mystery. His sense of smell could break down cigarette smoke into many of its components, and they were rank individually and worse collectively. He wrinkled his nose and shook his head. He could tolerate her smoking, but there was no way he could do it himself.

"She thinks she knows more about me than she does."

Titania waited for him to elaborate, but he didn't. She lit her cigarette and took a long drag, blowing the smoke sideways to avoid fumigating Lewis. That was fascinating, as she made her lips into a shape he'd never seen before.

She made a little chuffing sound and he realized he'd been staring at her lips for far too long.

"My ex thought that, too," she murmured.

Lewis started to protest—a lot of stand-up comedy was about "exes," and he knew that didn't apply—but his words died in his throat. Titania was looking at the river, lit by the lights on the moorings and the colored bridge lights on the Hawthorne and Morrison bridges. Her red tank top was vibrant in the soft light, softened at the shoulders where a few of her locs had escaped. She was out here talking to him because she thought they had something in common. Correcting her would ruin that.

"Hmmmph," he said. "Your ex was dumb."

Titania laughed an unguarded laugh that sounded like intelligence, delight, and something earthy. The thought that her laugh would smell like an overripe huckleberry flashed in his mind, which was weird enough to make him laugh with her.

"That's a passing grade, Lewis the Dishwasher. Tomorrow is my day off. I'm going to the zoo to stare at the bears. Would you like to come with me or are you worried the zookeepers will recapture you?" She ground her cigarette out in the steel can of sand beside the door. The label read "Hamburger Dill Chips."

Lewis' only mental image of a zookeeper was from a book about a monkey named George. The man in the book was easily tricked by the monkey. Plus, Titania could vouch for him like Rami had with the police. "I have a plan for evading the zookeeper," he answered. "Tell me how to get there and what to bring."

Titania retrieved her own glasses for the rest of the night, sparing Lewis any more possible contact with Dr. Perkins. When she left, shortly after 2AM, she said, "See you tomorrow." Lewis nodded and waved a hand at her, unconsciously making the harthoth gesture for a brief parting, a semi-circle starting and ending at chest height. She smiled and mimicked it before allowing Bill Ben to walk her to her ride.

"Yo, Lewis, Titania doesn't warm up that quickly to anyone. How'd you manage that?" Bill Ben asked, peeling off the night's cash wages and handing it to him.

"She likes my shoes," Lewis deadpanned.

Bill Ben laughed and shook his head. "Take tomorrow off, man, I can get Jaxopher some extra hours. He's been asking for an extra shift to get some shit for his Sentra."

Lewis nodded. It would be nice to have a day off, if he were honest. Having a job was great, but it took up a lot of his time. He had a pressing question on his mind, though. "When's the stand-up coming back?" he asked. Numbknots hadn't had another open mic night yet, and there wasn't anything up advertising one.

"Oh, I do that about once a month. We did it more often for a while, but got so many repeats, I decided to spread it out. You like stand-up?"

"It's my dream," Lewis blurted. He immediately wanted to stuff that aspiration right back where he'd pulled it from, but Bill Ben didn't laugh.

"Oh, really? Cool."

Lewis' sleep that night was a series of nightmares about his clan rising up out of the back of the bar and lighting him on fire on the stage. The rumble of the bus waking him was a relief.

He wasn't supposed to meet Titania for hours, so he rode over to Reed and used Tom's dorm showers. Tom wasn't in his room, but the other students in the Asylum Block had seen Lewis enough to avoid eye contact like he was any other Reedie. His beard and hair were a little shaggier than he thought they should be, so he waited for Tom in the common room.

"Hey, you." Chloe plopped down across from him. "How's it hanging?" She swung her pack to the seat next to her and put both feet into her chair, looking like a ball of potential force.

"Things are good." They really were.

"You still working at that place? What was the name again?"

"Numbknots Yachtery?"

"HA! Now I know where you work!" Chloe gloated. "That wasn't even challenging."

Lewis groaned. So much for keeping things separate. Dr. Perkins *and* Chloe knew, he might as well get a t-shirt and wear it everywhere. "Yeah, okay. Keep it to yourself, though, it's supposed to be a secret."

"What's a secret?" Tom said loudly, sliding into

a seat next to Chloe. His lips and nails were black today.

"NOTHING. I need a haircut and beard trim."

"Yeah, that's no secret," Tom said. "Come on."

Sitting in Tom's desk chair while the young man fine-tuned his fast-growing facial hair, Lewis decided not to tell them about his trip to the zoo with Titania. Tom would probably go overboard with preparations, which was okay, but Chloe...well. Whether she would be amused or angry was a toss-up. Better not to toss anything her way at all on that. They spent the next hour talking about the current speculated relationships between the librarians at a level of detail that was both intrusively graphic and academically interesting.

"You wanna come to class with me today? Dr. Perkins asked when she'd see you again at breakfast this morning." Chloe was getting ready to leave.

Lewis felt a cold sweat. "No thanks. I need to get back across the river," he barked. Dr. Perkins was much too interested in him now.

"You are the only workaholic dishwasher I've ever heard of, Lewis Clark. Come back when you have a day off, okay? We'll go poke your big Canadian finger in Philippe's eye over the definition of feral as it pertains to humans, or something." Chloe gave him a peace sign and headed out. Lewis followed after thanking Tom, a gesture the young man waved off.

Lewis had arranged to meet Titania at the Oregon Zoo in the afternoon. His TriMet pass got him from bus to bus, and then on the light rail train to the zoo. He liked the train. He waited at the gates, dodging families with gigantic strollers and toddlers refusing to sit in them. Since he didn't have a great handle on human time, it was a long wait watching the giant clock on the train station.

Titania finally arrived in a small car with a little neon sign in the window. She thanked the driver and scanned the crowd, smiling when she saw Lewis leaning on a traffic barrier. She was wearing a long, flowing floral skirt and another tank top, this one black. Her locs were tied back with a piece of leather, and small round sunglasses hid her eyes.

"Let's go," she said, patting him on the shoulder and walking past. "You look like you got all dolled up. You must not be from around here."

"I'm not."

They each paid for one ticket and wandered into the traffic pattern encouraged by the pathway, through the Great Northwest exhibit. Lewis felt uneasy as he watched the bears tear apart a large cardboard box. It was both natural and unnatural behavior. He wondered what he would do if he was in a cage for conservation and study.

Titania picked up on his unease. "You afraid of bears?"

He laughed. "Oh, no, I can handle a bear. I was just putting myself in their place, I guess."

"You can handle a bear? Like…physically?"

"Yeah. I mean, in Canada where I'm from, we have bears. They sometimes try to get into our houses or eat our food. We have to be able to convince them it isn't worth it."

"Huh. Canadian, huh? I wouldn't have placed the accent in a million years."

"The accent? I don't have an acc—"

"OMIGOD, TAMMY! Is that you?"

CHAPTER 22

A woman in her late fifties with gray hair in a sensible, short cut and fashionable clothes was making her way directly toward Titania at top speed. Titania looked like she would rather be eaten by the bear. She put Lewis between herself and the woman, trying to hide behind his one-inch-taller frame. It did not work.

"TAMMY! It is you! Come out here!" The woman did a little dodging dance, trying to catch Titania, but only succeeding in making Lewis the unwilling filling in an awkward sandwich.

"Tammy. Stop that! I haven't seen you in months, maybe years, and this is what you do. I guess you haven't grown up, have you? And who is this man? Did you get married without telling me?" The woman appraised Lewis critically. "I can't say I think much of the outside, but maybe he's got a nice personality."

Titania stepped out from behind Lewis and squared her shoulders. "Please. This is my friend, Lewis, from work. Lewis, this is my mother, Sandy."

Her voice had a slight tremor.

"Work? Where are you working? It must not be a good job, if he works there, too." Sandy pointed a dismissive finger at Lewis. "After all that money we paid for that liberal college. Your sister went to a state school, and she's got a good job right in downtown."

Lewis watched Titania deflate. Her shoulders rounded forward, and she looked at the ground, letting out a slow breath that dissipated all her momentary confidence into the air.

"Well, now we're here. I was supposed to meet Marilyn, you remember her from when we lived in Lake Oswego, right? She called at the last minute and said she had food poisoning. It was probably just an excuse, but I already had tickets. We can spend the afternoon catching up, assuming Louie didn't have some intellectual conversation planned." Sandy rolled her eyes, just in case her disdain wasn't obvious. Titania looked like she wanted to evaporate where she stood like a little puddle of Everclear. She shrugged.

Lewis would not have guessed in a million years that Titania was the Elko of her clan. He squared his own shoulders. He'd put up with the harthoth bullying him for 37 years because it left him free to do what he wanted most of the time, but that didn't mean he'd enjoyed it.

"My name is Lewis," he growled. Sandy's flapping mouth finally shut. "Today is my day off, and I was looking forward to a very educational trip to the zoo, which I have never seen before. *Titania* will be very busy explaining it to me, because I'm from Canada. The only animal I've ever seen in my life is a moose. Lots of mooses."

Sandy opened her mouth again, something skeptical creasing her face.

"Honestly, I might pass out when I see an elephant. I plan to cause a scene no matter what," he continued loudly. "I suggest you make other plans with *Titania* that don't involve me. She'll let you know when it's convenient for her."

Titania was watching him with wide eyes. He raised an eyebrow.

"Oh, yeah, I'll call you later," she told her mother, who obviously didn't believe her.

"Tammy, I do not believe that for one second. You give me your number and I'll call you when you're not *otherwise engaged*." Sandy managed to make the last two words sound as bitter as vinegar.

Titania froze.

"Oh, sorry, I broke the phone yesterday," Lewis lied. He realized that wasn't quite right. "I mean, I broke her phone. I was demonstrating some cool hockey moves and used it as the ball." He mimed swinging a bat, and both women looked confused. He folded his arms and smiled a big "I-just-told-a-huge-weird-lie-that-you-can't-refute" smile, daring Sandy to try. He was on unfamiliar ground, literally, but telling someone's mother the absolute untruth to get out of something was a comfortingly familiar trail.

Sandy decided to live to harangue another day, but she couldn't resist another dig. "I am disappointed, Tammy, that you can't make time for me even when we happen to be at the same place at the same time. I will expect you to make this up to me. You can come to the reunion. Your sister comes every year and brings the best marionberry pie. You can buy some chips again."

Titania made some peacemaking noises and submitted to an aggressive "hug." Sandy left without another glance at Lewis. He could tell he'd made an enemy, but he wasn't sure how much it mattered. He'd worry about that if he ever had to be in the same place with her again.

They watched Sandy hustling away, her stomping walk exemplifying her trampling personality. It took an age for her to disappear from view.

"She seems terrible," Lewis said, not thinking.

"She is. I've been to so much therapy," Titania agreed.

"Tammy is pretty, too, but I prefer Titania," he said, still not looking at her. "I changed my name when I came here, too." The confession felt very intimate despite the crowd wandering in all directions around them. It scared him a little.

Her quiet laugh surprised him.

"What?" he asked, turning to look at her face.

Smiling broadly, she shook her head. "I never would have guessed Lewis Clark isn't your real name. What is it?"

"Oh, Lewis is my real name. I just didn't know it

until I got here."

"Fine, keep your secrets." She punched him lightly in the arm. "Now that you've slain the dragon, the zoo might seem a little tame. You still want to ermagherd over the elephants?"

"Yes, if that means I get really excited and talk too long about it."

"That's exactly what it means. Come on." Titania grabbed Lewis by the hand and led him to the pachyderms.

CHAPTER 23

The elephants did inspire awe, but the thoughts Lewis had were more complicated than amazed. He spent a long time watching them manipulate the feeding stations in their enclosure. They were able to get a small amount of food every few minutes by performing a sequence of tasks. This seemed like a very diminished life for such an intelligent animal. He imagined being restricted to performing small, repetitive tasks for his food.

"They must be bored," he muttered.

Titania studied him for a minute. "How so?"

"They do the same thing over and over for the same reward."

"Kind of like tending bar, right?" There was an edge to Titania's reply.

"No, you have a choice. You choose to work at Numbknots. The elephants can't tell the zoo they quit and go look for a different job."

"If the elephants are going to be here, it's better they have something to do, though, isn't it? Conservation programs used to just cage the animals to keep them alive. It was pretty bleak. Imagine we locked you in a room and studied you, but gave you nothing to do."

Lewis conceded the point, but he couldn't shake the uneasy feeling. Zoos were probably not going to be his kind of thing. They also smelled really weird. He could track animals by scent on Mt. Adams, but here there were too many animal scents all on top of each other. Predators and prey and several different continents mingling into a weird soup worse than the garbage. His instincts told him he was going to be eaten any second by a bird from South America.

Titania was definitely his kind of thing, however, so he took the opportunity to ask her about things and let her talk. She told him about a difficult childhood with a mother hellbent on destroying every reminder of her ex-husband, including the child who'd inherited his curly hair and free spirit. The stepfather who believed his monetary contribution entitled him to the last word on everything. The perfect, golden sister who obediently did all the right things. The degree in marketing from the prestigious school, and the subsequent realization that she hated marketing, and businessmen, and her mother.

"You're a little too easy to talk to, Lewis," she finally said as they hiked up the hill to the exit of the zoo. "You know my whole life story, and I know your name is supposedly Lewis at this point and you're allegedly from Canada."

He enjoyed her curiosity. "Yup. That's right."

She grabbed his hand again, pulling on his arm. "C'mon, you have to give me something. Your mom was a logger. Your dad ran a stable of prostitutes. You have a pack of brothers and sisters, and they're all working in circuses as bearded ladies."

Lewis laughed. "No." Thinking of Manura, he sobered. "I left my family because they didn't need me for a long time." He didn't add that they finally did need him.

"I bet their dishes are piling up," Titania said in conciliation, letting it go for now. "You hungry?"

Lewis was hungry. They took the MAX train downtown and found a brewpub in the center of the city with outdoor tables. The menu had things Lewis recognized and things he didn't. Titania ordered a hefeweizen and veggie burger with everything. Lewis told the server he would have what she was having.

The drinks came, golden liquid clouded with fine white particles and a lemon on the side of the glass. Lewis realized this was beer. He'd seen people at the lake with it and heard a lot of jokes about it. Numbknots was a microbrewery, so obviously he washed a lot of pint glasses with an inch or two of beer left in them. He'd not once been tempted to have a sip, though. His experience with coffee had been too awful.

Titania squeezed her lemon into her beer and put the rind aside. Lewis did the same, thinking it might make a difference. Titania took a long pull from her pint, sighing in contentment when she'd finished. "That first sip is always the best, isn't it?" she murmured happily.

Lewis stared at his glass. He picked it up and braced himself. Titania had no idea how "first" this drink would be. Expecting to be orally assaulted, he grimaced and took a tentative drink.

He didn't realize he'd moaned aloud until he opened his eyes, saw Titania's smirk, and raised eyebrow. The flavor of beer turned out to be very unlike coffee. It was sublime. He could taste the citrus, cutting through the bready hefeweizen, but it was just a note of the whole symphony. As a highly carbonated style, it was dancing and fizzing as he drank another, longer pull. He coughed a little and set the glass down, now a third empty.

"Good?" Titania said, smiling.

"Why does anyone drink coffee?" he exclaimed. "It's just crazy. This is so much better."

Realizing he was serious, Titania answered. "Drinking a lot of coffee is called being productive. Drinking a lot of beer is called being an alcoholic. Only one of those is socially acceptable. Have you never had a beer before?"

"No. It's amazing." Lewis took another drink. The first sip had been wonderful, but it kept improving. Prepared for the bubbles, he let it rest in his mouth for a moment before he swallowed, getting the full profile of the beer. "I should have stolen one of these years ago," he murmured, shaking his head.

"Stolen? Do they not sell beer in Canada?"

"Not where I lived. We didn't really have money."

"You're making me think you lived in some primitive society, Lewis. Or a cult. It was a cult, wasn't it?"

Lewis gave that serious thought. "I honestly don't know. Maybe it was, in a way." He drained the rest of his beer. He was already feeling the effect of the alcohol thanks to his empty stomach, and the feeling was pleasant and freeing. His head felt light, floating just a little bit above its real position. "It wasn't fun, I can tell you that. No one ever laughed. Not once."

"What?" Titania was genuinely shocked. "That can't be true, people are hard-wired to laugh."

Lewis shook his head emphatically. "Nope. Not once. Except for me. I used to listen to these radio broadcasts, and I would tell jokes, and you know what? I was the only one laughing."

"Maybe they just didn't get that kind of humor. They must have laughed when somebody fell down, stuff like that. That's universal."

"They live in a different universe. Everything is serious all the time. That's why I left. That, and they wanted me to—"

"Here you go, two veggies with sweet potato fries," the server interrupted. Titania impatiently accepted the food with a hasty thanks and shooed the server away, but the moment had broken.

"What did they want you to do, Lewis?" she asked casually.

Lewis was eyeing his empty beer glass with suspicion. He'd very nearly blabbed details about his origins he'd had no intention of sharing. He'd heard a million jokes about drinking, and he suddenly understood them on a level he'd never before appreciated.

He thought carefully about how to put that line of conversation to rest while still telling the truth. He didn't want to lie to Titania any more than he already had.

"They wanted me to be someone I'm not." Truth, if not the whole of it.

CHAPTER 24

Titania didn't pry, exactly, but the rest of the conversation had a lot of open-ended questions and inviting silences. The food was surprisingly familiar. Meat was part of the harthoth diet, but not the center like it seemed to be for most humans. There was a small cup of tangy sauce to the side he didn't care for, but everything else was great.

"Another hefeweizen?" the server queried during her mid-meal check-in.

"No, I don't think I should," Lewis declined. He was feeling the effects of the first one still.

Titania smiled at him and shook her head. "No, thanks." The server, a young woman with magazine perfect makeup and long hair nodded and moved along. "That hit you pretty hard, huh?"

"I feel a little funny, I guess. Lighter, but not entirely in control," he confessed.

"That is called a 'buzz,' and you should just enjoy it since we're not driving. You know Bill Ben is a master brewer, don't you?"

Lewis hadn't really explored the "Brewpub" angle

of "Numbknots Yachtery and Brewpub." Titania explained the concept and the basics of brewing but deferred some of his questions to Bill Ben. Before he knew it, the plates were cleared, and the check appeared. Since the server set it in front of him, he picked it up and looked at the total. He had more than enough to cover it, but it was a whole evening's work.

"You want me to get half?" Titania asked.

"No, I have enough." He pulled a wad of twenties out of his pocket and sorted out enough to cover it plus and extra twenty. Titania was frowning at his pile of money. "What?"

She shook her head. "I guess you didn't have thieves in Canada, either?"

"Just me," he admitted without thinking.

"Just you? What did you steal?"

Mind racing through his quickly receding buzz, Lewis seized the first word that wasn't a physical object. "Knowledge. Couldn't get enough of it. Lock up your books or I'll come after them and steal all the learning."

Titania laughed. "A modern-day Prometheus? Did you take fire back to your people?"

Lewis was stricken and didn't hide it quickly enough. He focused on stuffing his cash back in his pocket in the uncomfortable silence. The light-hearted mood was broken.

The server swooped in to take the check and asked if he needed change. His assurance that he didn't was met with some surprise. It was probably too much, but better than not enough.

The conversation on the way to the bus stop was less easy, and Lewis didn't know how to ease the awkwardness. He couldn't explain, and Titania was guarded. The good-bye was brief and impersonal. "See you tomorrow, thanks for the meal!"

On the bus back to Reed, Lewis examined his disappointment. He wasn't sure what he had to be disappointed about. Chloe reacted in much more dramatic ways, and he'd felt confused, but not disappointed.

As he trudged into the canyon, taking his circuitous route that avoided giving away his spot in the rhododendrons, he put it aside for now. He was sleepy, and he didn't have anywhere he had to be, and a long nap in the warm evening air was calling.

Lewis woke up sometime in the middle of the night because of all the giggling. His mouth tasted like he'd chewed bark and he opened and closed it a few times to ease the dryness. Another reality of beer, he guessed.

Around him in the canyon, he heard running footsteps and laughter. A young voice called out, "Come out, you bastards, and get lit!" More giggling from several directions. The source of the yelling crashed toward the others, and Lewis could make out a flashlight beam bobbing away from him. He smoothed down his hair, rubbed his eyes, and quietly crept out to the pathway.

"OOOF!" A student-turned-projectile ran into

Lewis and knocked them both down in a heap. Disentangling, Lewis could see who'd bowled him over in the dark, but the student couldn't see him and was panicking.

"Tom, Tom, calm down," Lewis hissed. "It's me, Lewis."

Tom's body slumped in relief. He was face-up on the ground. "Shit, Lewis, I thought you were the ghost."

The loud voice called, "FEE FIE FOE FUM, I SMELL THE BLOOD OF AN ENGLISH MAJOR!" More giggles erupted, more crashing around and wildly swinging light.

"Oh shit, he's gonna get me," Tom said, and then broke into his own giggles, scrambling up and running off down the path.

Lewis' instinct was to melt away into the woods until whatever this was ended. It was loud and chaotic, but no one seemed to be in actual danger. He silently made his way to a large tree on the canyon slope and climbed to a comfortably angled branch to sit and watch. The game was a much more entertaining to the students than its mechanics suggested, chasing each other in the dark with a flashlight. When they passed more closely, the glowing tip of a joint flared and the skunky smell filled the night air.

They played tag in the dark woods for nearly two hours before someone yelled, "I'm going in! I have to lead discussion tomorrow!" Lewis swung down from his branch and headed for his place to get a few hours more sleep. A figure stepped into his path.

"That you again, man?" Tom's voice was a little mushy, slow.

"Yeah, it's me. You okay to get back?" Tom was wobbling.

"I'm really glad I found you, because I don't know if I am." There was a thud and Lewis rushed to his friend's side.

CHAPTER 25

It was easy to pick up Tom and carry him. Navigating with his better-than-human night vision, Lewis had him back to the Asylum Block in just a few minutes. Locked. He rifled through Tom's pockets for anything that would open the door, finally finding his student ID on a lanyard under his shirt. The door opened with a loud click. The common area was a mess, the remains of a pizza orgy on the tables, and two students were asleep on the couches.

Tom was breathing and making mumbling noises at any more abrupt shift in position, but he was limp. His room was locked, and Lewis couldn't find his key, so he took him back downstairs. He didn't know what to do next. Some urping noises from Tom gave him an immediate idea, and he held a trash basket under the boy's head while he vomited.

The stench was terrible and full of information. There was a synthetic smell to it that Lewis didn't recognize and instantly hated. Poison. It smelled like Tom had been poisoned. Without access to any of the harthoth leaders, he had to make his own judgment call.

Ripping the access pass off Tom's neck, he sprinted out the door and to the flower beds at the front of the library. Tearing off handfuls of verbena leaves until he had a good-sized wad of them, he ran back to the sink in the common area. Tom's skin was pale.

Using his fingers and a dirty pizza plate, Lewis crushed the leaves until they were a lumpy, green sludge. Holding Tom's head up with one hand, he forced some of the goop between his lips, massaging his throat to encourage him to swallow it.

Tom's eyes flew open, and before any of the verbena made it down, the rest of his stomach contents came up. He looked at Lewis after the heaving subsided with some suspicion. "Water," he croaked.

He sipped an experimental amount, then swished some around in his mouth and spat it in the wastebasket. "What the fuck was that, dude?" he asked.

"Ancient medicine."

"Please let me die next time," he mumbled. Fumbling in his pocket, he found his key and Lewis took him to his room and settled him with a trash basket and glass of water. Tom looked a little better, and his breathing was regular, so Lewis closed the door behind him and went to stare up at the leaves of his rhododendron until dawn.

Tom wasn't at breakfast, but Chloe was. She looked tired, but her energy got big and anxious when Lewis told her about the previous night. "Why didn't you come and get me?" she demanded.

"Because I don't know where you live?" Lewis replied.

"Okay, that's fair, but I'm going to show you right after we go check on Tom." She put her untouched breakfast on the scrounge table and trotted to Tom's room. She knocked loudly and called his name for several minutes before he opened the door.

"Good job not being dead, though I hear you had to have some help," she said, pushing Tom's bleary-eyed, noxious smelling, but not dead body aside.

Tom sighed and shrugged. "I guess my chemistry experiment was less controlled than I thought."

Chloe banged the window open and turned, arms crossed. "We talked about this. You're lucky Lewis was there, or somebody would be finding your corpse in the woods this morning."

"Given the choice, I might have picked that. What did you do last night, Lewis? My mouth tastes like I was grazing." His eyes popped open. "I wasn't, was I?"

"Not much," Lewis deadpanned. "It was the mooing I would be embarrassed about."

Chloe lost her battle to stay fierce and giggled. The sound was a balm over them all. Tom sat heavily on his bed, and Chloe and Lewis took the hint to let him rest.

Chloe lived off-campus in an old two-story Victorian house she shared with two other Reed students. Maureen, who Lewis had met before, said hello but Lilith was in her room. Chloe gave the impression Lilith never came out of her room. The furniture was threadbare and there was a respectable amount of grime on the hardwood floors and counters. It wasn't completely absent the smell of marijuana, but it was one note in a symphony of gently decaying house and shampoos. Strings of small lights were everywhere, making the gloomy corners seem more cavernous.

Lewis sat carefully in a tan upholstered chair, self-conscious about being a guest and his personal state, which wasn't great after the Tom episode and sleepless night. He suspected there was vomit on his clothes somewhere, and his fingers were still greenly herbaceous.

The women exchanged some information about the trash pickup and schedules, then Chloe sat across from Lewis. "You look like shit."

"Yeah, I was just thinking that."

"I'd let you shower here, but we have a rule about that. No boys upstairs and you don't let someone else's friends in where they aren't here. Keeps the peace with Lilith."

Lilith was sounding a little scary. Lewis nodded.

"If you need me, or come when I'm not here, you leave a note over there." There was a large whiteboard by the front door with the remnants of lists and notes on most of it.

Chloe must have seen the something in Lewis' face then. "Spit it out."

Lewis swallowed. "I can't really do that," he confessed. "I don't know how to write."

CHAPTER 26

Chloe sat back and looked at him through narrowed eyes. "You don't know how to write? You can't even leave a note?" Lewis shook his head. "What kind of schools do they have in Canada?"

"It was kind of informal."

"How do you do anything? How did you fill out a job application?"

"I didn't."

"How did you get a job then?"

"It was kind of informal."

Chloe stared. "So...can you? I mean, was there some reason you didn't learn, like your hand doesn't work or something?"

Lewis smiled. "My hands work fine. There just wasn't anyone to teach me or anyone to write anything for."

"You are sounding less Canadian and more feral by the minute. How do you learn to read if there's no one to write anything? Not even your name?"

"Nope." Lewis wished she would drop it. There was no good explanation that didn't force him to explain more than he was willing to.

After a brief, heavy silence, Chloe relented. "I know that this is all related to 'Canada,' but either you want to tell me or you don't. I'm going to assume you grew up in some kind of cult. Come with me." She hopped up and trotted to the white board. She printed his name with a smelly dry-erase marker, L-E-W-I-S. "Now you copy it."

Lewis took the marker and made two lines, his first letter. The pen felt awkward in his hand, and he could tell he was holding it wrong.

"Are you right or left-handed?" Chloe asked.

"I don't know."

"What hand do you eat with?"

"Oh, my right." He switched the chunky pen over. It felt more natural. He made another L, then finished the word. His writing was sloppy next to Chloe's neat block printing, but it was his name. He tried again, and it looked better.

Chloe clapped her hands in delight. "Good job! Now we start with the alphabet."

Several hours later, Chloe had missed all her classes and Lewis could write most of the upper-case alphabet. Z and S gave him some trouble, but he could print his full name and leave a rudimentary note about meeting at Tom's room.

"This must be so much easier because you already know how to read," Chloe mused.

Lewis was exhausted and his hand hurt. "I guess." He knew he never wanted to hear that damn alphabet song again. "I need to get to work. Thank you for this," he said, pointing at the mess of papers and pencils on the kitchen table.

"You owe me a better explanation sometime, but I can wait." Chloe shuffled the papers together. "Maybe you should write me an essay. 'What I Did Before I Was Lewis Clark.'"

Lewis felt guilty for withholding so much when she'd just spent her day helping him. "Maybe I will," he murmured. Chloe's small smile told him she'd heard even if her tidying didn't slow.

He rose to leave, but didn't get out the door before Chloe had pressed a new notebook and several pens and pencils in his hands. "Practice," she commanded. He nodded and tried to take the items, but she didn't let go right away. Chloe looked into his eyes, searching. Lewis felt nonspecific panic.

The awkward moment was broken when a slight figure in black lace glided down the stairs and said, "Who's the lumberjack? His energy is disturbing me."

Lewis got away from Lilith with his soul intact by leaving without another word. The day was warm, the kind of late spring day that promised everyone would feel overdressed and hot. He had just enough time to scrounge some food and hide his things before heading across the river.

He was dreading work a little, a new feeling for him. Titania would be there, and he wasn't sure what she would do. He wanted to tell her that things were good, fine, he just had a lot of history she didn't know. He wanted to tell her how much he'd enjoyed seeing her outside work. He wanted to talk about beer. They'd left things on such a strained note, he wasn't sure he could.

His bus pass didn't work. He tried it several times before the bus driver finally told him it was expired. "It's June, buddy! Go renew it!" The woman, short and scowling, pointed at the machines. Lewis mumbled an apology, embarrassed, and pushed past a woman with a baby and folded stroller to get off. She clutched her baby tightly to her, turning her head away from him.

He went to the TriMet kiosk and put his pass in the slot. Without too much trouble, he managed to press the right buttons to renew his pass for a month but couldn't figure out how to pay for it.

"You put the money in there," the man behind him said, stabbing his finger at the slot.

"Oh, thanks," Lewis mumbled. He got his pass back and went to wait for the next bus across the river. He was exhausted. Tom's bad drug trip, no sleep, and day of remedial writing lessons were catching up to him. He leaned against the glass wall of the bus shelter and closed his eyes.

When he opened his eyes again, it was early evening. A pamphlet about Jesus was tucked into his open hand, and he smelled even worse. He was late to work for the first time, smelled like he'd been on an all-night bender, needed to pee in the worst way, and was going to Burn in Hell if He Did Not Repent, according to the paper. He crumpled that up and shoved it in his pocket.

He couldn't blow off work. Bill Ben could decide their informal arrangement wasn't worth it if he did that. He looked down the street and didn't see a bus coming. He sprinted the other direction along his normal bus route, not caring that his top speed was clearly inhuman. His lungs filled and expanded, and he felt some of the tension release. He was halfway across the Hawthorne Bridge before his normal bus passed him.

Slowing outside Numbknots, he turned the corner to find Titania was outside smoking.

"Oh… hi," he stammered.

"Hey."

Lewis fiddled with his sweat-soaked flannel and smoothed his damp hair. He needed to run himself through the dishwasher.

"You're late." Titania stubbed her cigarette out in the pickle can. She was wearing her hair in a bright purple headband, but her tank top and jeans were plain black.

"I know. I had an unplanned adventure last night."

"Oh. She have a name?"

Lewis blanched. That assumption had never occurred to him. "Yeah, his name was Tom and I had to save him from dying in the woods."

"I'm sorry," Titania said. "I'm being an idiot."

"As an idiot, I can say you're not."

"Yeah, well, you're not an idiot. I'm the one who

ruined a perfectly nice day yesterday with my big mouth."

"I think your mouth is a great size."

Titania burst into surprised laughter. "Oh, you do, do you?"

Lewis didn't know how to respond to that.

"After your shift, come have a beer and tell me about your friend." Titania went inside, holding the door open for Lewis to follow her.

CHAPTER 27

"Shit, Lewis, I thought my magical dishwasher had disappeared," Bill Ben said when he saw the dish room occupied and humming. "Everything good?" His expression was concerned.

Lewis knew he looked terrible and smelled worse. "I missed my bus, so I ran," he answered without slowing his dishwashing.

"You what? From where?"

"Across the river." Lewis was deliberately vague, even though his lives seemed destined to collide.

"Huh. Okay. We'll talk later." Bill Ben turned his attention back to the kitchen, yelling for one of the line cooks to "get a hustle on."

The pile of dishes was a solvable problem. Lewis steadily worked his way through them, letting the clouds of steam and disinfectant roll over his tired body, emptying the dishwasher and his mind at the same time. Once he had the backlog worked down, he went out to the bar with a rack of clean pints.

"I tell my kids all the time to turn off the lights! Turn off the lights! What do you think, I'm made of electricity? And you know what the teenager says? 'Actually, you kind of are made of electricity, because if your body didn't have any electricity, you'd be dead.'" The restaurant was packed, and this got a decent laugh, but it wasn't bringing down the house. "So, I tell him again to turn off the lights, is he trying to kill me?" Bigger laugh this time, but the comedian was following a line the audience wasn't completely committed to. He seemed to realize it and abruptly switched into a riff about berries that surprised people back to full attention.

"It's comedy night!" Lewis exclaimed to Titania as he set the rack down.

"Yeah, sure is. Happens a lot around here."

"I want to do comedy," he blurted.

Titania paused her work to study him. "Really? Why aren't you out there on open mic night?"

Lewis had expected to be told why he couldn't do it. The challenge made him shy. "I don't have material. At least, not material that would work here."

"It might work better here than in your Canadian no-laughing zone."

Lewis considered that. "It still wouldn't work. People wouldn't get the situations, I guess, because it's so different."

"Then write some more material. Open mic will come around again in a few weeks. I'm sure Bill Ben would give you time to go on."

Lewis shrugged and went back to the dish room. Titania was making is sound so easy, and he knew it wasn't like that. He wished he could sit out in the audience tonight and watch. Even if the headlining comedian wasn't the best tonight, he could learn from what was working and what wasn't. He listened for the big laughs from the dining room and wished they were for him.

"Hey man, come with me." Bill Ben was at the door of the dish room watching Lewis finish up the scrub down on the sink. Instead of heading to the office for his regular payout, they went through the empty restaurant to the bar where Titania was prepping for the following day. Passing through a door at the back, they entered a portion of the building Lewis hadn't seen before. Huge overhead vats dominated the space, and the smell of yeast and fermenting grain overwhelmed Lewis.

"This is where the alchemy happens," Bill Ben explained. "Titania said you had your first beer yesterday and were curious about the process. I brew out here for the restaurant. Grain, yeast, water, and hops. Sometimes a seasonal fruit when I get bored. Pretty soon, I'll be able to do a nice strawberry blonde ale."

Lewis was taking it all in. His first impression was that it took a lot of metal to make beer. As he acclimated to the smell, defining the different notes and blending them back to a whole, he took in a deep breath.

"Yeah, right?" Bill Ben did the same. "Smells like life."

Lewis laughed. "If you mean it's complicated, yeah, just like it." Bill Ben laughed with him.

"Anyway, if you want to help out here, learn something, I work on the beer in the mornings before we open for lunch. Just knock at the side door that says 'No Admittance.'"

Lewis nodded.

"For now, let's go sample the latest brown ale I made. I called it Dingdong because of the chocolate notes, but let's see what you think."

Titania poured three pints and set them at a high table with four chairs. The restaurant was down for the night, road noise taking over for the hum of diners and staff. The ale was strong and bitter, with a finish that tasted slightly smoky. Lewis sipped his slowly. Bill Ben explained at length how he'd made the beer, provided so many details they washed over Lewis in incomprehensible waves. Titania made pleasant noises and stole worried glances at Lewis.

"Bill Ben, that is really fascinating, but I think Lewis is about to collapse," she interrupted when the dissertation on specific gravity got especially hot and heavy. The gravity of the earth was affecting Lewis' eyelids.

"I'm fine. I just need some sleep. Last night was a little wild."

"You said. Your friend almost died?"

"What? Is that why you were late?" Bill Ben was suddenly very concerned.

Lewis explained the Tom situation at a high level,

assuring them his friend was okay, just hungover.

"Christ," Bill Ben mused.

"I can talk to him, if you want," Titania offered. Lewis gave her a questioning look. "I have ... experience with that kind of thing." She rubbed her hand on her forearm, not smoothing the rumpled roses tattooed there, but soothing the nerves underneath.

Lewis thanked her and pushed his half-finished beer away. If he didn't get out of here, he would fall asleep on the tabletop. He said his good-byes and wandered into the night, desperate for rest.

Since the buses were long shuttered for the night, he wandered aimlessly from pool to pool of yellow lamp glow until he realized he was on Burnside. Stumptown Ethical Atheists Mission was also closed, but the night button worked, and Eve peeked out around the door after a few minutes.

"Lewis! Good to see you!" she exclaimed, despite clearly being woken from sleep. Her gray braid was frizzily nestled against the shoulder of her lavender flannel pajamas. The shirt said she was the World's Best Grandma.

Lewis took a deep breath and stared down the stairs. He desperately needed a shower, a meal, and probably somewhere to sleep that wasn't a bus shelter. He steeled himself and descended into the mission, telling himself the darkness below and the darkness above were the same thing.

CHAPTER 28

Lewis opened his eyes and panicked. There was no light, and he didn't know where he was. Every smell was wrong, even his own body. He smelled the sourness of days of sweat, his breath was like death. He pushed himself violently up and sprang from the cot, flinging the thin blanket aside. He could feel the earth pressing down. He hunched over, squeezing his eyes shut in anticipation of the crushing weight of the building above him. He stumbled forward and tripped over another cot and sent it clattering in a heap across the floor.

He made a terrified noise, swinging his arms wildly, blindly.

SMACK! One flailing hand found a landmark, unmistakably the side of someone's face.

"OOW! LEWIS! YOU'RE OKAY! STOP!" The man grabbed his arm, trying to calm him down. Lewis responded with an uncalm shove that sent his would-be savior backward onto the floor.

"LEWIS! STOP!" Another voice joined the first, Eve's, and it was enough to get through to him. He realized he knew the first voice. He'd just pushed Rami down. He stood, heaving breaths in and out, blinking, seeing the room, Rami, Eve, and several other people he'd woken from sleep. Their faces were annoyed or resigned. Outbursts in the mission were not welcome, but they weren't a novelty.

Rami got up off the floor and approached Lewis, keeping his hands to himself this time. He was in street clothes with his long hair loose, disheveled from the fall. He rubbed his cheek. "Come on, man, let's get you out of here so these folks can get back to sleep." Eve stood back against the wall, letting Rami take the lead, then following Lewis out of the room. She closed the door behind him with a quiet click.

Low lights were on in the hall. Lewis followed Rami back to the cafeteria, but he didn't take a seat. The stairs out were calling. His breathing was still ragged.

"So." Rami leaned against a table a few feet away. "You want to tell me what's going on? You look and smell like shit, and you woke up in some kind of mental health situation." He was calm, but his manner was less friendly than commanding. This was clearly not his first "mental health situation."

Lewis tried to calm his breathing and got it under control enough to breath a small, "Sorry." Eve exchanged a small nod with Rami and slipped out of the room.

"I'm gonna ask this once, and I expect a truthful answer. Are you on something? Did you take drugs?"

That was absurd enough to shock Lewis back to some semblance of reality. "No!" he barked. "That was Tom. I just had a beer."

"One beer? Tom?" Rami's deep voice was thick with skepticism.

"Okay, two, but only one at a time. I didn't even finish the DingDong one. It was too thick."

"Ding what?" Rami's posture softened. "What are you talking about?"

Lewis let out a deep breath. His body wanted to bolt up the stairs, but the opportunity to let out some of the last two days couldn't be ignored. He pulled out a chair and poured out his story. He only left out things that would reveal his biggest secret.

Rami's face when through a full range of tragic and comic expressions. "So...you went on kind of a date, had a beer for the first time, saved your young friend from an overdose, learned how to write, slept in a bus shelter, and worked a dishwashing shift at a place where you are going to learn how to brew beer." He shook his head and chuckled. "You remind me of me," he murmured.

Lewis was relieved his friend wasn't mad. "Yeah, except I don't think it was a date. So, I came here to sleep, but I don't like being underground. In my culture, it's forbidden."

"Your culture? Canadian?"

"Well, the specific people I grew up with. I guess you would call it a cult."

"Okay, I can work with that. You can just tell people you're claustrophobic."

"Oh. Okay." Lewis sighed. "I really need a shower and some clean clothes. And about a day of sleep, but not here. I won't be able to sleep here."

Rami got up and walked past him, clapping him on the shoulder. "Go clean up. I'll explain to Eve. She doesn't like drugs, but your weird life is what it is without chemical enhancement."

Half an hour later, in clean clothes and reeking of the pine shampoo, Lewis made a better apology to Eve for the ruckus and left. Rami walked him to the bus stop and stayed until the early routes started. In the light of dawn, his face showed some swelling and redness from Lewis' blow.

"I am so sorry about that," Lewis said, pointing to

his own cheek.

"Naw, I've had worse. Just don't try it again, or I'll have to use the kung-fu of my people on you." He paused, clearly weighing his next words, deciding. "You are handling this transition pretty well, Lewis, but it would probably be advisable to be more deliberate about what you do and reveal."

Lewis couldn't get another word out of him after that cryptic statement. The bus came and carried the harthoth across the river to Reed. He walked to the canyon still thinking about Rami's words. He didn't feel he'd been particularly careless with what he told people, but he knew a lot of information had been disclosed in other ways.

His spot in the rhododendrons felt safe. He looked up at the leaves, his head resting on his hands, and thought about what to do next. All the people in his life here had claims on him now, he realized, because he'd opened himself up to them. Fled the expectations of an old life to build bewildering new ones in a place he barely understood.

A pang of homesickness surprised him. Thinking of his mother, and Manura, he hoped they were okay. He knew his absence didn't make a difference one way or the other, but he didn't want bad things for them. He just didn't want their things for him. He wished he could tell them.

As he drifted into sleep, a thought snapped him back to wakefulness. He couldn't tell his family anything from here, but that wasn't the only way to put those thoughts into the world. He dug in his things for the notebook and pencils Chloe had given him. On the first page, in laborious block letters, he printed:

FAMILIES ARE HARD. THEY EXPECT YOU TO

DO WHAT THEY SAY, AND THEN THEY EXPECT YOU TO DO WHAT THEY DIDN'T SAY, TOO. BE RESPONSIBLE MEANS BE LIKE ME. BE QUIET MEANS LISTEN. BE MORE LIKE YOUR BROTHER MEANS WHY DIDN'T I STOP AT ONE?

As a joke, it wasn't the worst, or the best, but it was first. Lewis smiled and drifted off with his notebook splayed on his chest.

CHAPTER 29

Lewis managed to wake up on a schedule that got him to the bus stop to get to work on time, but he was absolutely ravenous. There were some strips of dried meat in his pack that were a little worse for wear, but they were better than nothing.

He had to fast-walk through campus to the bus stop. He had one of his bags this time, carrying his notebook and pencils in case something funny occurred to him on the bus ride.

"Lewis! Lewis Clark!"

He turned to see Dr. Perkins hurrying after him. He considered sprinting away at top speed, but she reached him before he made up his mind. He tried to look like he was in a hurry.

"Hi! I was just wondering if you'd heard from Jack recently. I sent him a message and haven't gotten a reply. I know his internet is pretty limited, but it's unlike him to ghost people."

"Jack?" Lewis didn't place the name immediately.

"Dr. Miller? Jack?" Dr. Perkins was probing now. She definitely had suspicions.

"Oh, yeah, I don't usually call him Jack, sorry. He's been hard to reach, yeah. I haven't heard from him either." Bald truth.

"Who else is supervising your project? What did you say it was, again?"

He knew he shouldn't say anything, make an excuse and run away, but more evasion was going to cause this woman to dig deeper. He could feel it. Thinking about conversations he'd overheard while scrounging, he improvised some big words.

"Sociocultural Implications of Illegal Employment and the Underground Economy."

Dr. Perkins was surprised by the answer. "What? Is that why you're working at that bar?"

"I don't think I'm supposed to talk about that," Lewis said as he took a few steps toward the bus stop. "I have to go now, bye." Dr. Perkins threw several more questions at his back, including one about his bag, what tradition was it modeled after? He kept walking, fast, and didn't look back.

He barely made the bus, and as it pulled away, he saw Dr. Perkins watching it, arms crossed and completely unsatisfied with his answers. He turned to a page in the back of his notebook and printed the name of the fictitious project he'd made up. He had no doubt it would come up again.

The bar was busy, and he was able to throw himself into the work and avoid thinking about all the ways he'd possibly compromised his cover. He decided he'd better learn more about Canada. Learning about a country from stand-up comics might leave a few knowledge gaps.

The next two days were blessedly uneventful, work and sleep. He felt recharged enough to brave the cafeteria, though he watched over his shoulder for Dr. Perkins while he walked through campus.

Chloe and Tom were arguing about whether staying on campus during the summer was pathetic or brilliant.

"If you go home, it's all parents looking over your shoulder and asking for 'quality time' every weekend. At least if I stay here, I can take one seminar and get them off my back." Tom's hair was blue and standing stiffly out from his head, matching his glittery blue eyeshadow.

"Get drugged out of your mind, you mean," Chloe retorted. She had short pigtails in, wearing a t-shirt featuring the hind end of a housecat, complete with butthole.

"Ooo, one point to Chloe," Tom sneered. He noticed Lewis standing next to the table with his tray full of leftovers and his face full of worry. He had the grace to look embarrassed. "She doesn't mean like the other night, Lewis. That was the result of a series of unfortunate decisions that will not be repeated. Not in that order, for sure."

Lewis sat down, keeping his face neutral. "My friend wants to talk to you about that."

"Your *friend*? Tell us about this development," Chloe demanded.

"My *friend* works at the bar, and she said—"

"*She?*" Chloe was leaning across the table.

"Titania. She said she has some experience she could share."

Tom shook his head while Chloe processed this new information. The look on her face made Lewis want to change the subject as quickly as possible.

"I have my notebook!" he announced.

"Uh huh." Chloe was not so easily distracted.

"I wrote jokes in it!"

"Can I read them?" she asked, interested despite herself.

"NO." Lewis was shocked by the request he should have anticipated.

"Oh, come on," she wheedled.

"No. Not until I've worked on them. Besides, I don't think you're supposed to read jokes in a notebook."

"So, you'll perform them for us?" Tom asked, smirking. He knew he was stirring the pot.

"Yeah, I will," Lewis said. He stuffed a quarter of a bagel in his mouth. Around the glob of bread, he said, "Im fack, I wool do ih ohn sage."

"What?"

He swallowed, the clump slowly sliding down his throat. "In fact, I will do it on stage. At Numbknots open mic night."

Saying it out loud made his stomach consider rejecting the wad of bagel, and a chill went from his braid to his testicles, but now that he'd said it, it was going to have to happen.

"This, I will need to see," Chloe said, an

unreadable expression under her perfectly arched brows.

CHAPTER 30

Lewis was early enough to catch Bill Ben in the brewery before the lunch prep started. The smell was earthy and mildly unpleasant, like a heavily wet field in autumn. The tang of chlorine undercut the bready moisture hanging in the air.

The process was simpler than Lewis expected, but full of "magic." The grains were boiled, with hops added at "the magic moment" according to Bill Ben's description, and then cooled. After it had cooled, the wort was transferred to fermentation tanks and yeast was added. Another "magic moment" told the brewer when to move to conditioning. Roughly two weeks later, the beer could be filtered (or not) and packaged in kegs for the bar. There were a lot of science terms involved that might as well have been magic.

"I don't sell anything in bottles or cans, and I don't rent kegs, so I don't pasteurize," Bill Ben said. Lewis nodded, though he had no idea what pasteurizing would do. He imagined the kegs sitting in a field of grass with cows milling around. That did seem unnecessary.

"How did you learn to do this?" Lewis asked.

"I started at home in the bathtub. When I realized I had a feel for it, I took a class at the community college. Anybody can make a fermented drink, Lewis, but keeping the wee beasties under control is an art."

"Beasties?"

"Yeah, the yeast? They're alive. Little fungi, technically, not beasties, but they transform the beer by eating the sugars from the grains and burping and farting out gasses." Bill Ben laughed at the look on Lewis' face. "Food is weird, man, you don't even know. Some of the things I worked with in culinary school would curl your toes."

Lewis liked the sanitation area. It felt like his dish room. He realized he thought of it that way. "His" dish room, with pride in his work there. He had a brief pang, knowing his clan on Mt. Adams would never understand. He was proving himself in a way they couldn't grasp, in a place they didn't know about, doing something they wouldn't appreciate.

The shadow must have crossed his face, because Bill Ben clapped him on the shoulder. "You okay, man? You looked like you got bad news for a second."

"I'm great," he said. It was true, even if some regret was mixed in.

Jaxopher showed up for his lunch shift, so Lewis had a few hours to kill in downtown Portland. He walked uptown to Pioneer Courthouse Square.

Competing musicians busking created a cacophony of reggae drums and shrieking synthesized violin. It was a warm June day, the midday sunlight bright in a cloudless blue sky. His flannel was just a little too warm for the day, and his scalp felt damp with light sweat.

A man with a shopping cart piled high with black trash bags caught his eye and asked if he had change. A dog of indiscriminate breed and age sat on the sidewalk next to the man, sniffing the air in a testing way. The dog lifted one lip and gave a half-hearted growl. "Stoppit, Wolfie," the man said, pushing the dog's muzzle lightly away. Wolfie laid down but didn't take his eyes off Lewis.

Lewis didn't know how to respond. He realized he hadn't seen the man, not really, until he spoke. Now he stood and stared. There was a thick layer of grime on pale skin. Dark hair covered his head and most of his face, sticking out at angles. His beard was shot through with silver strands. He was thin under bulky layers of clothes. His boots were cracked and held together with tape.

"Well?" the man challenged. "You got something or just stop for the show?"

Lewis blinked. He fished in his pocket and drew out a twenty. Bill Ben was still paying him in twenties every night, and he had a big stack of them stashed away. He carried a few everywhere now. He held the bill out to the man, who snatched it before he could change his mind. Settling his face onto his chest, the man feigned sleep, ending the interaction.

He wasn't asleep, because he nudged Wolfie's muzzle again when a growl escaped, but Lewis got the hint.

Walking again, Lewis considered his own situation. He wasn't that far removed from living on the sidewalk like the man and his dog. What was the difference? He recognized his own luck, but he also had a back-up plan. He had a home of last resort if things went as bad as they must have for that guy. His living situation and under-the-table job were precarious, but he could crawl home and be taken back.

At least, he thought so. The thoughts of the morning, the foreignness of his life here in Portland intruded. For the first time, he considered the possibility he had it wrong. It might not be a sure thing. Would they take him back after he fled his responsibilities? How much of an outsider had he become?

Unsettled, he turned back toward the river and the dish room at Numbknots, ready for the steam and rush to keep him from thinking much of anything at all.

CHAPTER 31

The next morning, the cafeteria at Reed was noticeably empty. There were a few students scattered around, but the normal low hum of conversation was missing. The scrounge table was also very light. Lewis found Tom eating at a table by himself, wearing a lime green beret and matching shoes.

"Where is everybody?" he asked.

"Summer break. Most of them left yesterday—you must have been gone most of the day if you didn't notice."

"Does everyone leave?" That was going to complicate life for Lewis. No more free food and showers.

"No, I'm staying. Some of us would rather go insane here."

Tom wouldn't elaborate, so they talked about the summer and how Tom would fill the hours he wasn't in seminar. A part-time work-study job was going to justify his housing.

"The rest of the time, I will be exploring the

cosmos," Tom said, waving one hand in a semi-circle.

"Don't get lost," Chloe interjected, plopping down next to Lewis. Tom's face soured.

"Are you taking a seminar, too?" Lewis asked.

"No, I just stay so the lease on the house is secure. The other girls are getting their stuff out now. My parents wouldn't know what to do with me for a whole summer without a camp to send me to." Her tone was light, but there was something sharp underneath it.

"I guess I'll cancel my summer in the Alps, then," Lewis said. Tom giggled, but Chloe frowned at him.

"You aren't going anywhere, are you?" she asked.

Lewis shook his head, seeing her relax. He was a little surprised at how much it seemed to matter to her.

After breakfast, she followed him out of the cafeteria. "What are you doing today?"

Lewis had planned to head to the brewery, but he didn't have to be to Numbknots until his dish shift. He shrugged. "I don't have to be to work until later."

"I don't want to go home right now. I'd be in the way while they move all their stuff."

"Lilith has some help getting her coffin down the stairs?"

"Her army of bat minions will fly it down on their tiny rabid backs," Chloe deadpanned.

Their laughter broke some undefined tension between them. They wandered into Reed Canyon in the warming day, chattering about what Chloe would do with her days and what Lewis was doing with his nights.

Lewis realized they were getting close to his rhododendrons and stopped. He thought Chloe knew he slept out here, but he wasn't ready for anyone to know where. The thought of his one private place being known made him feel panicky.

"What?"

"I just remembered, I need to be at work early."

"Really? You just remembered that?" She didn't buy it. The tension descended again, thick enough to deaden her expression.

"Yeah." Lewis didn't elaborate.

"Fine. See you around." Chloe turned and walked back toward the college without another word.

Lewis felt like he should say something or run after her, but he didn't know what to say or do. She was hurt, even he could see that, but more lies would make it worse, and the truth would leave him exposed. He sighed and watched her go. He kept doing the wrong thing with her, but the right thing was elusive.

The restaurant was quiet, so he wandered out of his dish room with a rack of glassware, setting it down where Titania could easily put them away.

"Hey you," she said, smiling at him.

"Hey. Slow night?" There were two men sitting at the back of the room watching the television intently. When the golfer on the screen made a particularly bad shot, they winced in unison and picked up their beers.

"Yeah, it's just those guys, watching golf like they bet their houses on it."

"Do people do that? Bet their houses?"

"Some do, yeah, but usually only once," she answered.

Lewis had thought about what he was going to say at this moment for several days, including writing a little speech down in his notebook in big block letters, but all his prepared words flew out of his head.

"You have no work tomorrow?" he asked. Titania chuckled. "I mean, I could not work if you aren't working. We could not work together."

"I was planning on not working," she replied, nodding with exaggerated enthusiasm. Her locs bobbed. She was wearing a gold tank top and jeans with a torn knee tucked into high-top canvas shoes.

Lewis knew she was teasing him and didn't mind. He remembered the gist of his speech. "I heard the roses were blooming at the Rose Garden and wanted to see them, if you want to go with me. We can look at the roses together." Titania had a large rose tattooed on her arm, twining around one bicep. He'd overheard some elderly men talking about the International Rose Test Garden on the bus and found out it was near the Oregon Zoo.

Titania looked down at the bar for a moment, and Lewis knew she was going to say no.

"Sure. I have to change some other plans, but June is the best time to see the roses, especially on a day when I have no working to do." She winked at him and started putting the glasses away.

Happy that he'd managed to get the invitation out and ecstatic about the answer, Lewis trotted back to the dish room on deep fat scented air. Bill Ben looked up and grinned, shaking his head slightly.

At payout time, there was an extra twenty in the pile. "What's this?" Lewis asked. "Did I get a raise?"

"No, I'm sorry to say, you did not get a raise. That's a little bonus for you to spend tomorrow." Bill Ben pulled some paperwork in front of him and peered at it, making a show of doing business owner things.

Lewis knew he was dismissed, but his curiosity got the better of him. "Why?"

Bill Ben sat up and pushed his chair back. "I don't know how well you know Titania yet, but I've known her for a very long time. She's spent a long time trying to become herself, but she hasn't quite gotten there. I would love to see her embrace that."

Lewis wasn't sure he understood. "But why give me extra money?"

"I have a feeling you're a good tour guide, Lewis, in the land of becoming yourself. Or maybe you get lost together. Either way, it works."

Bill Ben went back to his busywork, and Lewis stood. If his boss wanted to be cryptic, he would. It wasn't going to make him turn down the money.

As he left the office, Bill Ben cleared his throat. Lewis turned. "By the way, Lewis, think about what you might need to do to work here legally. If things work out, you might want to stay longer than I think you had planned."

Lewis nodded, but his stomach suddenly felt sick. He hadn't thought anything needed to change if he stayed. Seeing how naive he'd been in those few words made him feel small and stupid. He left the bar and wandered along the river, walloped by the complication of the future.

CHAPTER 32

The Rose Garden was a jewel box with gemstones that perfumed the air like a circle of elders anointed in ceremonial oils. Rows of thorny plants labeled named "Honey Nectar" and "Thomas Becket" vied for attention with softer varieties like "Peace."

After a few rows, the flowers started to look the same to Lewis. The difference between a floribunda rose and a hybrid tea rose seemed to be nothing. The scent was a little overwhelming. He could pick out different flowers, hundreds of them, but they combined into an overwhelming wall of scent he had to try to ignore. Titania stuffed her nose in so many she couldn't be smelling them properly, but she persisted.

Lewis' attention was on Titania. She'd worn a gauzy white blouse which moved playfully in the small breeze. Her leggings were black, matching her headband and sandals. In his usual jeans and flannel outfit, Lewis felt like a weed.

"Look at this!" she enthused, pointing to a white bloom with a froth of ruffled petals. "This one is called 'Proud Titania,' Lewis." He made a show of smelling it, though he could have identified that one from a block away. The rose didn't suit Titania at all.

"I think they misnamed that one," he said.

"What do you mean?" She seemed disappointed.

"There's no mystery there. It's just a big white blob."

Titania laughed. "The Queen of Faerie probably isn't so straightforward. Maybe there are deadly bugs hiding in it."

Lewis grimaced. "I was thinking of you. Now I'm a little scared you have deadly bugs hidden somewhere."

"I might, watch yourself," she said, grinning.

The sun was behind her, making the outline of her body a shadow in glowing gauze. Her eyes were dark and brown like his, he realized. Lewis looked into them for a moment and forgot to breathe.

When he did remember to breathe, he took in a lot of air and managed to get something down the wrong way. The coughing was immediate and dramatic. An emotion he couldn't read passed quickly over Titania's face, then she whacked him on the back a few times.

They wandered the rows for a few more minutes while he cleared out whatever he'd inhaled.

"So, are you going on stage next week?" Titania asked with studied casualness.

"Next week?" Lewis hadn't known open mic night at Numbknots was coming up so soon. He had a lot of material written in his notebook, but it wasn't in any cohesive form. He hadn't tried any of it on anyone. He didn't even have it organized in types of jokes. He'd finished the book by the comedian he admired, and knew more from that about what he needed, but he didn't have a clue how to make what he had into what he thought he needed. Terms like "self-referential" seemed easy enough to understand, but doing it was something else.

Titania was looking at him expectantly. Suddenly, it was particularly important to him to do what she expected whether he knew how or not. "Yes, I am going to get up on that stage and tell jokes next week."

The rest of the afternoon blurred into an hour of panicked, distracted pleasantness. All Lewis could think about was getting back to his notebook and planning his act, at the expense of the beautiful day. Titania felt the vibe and asked if he was ready to go, making some excuses about her own chores to let him off the hook.

"Yeah, I should work on my material," he admitted. "It's a little rough." It was a lot rough.

"Let's ride the train back in. I don't feel like dealing with an Uber."

They sat together on the MAX, mostly in silence, watching lights flash by in the tunnel outside.

"You okay?" Titania asked.

Clearly, she was picking up on his tension. He chose a handy scapegoat. "I don't like tunnels. It's too much like being underground."

Titania frowned. "We are underground, though.

This is a subway. I think it's a really deep one, actually. One of the deepest in the states."

Lewis stopped breathing. He thought of the times he'd used the train without even knowing he was underground. What had he assumed? That there was some reason to have a big concrete casing on the train above ground? He felt an adrenaline spike and shoved it down. If he gave into it here, what would happen? He couldn't exactly run off the train, and stopping it would mean it *stayed* underground. He squeezed his eyes closed and forced himself to breathe in small, shallow gasps.

Titania grabbed his hand and squeezed it. "Hey, hey," she murmured. "You're okay. We're almost there. Hey."

Lewis took her hand in both of his and tried not to crush it.

"Try this," Titania said. "Breathe in for four, hold your breath for four, breathe out for four, hold your breath for four."

Lewis did a ragged version of box breathing until Titania told him they were above ground. He opened one eye, seeing daylight. He could smell his own sweat, and her hand felt slick in his damp grip. He let it go, wiping his palms on his jeans.

"I used to feel like that a lot," she said. "I felt like the next thing I did was going to be the biggest mistake of my life, even if I was just ordering coffee or taking a quiz. I did some stupid shit to deal with it."

Lewis took a big shuddering breath, embarrassed.

Titania's kindness had gotten him through the crisis without making a scene, but he wasn't sure what he should say.

"Last time I felt like that, I bolted through downtown Portland and got stopped by the police." Titania's eyebrows lifted.

"Look at you, then, you didn't even cause a scene. I guess the tour of the haunted Portland Underground is out, though," she teased.

"The what? Why would anyone do that?" Lewis was aghast. "Is it haunted by the people who died on the tour before you?"

Titania laughed, taking his hand lightly in hers. "Probably, yes. It's an unexpectedly long tour."

CHAPTER 33

When the train stopped, Lewis bolted for the door. Titania hurried after him. His panic made their good-bye awkward. After a clumsy, short hug, Lewis and Titania went their separate ways. He trotted to his bus stop and rode back to Reed, hurrying to his spot in the canyon. He had five days to get ready for Numbskulls at Numbknots, and his mind was racing with where to even start.

Looking through his notebook helped, but he needed another opinion. He wandered back out of the canyon and knocked on Tom's door.

The creature who opened the door didn't promise to be much help. Tom had transformed himself into a green-skinned alien in a leathery, strappy top with tight black pants. His pupils were half the size of his eyes, with just the smallest ring of iris showing around the edges.

"Ohhhh, hello, Lewis," he sing-songed. "I was expecting someone else."

"Aliens?" Lewis asked.

Tom laughed very hard at this, nearly falling over.

Lewis knew it wasn't that funny. As Tom struggled to collect himself, a trio of very loud young men in full costume came out of the stairwell and caught sight of Lewis at the door.

"Oh, Tommy, who's the bear?" asked a tall blonde dressed as a bumblebee. "I didn't know you invited a lumberjack. A ginger, too! Bzzzzz, bzzzzzz!"

"Shhhhhh, nooooooo," Tom said. "He's a *Canadian*." This made them all laugh again.

"Make him come with us!" squealed the squirrel around fake buck teeth, sounding like "uth."

Tom clapped his hands. "Yes! This is a wonderful idea! Lewis, you should come with us."

"Uhh...where are you going?"

"Out!" they all chorused at once.

Lewis smiled. Their exuberance was charming, but he really needed to work on his material. He also needed a shower.

"No thanks, guys, not tonight. I have to work on some things." The quartet pouted as one.

"C'mon, Lewis," Tom wheedled. "You just work all the time and never have any fun. Come with. When was the last time you did anything fun? Huh?" He was leaning on Lewis heavily, eyes slightly unfocused.

"I do fun things!" Lewis protested.

"Like what?" Tom asked, rolling his eyes. Lewis shrugged, not willing to go into his afternoon with Titania in front of strangers. "Okay, Mr. Mystery," Tom grumbled.

"That's Mr. Canada to you," said the blond, setting

off a round of giggling in the group. He put one hand on Lewis' arm. "If you change your mind, we'll be over at Dante's."

"Eventually, we'll be at Dante's," broke in the squirrel. They all laughed again at some private joke and crowded into Tom's room to do some "pre-gaming."

Lewis wandered out onto Woodstock Boulevard, seeing lights spilling out in the early summer night from houses and businesses. He'd come back later to get a shower when the boys were off doing whatever they had planned. Showing up in Tom's room in a towel seemed like it would be especially awkward with these particular friends there.

He couldn't help worrying about the last time Tom had been recreating with substances. Tom was out of it, and they hadn't even left his room. He sighed.

Lewis went into a restaurant advertising the best sausages in the world and ordered one with a beer. Sitting at a picnic table outside, he pored through his notebook, rewriting the jokes he thought would work on a page toward the middle. He hardly tasted the food and found his glass empty sooner than he expected. The beer loosened him up enough to try a few jokes out loud to himself.

"I don't take drugs, I'm weird enough without that," he muttered. "If I tried that, I might become so weird, I'd suddenly be normal. 'Hello, I'm Lewis, and I'll be your accountant today.'" He wasn't sure about the accountant bit. He kind of knew accountants were boring, but he didn't know what they *were*, not really.

"I don't take drugs, I'm naturally weird," he tried. "If I took drugs, it would make me so weird, I'd be normal. 'Hello, I'm Lewis and I have a stable job and get eight hours of sleep.'" He couldn't tell which one was better. Maybe they both stunk.

He thought of Tom again, and he felt his worry intensify. It was distracting. He sighed and closed his notebook. He picked up his dishes and put them in the bus tubs by the door.

He trotted back to the woods and stashed his notebook, changing his shirt for a clean one and grabbing some additional cash in case he needed it.

"How do I get to Dante's?" he asked the bus driver, a large black man with a stiffly pressed TriMet uniform.

"Dante's? Okay. You go back over the river and head down to Burnside. You know Burnside?"

Lewis realized he did—the mission and Powell's were also on Burnside. He nodded.

"Okay, it's in the 300 block, closer to the river. There's a big sign, you can't miss it." The driver shook his head. "They're gonna eat you alive," he muttered as Lewis walked to a seat further back.

The atmosphere at the club was raucous. The marquee proclaimed "Glitter DaFunk and the Funkelles" were playing for a limited engagement. The line outside was short and sparkling with a mixture of costumes, sequins, and mismatched

Portland casual. Lewis paid the cover and went inside, choosing to stand by a long bar running the length of the balcony level. A woman of indeterminate age wearing black spandex with impossibly long eyelashes asked what he wanted to drink.

"A beer?"

"What kind of beer, sweetie?"

"An IPA?" he guessed. A second beer seemed acceptable in the party atmosphere.

"Okay, sure. Be right back." She brought a glass of wheat-colored beer with a short head and took his money. He gave her back two dollars from the change, and she smiled brightly. "Thanks, sweetie. I'm Donna. I'll be back around when you need another one. You been here before?" Lewis shook his head. "You know what this is about, right? Cabaret?" Lewis shrugged. Donna chuckled. "Oh, this will be great! You enjoy!"

Lewis was less interested in the entertainment. He scanned the room for Tom and his group. After a minute or two of wondering if they were even there, he spotted them at a table down by the stage. He was relieved. He considered joining them for a moment. The bumblebee chose that same moment to let out a long ear-splitting howl. Maybe not.

A fanfare sounded and the house lights dimmed. The show that followed was in turns marvelous and bewildering to Lewis. Tom and his gang were close enough to interact with the performers, hooting and yelling answers at the stage, and everyone seemed not just to tolerate this but expect it. The third act in was a drag queen with a comedy set, and Lewis hung on every word and gesture. Lola Canola was vibrant, filthy, and funny, a tall, dark brunette with aqua sequins in every place her shiny, oiled skin wasn't on display. After all those years of listening to comedy on his little radio, Lewis was finally seeing the real thing, and it was transcendent and intimidating. He'd thought the open mic night was a high level of performance, but there was a gulf between that and capturing an audience this way.

He realized he should be comforted. Amateur night at Numbknots wouldn't be professionals like Lola. The audience at Dante's was something else, too. They were there to have a good time, hell or high heels. Lola left the stage with the mic in one hand and sashayed over to the table where Tom's group was sitting.

"Hello, boys," she cooed. "I see you got my memo. I really need to get *buzzed* tonight."

Lewis laughed at the reaction of Tom's friend. With the spotlight on the table, he could see him well. He couldn't see Tom, though. Tom's drink was tipped over on the table, a puddle of liquid shining like quicksilver. Tom was not in his chair. Nor was he at the bar, or anywhere Lewis could see. All of his friends were at the table with Lola.

Lewis felt his stomach twist. It could be a trip to the bathroom, but the spilled glass gave him a bad feeling. He left his unfinished beer on the balcony bar and pushed through the crowd down the stairs.

CHAPTER 34

The crowd was thick, but fluid. Lewis was downstairs before Lola Canola left the table of Tom's friends.

"Oh, sweetie, who are you?" she purred, giving him a long look up and down. The spotlight glared.

"That's Lewith the Lumberthack!" the squirrel lisped, his plastic buck teeth crooked.

"Oooooo, he's a hairy one, isn't he?" Lola took a few small steps toward Lewis, carefully managing to stay in the circle of light. "How do you keep that beautiful hair combed? Need some help?" Lola let a hand glide down Lewis' shoulder, flipping his loosely tied queue with one long fingernail.

"No, thank you," he said into Lola's microphone. "I combed it yesterday."

The crowd roared. Lola put on a pouty face, but Lewis could see merriment in her eyes. "Anything else I could help you with? Maybe you have a log that needs to be felled?" She turned and yelled to the crowd, "TIMBER!" The crowd was delighted.

"I'm not actually a lumberjack," Lewis confessed.

"I'm a dishwasher."

Lola smiled with real warmth. "Well, Lewis the Not-actually-a-lumberjack, we all start somewhere. Good luck with that, honey, you can scrub my cups anytime." She gave Lewis an exaggerated wink and moved to the next table.

Tom's friends stood and grabbed him, laughing and delighted he'd made it after all.

"Tom said you wouldn't come!" the bumblebee exclaimed.

"Where is Tom?" Lewis asked, struggling to be heard over the continued crowd noise.

The guys looked around as if it had just occurred to them to wonder where Tom was. Lewis felt himself getting angry. If he'd taken Fliggo the harthoth out in the woods, knowing he wasn't very bright, he wouldn't let him wander off without noticing.

"Bathroom?" Tom's unicorn-themed friend shrugged.

Lewis looked for the bathrooms. Bumblebee grabbed his arm and pointed toward the back.

The men's room was wall to wall blackboards with everything imaginable scrawled on them, from real art to the mundane assertion that "Jimmy wuz here." It was also empty. The stall doors all hung a few inches open.

Lewis ducked back into the hallway, scanning both directions. Donna walked by with a tray of drinks, most of them pink, and took a step back when she realized it was Lewis.

"Everything okay, sweetie?" she said. The worry on her face mirrored his.

"I don't know," he said. "My friend, Tom, is missing from his table. His friends don't know where he is." When Donna didn't immediately spring into action, he decided to elaborate with something he'd heard Chloe say. "He's on drugs. He makes bad choices."

Donna nodded. "Okay, what does he look like? I have to get these drinks out, but I'll see if he's in the crowd somewhere."

Lewis brightened. "Oh, that's easy. He's green."

"Oh, the green alien boy? That's your Tom?" Donna grabbed his arm with her free hand. "He went out the back." When Lewis didn't react appropriately, she added, "Not by choice, sweetie. He was escorted out when he wouldn't stay out of the kitchen." She thought for a few seconds and made up her mind. "Stay here." She hustled out to the floor to deliver her drinks.

Lewis nearly bolted for the back during the two minutes it took for her to return. She handed her tray to another server and led Lewis toward the back.

"I'll let you out the back so you don't have to go around or set off the alarms. He's probably gone by now, but you can check."

"Thanks."

"Sure. A lot of these kids make bad choices. I'm glad someone is looking out for this one." Donna punched a code into a panel and let Lewis out into the dark alley. A dingy lamp cast a pool of light that gave up a few feet away.

As the door clicked shut behind him, Lewis was glad for his night vision. As the perfumed air of Dante's backstage waned, the alley stank of urine, vomit, and dumpster. Lewis' instincts were screaming. Tom might have stumbled off to who knows where, but it was just as likely he hadn't made it far. Looking behind dumpsters and calling Tom's name softly, Lewis searched the alley.

He was starting to believe Tom had wandered out of the alley when he heard something behind a pile of empty crates. The crates were having a tiny, localized earthquake. He ducked his head around, expecting to see an animal digging at the stack.

Tom was lying on his side, his face in a puddle of rejected alcohol and bar food. His body was seizing against the crates. Lewis had never seen a seizure, but he didn't need prior experience to know it was critically bad.

He picked Tom up and stood in the alley, holding the slight, trembling body in a wash of blank panic. His friend needed a hospital, he knew that much, but he had no idea where one was. There was one place he could take him for help.

It was only a few blocks to the Stumptown Ethical Atheists Mission. It was still early enough in the evening for the front door to be unlocked, and he managed to awkwardly turn the handle without dropping his burden. The seizure had stopped, but

Tom's body was limp now. He seemed on the verge of something worse, his breathing slower. Lewis' heart compensated by beating twice as fast as normal.

"EVE!" Lewis bellowed. "RAMI!" He flew downstairs, nearly knocking Eve over as she hustled to the entrance. There were a few stragglers from dinner, and the room smelled like roasted carrots and spices.

"Who is this?" Eve asked, quickly clearing a table. Rami hurried in from the kitchen, carrying a large red bag with a white cross on it. "What happened?"

"This is Tom. He took things. I don't know what. I found him in the alley at Dante's, and he was doing this." Lewis shook his body in an imitation of a seizure.

Eve nodded and grabbed Tom's head, peeling his eyes open and checking his pulse at his neck. "I think the Narcan, Rami."

Rami had the red bag unzipped into two halves and laid out on the table. He took a small spaceship-shaped item out and handed it to Eve. She stuffed it up Tom's nose and pushed the activator on the bottom.

"Now we give it a minute," she said.

"I'll get the ambulance," Rami said, pulling a phone out of his pocket and walking a few feet away. The diners had gone back to eating silently.

"Is he dying?" Lewis asked.

"Honestly, Lewis, maybe, and that is indescribably sad," Eve said, squeezing his arm. "Bringing him here was quick thinking. You gave him the best possible chance."

"The EMTs are on the way," Rami said. "It usually takes them about ten minutes to get down here."

Lewis was watching Tom. It seemed like his breathing was a little more normal, but maybe that was wishful thinking. "Is he better?"

Eve tried Tom's pulse again and listened to his breathing. "Yes, I think he's responding to the Narcan. That's lucky, since we didn't know what he took for sure. Rami, does he need another shot?"

Rami examined Tom's eyes and took his pulse. "It wouldn't hurt. He's still swimming around the bottom of the pool." Eve nodded and administered another dose.

Lewis felt helpless. All he could do was stand there, watching. He felt a flash of anger toward Tom's "friends," who hadn't stopped him from doing this to himself or realize he was dying in the alley while they enjoyed the show.

The EMTs banged the doors open at the top of the stairs, yelling identification and questions down. Rami bounded up the stairs to meet them, and the next few minutes were a bewildering blur of activity until they hauled the unconscious Tom up the stairs on a gurney. The snowfall of packaging and tape ends was the only evidence of the crisis. Eve bustled around picking it all up.

Rami hugged the petite woman lightly, and her body relaxed. "I wish they wouldn't do that," she breathed.

"Me too," Rami sighed. "Hey, Lewis, you want

dinner? A shower?"

Lewis realized he was wearing several layers of body odor, including vomit and fear. He nodded and headed for the room where they kept clean clothes. He was almost looking forward to smelling like he'd rolled in a dead pine tree.

CHAPTER 35

Rami was at a table when Lewis came out of the shower room in fresh clothes. He had a tray of hot food and a cup of coffee waiting. Lewis sat and pushed the coffee away, digging into the food as if he hadn't eaten the world's best sausage only hours earlier.

"You don't drink coffee?" Rami asked. His mellow demeanor was soothing after the crisis with Tom.

"No, that's worse than ditch water." Lewis would know, he'd tried to drink water around the campground at Takhlakh Lake. Ditch water was much preferable. Rami chuckled. "Will Tom be okay?" Lewis asked, half afraid he didn't want to know.

"He will probably live, this time, but I don't know about okay."

"What do you mean? Is he going to be different?"

Rami thought for a moment. "That's possible, but what I mean is that he might keep hurting himself if he doesn't figure out why he's doing it. Hiding from your problems, whether it's getting high or running away—it doesn't solve anything. It just creates more problems."

Lewis felt stung. "Sometimes the problems aren't your fault!" he exploded, causing Rami to sit back a few inches and narrow his eyes.

"I guess that struck a nerve," he said mildly.

Lewis decided to stop talking before he revealed any more of his own issues. Rami left to do something in the back and Lewis slipped out before any more truths could be laid at his feet.

He caught the last bus across the river and got off at Reed. He stood in a pool of lamplight for a long time, thinking about his next move. He desperately needed rest, but the idea of sleep was ludicrous. He turned away from campus and walked.

Chloe took a long time to come to the door. Her hair was a wild black tangle. In purple pajamas without makeup, she looked much younger. Her face creased in confusion as she tried to make Lewis' exhaustion square with his fresh clothes and pine scent.

"What happened to you?" she demanded, bringing him into the living room. Most of the furniture was gone, and Lewis sat heavily on the remaining couch beside her.

"It's not me," he answered.

Chloe's face crumpled. "That idiot!" she said, tears rolling down her face. "I knew he wasn't being careful." She grabbed a couch pillow and sobbed into it.

Lewis was alarmed by her reaction, and he wasn't even sure she knew who "he" was, though it was likely she'd guessed right. "Are you talking about Tom?" he asked.

Chloe snatched the pillow away from her face, slicing into Lewis with her look. "Of course we're talking about Tom? Who else do we both know? Who else would you feel obligated to inform me about in person? 'I'm sorry Chloe, but the second cousin of bus driver's grandma is dead?'"

Lewis blanched. He'd screwed this up without saying anything. He thought about Rami and Eve, how they had comforted each other after the paramedics left. He tentatively reached out a hand and placed it on Chloe's shoulder. "Tom is not dead, Chloe. Tom is in the hospital, and he will most likely recover." Her shoulder was trembling and sparrow delicate under his hand. He felt as crude and clumsy as his effort to comfort her.

Chloe pulled the pillow back and smacked it into his face. Hard.

"Why did you do that?" he spluttered.

"Why didn't you start with that? Instead, you come here IN CLEAN CLOTHES looking as if your only friend just died like it's some formal notification! Of course I assumed he was dead!" Chloe got up and stalked out of the room, muttering to herself.

Lewis wasn't sure if he should leave or wait or crumple in on himself until he no longer existed.

When Chloe came back ten long minutes later,

Lewis was still on the couch, holding the face-smacking pillow, but he was more irritated than confused. "Chloe—" he started.

"I know, I know," she cut him off. "I'm kind of waiting for that call, and I assumed. Tom needs a round in rehab. His parents might see it now, or they might not, and I'm pissed at him." She was still in her pajamas, but her hair was in pigtails and the smell of toothpaste lingered. "Wait." She looked Lewis in the eye. "How do you know about it? Were you with him?"

Lewis explained finding Tom behind the bar and the trip to the mission. The anger that had evaporated from Chloe condensed back over her in a luminescent cloud of rage.

"THOSE IDIOTS," she yelled. "I will get every single one of them expelled. No, no, I will kill them, and I will bury their stupid corpses under Hauser with the MG. I will…I don't know. It will not be good, I know that." Chloe punched another pillow.

"They aren't good friends," Lewis conceded. "They're just kids, though." He thought of some of the things he'd done at their age, his "teenage" equivalent, and sighed. For the first time, he felt separated from that younger self by something. Experience, loss, perspective, responsibility, he couldn't say. "So are you and Tom. Kids have to learn things the hard way."

Chloe was stock-still next to the couch, staring at him. "What did you just say?" she breathed, sounding as if she'd just lost all her oxygen.

"You learn things the hard way?" he tried.

"Because we're children?"

Lewis felt the danger, but he didn't know how to defuse the bomb. "Um. Yes?" The truth would shield him. Maybe.

Chloe was in front of him in three quick strides. She pushed him roughly back on the couch and leaned over him. Her mouth was on his before he knew what was happening, kissing him with more anger than passion.

Kissing, like laughter, was something the harthoth did not understand, and that included Lewis. The feel of Chloe's mouth on his set off a visceral reaction, a confusing mix of pleasure and disgust from the nerve endings in his face overwhelmed by shock and violation from his traditions. Lewis grabbed Chloe by the arms and shoved her away, trying not to use his full inhuman strength and barely managing not to throw her.

Chloe staggered back with a cry of pain that was clearly more than physical. Tears streaked her cheeks, glinting in the fairy lights.

"Chloe," Lewis said softly, "no."

The young woman hugged herself, rubbing her arms where Lewis had grasped them.

"It's *her*, isn't it?" she spat. "Your 'friend' from that bar."

Lewis felt the urge to protest, the words nearly came out of his mouth, but he realized it was true, at least partly. It wasn't the reason, though, and Chloe deserved honesty.

"No, it isn't that I like someone else. I just don't like you that way."

When Chloe grabbed the nearest object and hurled it at his head, he ducked and headed for the door.

"GET OUT!" she screamed, confirming his plan of action.

He heard something hit the door behind him and shatter. It felt like his heart. He'd saved Tom's life and lost both his friends all the same.

CHAPTER 36

After a night of staring into various darknesses trying to make sense of something, Lewis rode the bus across the river to Numbknots. Exhaustion made the scenery outside the window blur into one continuous shape. The bridges seemed even more chaotic than usual, like a row of increasingly half-assed experiments culminating in the Marquam's ugly concrete decks.

Bill Ben was in the brewery, sampling and testing his latest creation, a ruby ale he named "Lucy Loosey." He looked up when Lewis came in and set his equipment down on the stainless table.

"Dude, you look awful," he said, handing Lewis one of the barstools that served as the brewery's chairs.

"I feel awful," Lewis admitted, slumping onto the seat.

Bill Ben left the room and came back with a large glass of ice water and a hastily thrown together sandwich. He set it in front of Lewis and didn't speak until the food and water were gone. "What ran over you?" he asked.

Lewis felt a little better physically, but his mind was a mess. "I think I lost my two best friends last night."

Bill Ben's forehead wrinkled. "Like—they died?"

"No, no, well, one of them almost died, but the other one tried to kiss me, and I didn't know what to do."

"You didn't know what to do about your friend who was dying?"

"No, about the kiss. We don't do that in Canada."

Bill Ben chuffed a laugh until he saw Lewis was serious. "Damn, Lewis, you make Canada seem really unappealing. No wonder you left. So was Titania mad, or what? What was the misunderstanding?"

"Oh, no, it wasn't Titania." Lewis had an almost physical jolt of epiphany as several mental connections were made in circuits he hadn't realized were dark.

Bill Ben shook his head. "Your life is mysterious and way more complicated than I imagined. Do you need the day off to deal with it? I can probably scrounge around for coverage."

"No." Lewis said it with more force than he'd intended. "I mean, no, thanks, I don't want tonight off. I do need tomorrow night, though." The open mic night was looming over him, his lack of preparation making him queasy. He'd never said any of his jokes out loud in front of a person. It was terrifying, and it was the only anchor he had after the last 24 hours.

Bill Ben grinned. "You're really gonna do it, then? Titania said you were thinking about it. Man, I can't wait to see what you have."

Lewis was thrown off and irritated by Bill Ben knowing his business. The people in his life kept connecting in ways he didn't anticipate. He changed the subject, asking about the beer. He spent the rest of the morning blearily learning about brewing.

Bill Ben sent him for a nap at lunchtime in the office, which he sorely needed and wasn't long enough. He woke groggy and cranky. Titania tried to talk to him when she came to get the glasses, but he ignored her or answered in short grunts, pretending to be too busy with plate spraying to talk. He didn't know if he was supposed to tell her about Chloe or what he would say if he did. He broke almost a dozen plates trying to stack too many at a time and dropped an entire tray of glassware.

When he went to collect his cash at the end of the shift, Bill Ben and Titania were sitting in the office together, waiting for him with a beer and cheeseburger. He nearly turned and left without being paid.

"Get in here," Bill Ben said. Titania stood and pointed at the chair. Lewis felt a stirring of the old resentment at being told what to do, but his hunger overruled his resistance.

In the middle of his meal, they pounced.

"We are here—" Titania started.

"Lewis, you need to get your head out of your—"

Bill Ben cut her off.

"What Bill Ben *means* to say," Titania interjected, "is we noticed you were in a pretty bad mood tonight. You aren't yourself."

Lewis laughed, but it had a bitter tinge. "You have no idea," he said. Bill Ben and Titania exchanged a look. Lewis decided to tell part of the truth. "I haven't been able to practice my set in front of anyone. I went to do that last night, and ended up with an emergency and a *misunderstanding* to deal with instead."

"So do it," Titania said, leaning against the wall with her arms folded. Lewis could tell he'd upset her by being a jerk, but he could hardly look at her, thinking about how much he must have *misunderstood* her if he was so stupid about Chloe.

Lewis let out a long sigh. "I know, and I appreciate it, but I am so tired and I don't have my notes. I'll work on it tomorrow. It'll be fine."

Bill Ben shrugged. "No skin off my nose, the crowd kind of likes it when people bomb."

Titania glared daggers at him. "Lewis isn't the only one with his head up his ass."

"Yeah, well, I paid for a couple hundred dollars of broken dishes tonight, sue me," Bill Ben retorted. He sighed and turned to Lewis. "Man, I absolutely wish you all the best with that, but right now, you need to go wherever home is, sleep for about twelve hours, and come back fresh. You are so far off your game."

Lewis walked back to Reed Canyon in the dark, seeing everything and seeing nothing as his exhaustion threatened to knock him over. Under the rhododendrons, his sleep was fitful and wild with dreams he was in the harthoth clan meeting with clothes on, trying to get them off while the clan stared in silent disgust.

His notebook had several dozen pages of jokes and notes, amateurish in every sense. It was overwhelming trying to organize it into something coherent. He wished he could get help. He wandered over to the cafeteria to get some food and sat at a table with his scrawlings and the slim pickings from the scrounge. He laboriously copied them on a clean sheet in an order he thought might work, murmuring to himself.

"Hello, Mr. Clark. Working hard on your special project?" Dr. Perkins asked.

"Ah!" Lewis squeaked, scribbling a large black mark across the page before squashing his notebook closed in a mangled mess. This woman could give him a real challenge in a sneaking contest. "Sure, yes, hard at work," he said.

Dr. Perkins put on a bright and terrifying smile. "May I see it?" she asked.

"Nope."

"I thought since Jack seems to be unreachable this summer, maybe you would like some feedback. Or is he returning your messages?"

"Talked to him yesterday. All good." This was a terrible trap.

Dr. Perkins nodded as if she believed none of it.

"You may want to go talk to the registrar, Mr. Clark. While I can't access student records without a good reason, they couldn't even confirm you exist. There must be an issue with your paperwork."

Lewis played with his notebook for a moment, unsuccessfully smoothing the cover. "Thanks for letting me know," he answered. "I'll get that sorted out right away." He needed Dr. Perkins to go away. This was not helping.

Dr. Perkins smiled again, but her eyes were narrowed. She knew something was rotten, but she hadn't figured it out yet. She left him alone with his spiraling, compounding anxieties.

Lewis was able to get into Tom's building for a soap-less shower. There was no sign of Tom, but his room still had the crisscrossed "Caution" tape on the door. Lewis wished he knew how Tom was doing. There was no way for him to find out.

On the bus over the river, he practiced his set. It was only a few minutes long, but that was enough for a first timer. Along with the nerves, he felt the elation of following in his hero's footsteps. Tonight, he was going to perform stand-up comedy in front of an audience. People who actually knew how to laugh would watch him, and they would laugh because he *made* them laugh. His jitters and his wholly unearned beginner's confidence made his stomach hurt while everything around him was brighter, more beautiful. Even the Marquam Bridge had a good abutment day.

He was incredibly early, several hours. The stage wasn't set up and the sign-up list wasn't out. He sat at the bar and nursed a lager. Bill Ben saw him and smirked at his eagerness.

When the list finally hit the front podium, Lewis scrawled his name in big letters in the first slot. The hostess, a slight, pink-haired college student from Portland State, smiled and said, "Nice. Can't wait."

Lewis was still hunched over his notes at the bar with a quarter of his very warm lager when Titania came on shift. "Hey, you want a fresh one?" she said.

Lewis startled up, finding himself looking directly into her coffee-colored eyes from eighteen inches away. She was wearing a black button-up shirt tied in a knot over her stomach with black leggings. Her locs were tied back in a red bandanna. He forgot to breathe for a moment until Chloe and her failed kiss barged into his mind. He sucked in a breath and fell backward off his stool.

"I'm okay," he said, righting his stool and standing. He was fine, a little fall wasn't anything to his harthoth body. Titania was already halfway to him, looking worried. She put a neutral face on and came back on her side of the bar.

"Maybe you've had enough?" she said dryly.

"Oh, it's not that," Lewis muttered. "I guess I'm jumpy."

Titania poured him a soda anyway and cleared his pint glass. Lewis took a small exploratory sip and found the soda chemical and overly sweet, but the coolness was soothing. She punched something into the order system and a server came out with a veggie burger and fries ten minutes later for Lewis. The food settled him a little.

"When do you go on?" Titania asked after his dishes were cleared.

"First!" he announced, proud to be on top of things.

Her eyes widened. "Wow, brave," she said, but wouldn't elaborate. The brewpub filled up quickly as early evening brought downtown workers in for happy hour and grievance trading, and she was slammed. The mood was loud and excited. As people signed up on the sheet, they would join tables of supporters and friends ready to cheer them on. Lewis felt his earlier confidence ebb.

"Hey, buddy, you're on in a few," Bill Ben said, taking the empty stool next to him. "You ready?"

"I guess so." Lewis felt sick.

"Listen. There's something special about you, man, I knew it when I found you digging through my dumpster. I don't know how this is gonna go tonight, but you go out there and give it your best and see. Worst thing that happens is you're still the world's best goddamn dishwasher."

As weird as that pep talk was, it worked. Lewis nodded. Bill Ben clapped him on the shoulder and went back to work. The MC, a man with spiked hair, eyeliner, and sarcasm, warmed up the crowd with a few jokes about the "Numbknots" name, always easy to do, and introduced the first "victim."

"And tonight, we have a first timer here at

199

Numbskulls at Numbknots, Mr. Lewis Clark! Will he blaze new trails or die of dysentery?" Applause and mild laughter filled the room as Lewis walked on stage still clutching his abused notebook. Titania gave him an encouraging smile.

He stepped up to the microphone, getting too close and causing some feedback. "Sorry, sorry," he mumbled. The lights were blinding, and he couldn't see the individuals in the crowd. It was a mass of humanity, the hundreds of different scents mingling and separating.

"I grew up in Canada," Lewis said. The crowd noise quieted as he paused. He felt the pause stretch out too long. He whacked his notebook against his leg and tried again. "I grew up in Canada. I moved here recently and found out things are pretty different. Like, instead of hockey, you guys have baseball. I did some research on baseball the other day, because I assumed they were the same, but it turns out, baseball is hours long and no ice at all. In fact, if the field is covered with ice, you cancel the game! Weakness. In Canada, we bring the bad weather indoors to play in!"

Scattered chuckles greeted what was arguably the strongest joke until his closer. Lewis felt his skin flush as sweat traced electrical tracks down his back. He took a deep breath and plunged ahead.

CHAPTER 37

In the next few minutes, Lewis found out what it was like to go on first with an entirely mediocre and sometimes baffling set. The audience tried so hard to follow him, some of the women were nodding and smiling as if he were reciting his first ceremonial chant as a tiny harthoth. He felt like he was doing comedy for all the aunties. His spirits sunk with every indulgent ripple of laughter.

"Bridges are weird, right, and Portland has so many different kinds. It's like the city leaders went out of their way to make an unmatched set. Then they got to the Marquam, and said, 'Fuck it. Concrete.'"

Laughs from a few of the men on that one. Lewis wasn't reliably connecting with any group in the audience. His set was as scattered as the laughter. He was dying. He mumbled a joke and ruined the punchline. A rumble of conversation began at the tables as people gave up

"Wrap it up!" a man yelled. His friends turned and hushed him as soon as the words were out, but the punch had already landed more effectively than most of Lewis' material.

"Okay, yeah," Lewis stammered. "Don't set your hair on fire." A couple of the aunties applauded his comeback, weak as it was.

"Speaking of hair," he said, removing the tie from his braid. "You might have noticed I have some." He pulled the braid out, leaving the three large strands intact. "Bet you never saw someone get swallowed by his own hair."

This was tricky, and the only physical comedy he had in the set. He flipped his head down and fluffed his long hair into an enormous, coppery mass. The confused audience was quieter while he did whatever this was.

When he had everything exactly right, Lewis stood up quickly, giving his hair a violent toss toward the ceiling with a jerk of his head. As he'd hoped, the strands took a second to float down and conceal his entire head. It was something young harthoth did to impress each other. The longer it took your hair to settle, the more skill you claimed. He was the undisputed champion of his clan.

There was an audible gasp from a few people, then a light round of applause. Lewis parted his hair in front of his face and thanked them. He forgot to remind them of his name, walked the wrong direction to get offstage, and had to walk across the entire stage again to get away.

Once offstage, he kept walking, holding onto his hair with both hands. He walked right out the front door and onto the sidewalk. Quickly plaiting and containing his red hair as he moved, he put four blocks between himself and Numbknots before he felt safe enough to stop. There was an open wrought iron and wood slat bench facing the water. He sat, staring across the river canyon to the other half of Portland, and further, the mountains. It was a clear day, and Mount Hood stood enormous in the distance, a volcano cloaked in snow. The late setting summer sun behind him cast peach and lavender tones to the blue sky and snow-topped peaks. It was straight out of magazine advertisement for peace and tranquility. It was the opposite of his internal scenery.

He closed his eyes and breathed in the smell of grungy water and traffic. His heart was still racing, and he could smell his own sweat, acrid and sharp. He couldn't remember much of what he'd said and done on stage. He did know it wasn't great. Most of the positive audience reaction was sympathy. He certainly didn't feel triumphant.

He didn't know what to do now. He could go back to Numbknots and watch the rest of the show, or he could go to the mission, or he could go home and sleep. The existence of options made him feel slightly better. Going back to Numbknots was out without much consideration. He couldn't face the crowd again after he'd mostly bombed his set. He found he didn't want to be alone in Reed Canyon, either. Too much had happened in the last couple of days. The mission made him think of Tom, too, and he decided not to relive that tonight.

He decided to get on a bus and see where it took him. Getting deliberately lost was a terrible idea, but he was confident he could find the river and his way back home eventually. He craved the anonymity of public transit after being so exposed. He boarded the first bus that stopped near Naito Parkway and sat alone in the back. Only a handful of riders were on this bus this late in the evening, but he was comforted to be with people without being with anyone.

CHAPTER 38

He was on Bus 16 heading north. The reader board inside said it went to Sauvie Island. Lewis had never been to an island before. Might as well conquer another first. The route followed the river on the right and Forest Park on the left for nearly 20 miles. Lewis let the rumble of the travel wash over him until he was close to a hypnotic state.

"Last stop!" the driver called over the speaker, and Lewis got up to leave. He was alone except for a tired looking middle-aged woman in the front. She hustled herself off and strode briskly away, clutching her purse. Lewis thought about following her, but when she glanced back to see if he had, he went the other way.

The night air was cool and the island smelled of the water and growing things. On the breeze floated the scents of ripe strawberries and flowers. A sweet undercurrent of things not yet fully matured promised abundance all summer long. Lewis felt his mouth water. On Mt. Adams, there were alpine strawberries and wild huckleberries if a harthoth knew where to look, but they yielded a few handfuls of tiny berries during their short season. This was something entirely different.

He followed the scents, trotting at a good pace, until he found a farm with a giant plywood sign proclaiming "U-PICK OR WE-PICK" strawberries. The gate was closed, but he found it easily scaled. Avoiding the outbuildings and driveway, Lewis headed into the fields of strawberries. The ground was crumbly and damp, but not muddy, so he kicked off his shoes and let his feet feel the soft earth. It felt so good to walk freely.

He reached the rows and bent down, using his night vision to find the most perfect strawberry, large and yielding slightly to his fingers as he plucked it. He smelled its sweetness as he raised it to his mouth. As he bit off the end of the berry, red juice stained his lips and fingers. The flavor exploded in his mouth, mellowed to the edge of savoriness with a lemony tang underneath. He sighed a soft sound of complete pleasure.

He ate several more, indulging in only the best, most perfect fruit. He realized he was starving after skipping dinner. He wanted to sit on the ground and stuff strawberries in his mouth until he was sick. The night was peaceful, quiet, and he suddenly did feel sick. Homesick. He was surprised by the strength of the feeling. What was he doing, pretending to be human, pretending he could be a comedian, pretending he could live under a bush and have a normal life—it was ridiculous. He felt embarrassed by it all, all the pretending. He was supposed to be living in a wilderness, connected to the earth.

His clothing felt suffocating. He tore at the buttons on his flannel shirt, finally giving up and tugging it over his head. He shimmied out of his pants and underwear, flinging them all in a pile on top of his shoes. The moon was just a sliver in the sky, the darkness hiding him while he saw everything in perfect clarity. He wasn't human, he was harthoth. He raised his head to the sky and let out a long, mournful cry across the fields of strawberries.

In one of the buildings, lights flipped on. He heard a door open and a command. "Get 'em, Danger!" The heavy breathing of a very large dog with jingling tags advanced toward him very fast. A clearer signal to move on from the moment was hard to imagine. The dog wasn't barking, which was somehow more terrifying. A flashlight bobbed behind the dog, much slower but just as agitated. "Get out of here, hippie!" the old man yelled as the flashlight exposed Lewis in all his unprotected glory.

He had the presence of mind to grab his clothes and shoes before running at full harthoth speed out of the farm. He could hear the dog trying to match his speed and almost managing it.

"Holy shit, Danger, that one's fast!" yelled the farmer. "Come on back, girl!" He whistled and the dog obeyed immediately. Danger wasn't a spoiled pet, she had a job and it was chasing off hippies. Job done, she loped back to her owner and sat for praise. Lewis was over the fence before he looked back. The flashlight bobbed back to the house.

Lewis walked down the road a few hundred yards before he struggled back into his clothes. Dressed, he walked down the road and thought about his evening. It had held such promise. Then, not content to have embarrassed himself on stage, he ended the evening streaking through a farmer's field chased by Danger. A smile tugged at his lip, then a chuckle burbled up. He kept imagining the farmer watching his hairy ass running out of the field at superhuman speed, and he laughed alone in the grass by the side of the road until his face and sides hurt.

After sleeping rough in an undeveloped part of the island, he caught the first bus of the morning into Portland. Seeing his reflection in the bus window, he tried to get the leaves out of his hair and beard and clean the strawberry juice off his fingers and face. His efforts made two other riders move further away from him, so he stopped.

He didn't see any reason to head for the canyon, so he wandered down to Numbknots and sat down by the brewery door in the grass to wait. It was mild and sunny, but clouds were coming in from over the mountains, promising a shower. He would have to head over and make sure his stuff wasn't exposed before that happened.

"I heard you had an interesting night," Bill Ben

said, strolling up with his keys in his hand.

"Yeah, I guess I didn't realize the farmer would get that mad about a few strawberries. It did say 'U-pick,'" Lewis replied.

Bill Ben laughed, shaking his head. "Dude, that is a remarkably interesting non sequitur, which I will ask you about later, but I meant on stage. Titania said you walked straight out afterwards and didn't come back."

"Oh, yeah, that," Lewis mumbled. He'd been successfully avoiding thinking about it. The loneliness of the night hit him again. "It didn't work."

"Whoa, man, I think that's a little harsh." Bill Ben opened the door and ushered Lewis through it. "Maybe it wasn't great, and the way Titania described the hair thing was super weird, but there have been bigger disasters." He grabbed his notebook and began noting instrument readings. "There was this one guy, he came on with a puppet of his hand. His entire act was hand-related jokes involving a fake version of his hand, on his hand." Bill Ben glanced at Lewis and chuckled. "Yeah, the audience had that exact same look on their faces the entire time. I couldn't watch your whole bit, but I did hear a laugh or two. You'll get 'em next time when you're over your jitters."

Lewis did not believe him.

CHAPTER 39

Lewis made a quick trip across the river between shifts to check on his belongings in Reed Canyon. The clouds were rolling in dark and thick, promising a summer thunderstorm and soaking rain. He'd accumulated more belongings than he realized. He stuffed as much as he could in the bags and hung them upside-down. He draped his extra clothes on branches. It would be like washing them, he decided. He hadn't really done that yet, just picking up new ones at the mission, but it was past time.

He decided to take his books with him. He didn't look inside his notebook. The confusion and embarrassment of his performance still stung. Looking at his belongings hanging from the rhododendrons, it felt alien again, a shadow of what he'd felt in the strawberry fields. He shook it off in favor of movement.

Loping across campus to catch the bus, he caught a glimpse of black hair and a bright t-shirt heading toward the Anthropology building. He almost called out to Chloe, and she must have sensed his eyes on her, because she turned. When she saw Lewis, she quickly turned and kept walking.

The first few fat raindrops were cool on his flushed face. He didn't know what he would have said, anyway. He caught the bus and watched the downpour outside. Lightning and thunder punctuated the sheeting rain as it crashed against the sides of the bus. Standing water on the road flared into plumes that reached his window, dirty water sluicing against the glass in a startling slap.

He felt it. Chloe. He'd messed up with his clan in the past, but they were so few, and living so closely together, it always worked out eventually just because they would have to sit a few feet away from each other on a regular basis. Chloe could simply never speak to him again. The human world was fraught with the possibility of being discarded.

Lewis walked into Numbknots in defeat. The kitchen staff acknowledged him as usual, but no one mentioned his foray into the front of the house. The dish routine and steam didn't cheer him up like it usually did.

Titania came back with glasses after he'd been sadly stacking dishes for an hour. "Hey you," she said, "you did a good job last night." Lewis looked up, and what she saw in his eyes made her suck in a breath. "Oh, hey, it wasn't that bad, hey." She put her tray of glasses down and drew him into a hug.

The contact almost broke him. He'd had some physical affection as a young harthoth, of course, but as he matured it evaporated. The clan leader and her family were considered outside and above the rest. Casual gestures did not happen, even with the disappointing second son. Maybe especially. He held his breath and leaned into Titania for just a moment before pulling away. Her hands stayed on his arms.

"It wasn't the best comedy set ever, but it was your first time, and—"

"It was bad." He said simply. A busser brought another tub of dishes in and Titania snatched her hands away. They stood in their awkward tableau until he left.

"Well, it was a little…weird," Titania admitted. "It was, I don't know, like you were playing the part of a comedian, and you had several different scripts." She saw his confusion and sighed. "Let's talk about it after shift and I'll see if I can put my words in a better order." She leaned in to plant a light kiss on his cheek and fled the dish room without another word.

Lewis raised his hand to the place where Titania's kiss was sparking on the bare skin above his beard. His first impulse was to wipe it off, but his second impulse was entirely different. For no reason, he thought of the strawberries on Sauvie Island.

It was a long night with people staying well after closing. Bill Ben's office was empty, and he found his boss at the bar with Titania. There were three full pints sitting there, untouched. Bill Ben kicked a stool out and Lewis sat. When he opened his mouth to speak, Titania shushed him.

"I have a toast," Bill Ben declared, lifting his beer.

"Here's to your next comedy set, Lewis." His look stopped the protest forming on Lewis' lips. "Clearly, you did not realize that everyone sucks the first time they try everything, due to your supernatural gift for washing dishes, but it's true. The only way to not suck is to be too stupid to quit. So here's to you and your future stupidity, which T and I fully expect and support."

Titania was frowning at Bill Ben. "Wow," she said, before clinking her pint along with the men.

Lewis was smiling despite himself. Bill Ben's toast resonated with him more than Titania believed, but it was irrelevant. "I don't think so, but thank you. I don't know what I would do differently that would help. That was the best stuff I could come up with."

"Nobody's going to make you go up there again unless you want to," Titania said. "But I thought about what was off, and I think you just weren't yourself. You weren't authentic, you know?"

Bill Ben could see Lewis didn't understand. "I'm gonna tell you a story, Lewis, and you cannot repeat it, okay?" Lewis nodded. "Sit back and wonder," he paused dramatically, "at the tale of how I came to be called 'Bill Ben'!" Titania made a small mock gasp and covered her mouth with her hand.

"You see, my parents were hippies, and not the kind of trendy hippies you see downtown. We lived on five acres and everything we ate come from our property. I didn't wear shoes or get a haircut until I was five. Real hippies.

"So anyway, they were really into two things: marijuana and Tolkien. A couple of weeks after I was born in the bathtub at home, they conceded I should probably have a birth certificate and carted me into town in the old Volkswagen bus. After showing me to the clerk at the Health Department, they gave her all my information through a little window. They were, by their own admission, high as fuck to take the edge off going into town.

"The clerk got most of the information right, but she was not as into Tolkien. When my parents told her I was named 'Bilbo Peregrine Starwielder,' she transcribed that as 'Bill Ben Paraguay Stanfelder.' No one bothered to double-check, because the goal on both sides was to end the transaction as quickly as possible.

"When my birth certificate showed up in the mail, my mom says she laughed until she cried. They immediately started calling me 'Bill Ben' as a joke, intending to go fix it, but it never happened. After a while, everybody thought Bill Ben was my name, and it legally was, so it seemed less and less important to do anything about it."

Lewis did not get what that had to do with his situation and said so.

"Ah, yes, the point. See, when I was in high school, my dad asked me if I wanted to change my name since it wasn't really 'my' name. He said I could change it to anything I wanted, not just 'Bilbo,' since they had cut way back on the pot and saw their original choice might not have been inspired after all. I could pick just Bill or Ben, for example.

"I was so offended by that offer, I stormed out of the room. My name was weird, and sometimes embarrassing, and don't get me started on the teachers with middle name seating charts, but it was and is part of the core of me.

"I suspect you've done a lot of reinventing here, Lewis, and lost some of yourself in the process. The kind of generic act I think you cobbled together suffered for it."

Titania was nodding. "I agree with Bilbo," she said, earning a dark look from Bill Ben. "People connect when the comics are revealing something personal. I've watched a lot of bombs, and some really spectacular acts, and the difference...some of it's timing and skill, and some of it is some intangible thing that boils down to opening yourself up. Who you are may be awkward and deeply weird thanks to your Canadian cult or whatever, but I bet it's more interesting than jokes anybody could tell."

"And no puppets," Bill Ben added to Titania, cracking them both up.

Lewis almost told them then and there about his origins, his family, his real name, and his current status in the world, but he was too scared of losing what he had left of the life he was making. He nodded and smiled. He sipped his beer. He felt exposed.

CHAPTER 40

The world dried out and turned warmer over the next week. Lewis did his best to be satisfied with a smaller version of his ambitions. He knew enough about beer to brew it himself now. His dishes sparkled. His hair grew unruly without Tom to help tame it. His banter with Titania stayed friendly, but it seemed like she was waiting for him to say something. What, he had no idea, and his impulse to tell her everything made him cautious.

Reed Canyon was starting to feel less like home and more like hiding now. He no longer ate at the cafeteria to avoid running into Chloe or worse, Dr. Perkins. He took a long, circuitous route to the bus stop. He did occasionally sneak into Tom's dorm block to shower, but every time felt more fraught. He couldn't carry all his stuff with him everywhere, but he didn't have a better place to put it. His previous contentment was gone.

He didn't have any idea what to do about it, though. He had a pile of money, but he was catching on to the fact that a wad of twenties was not the right currency for some things. He was also spending more buying food now that breakfast and lunch weren't free, so it was growing more slowly.

On a day Bill Ben ordered him to take off, he rode into downtown anyway, wandering through the busy city blocks, going into stores and coming back out without buying anything. One store was focused on shoes in garish colors and strange-feeling clothing in equally vivid bad taste. He walked around marveling at why these things existed until he realized one of the perky, pony-tailed retail "athletes" was following him and rearranging clothing that was already arranged. He knew the feeling of being expected to do the wrong thing any second.

"I'm not going to steal these," he said, holding up a pair of lime green running shoes and startling her into embarrassment. She spluttered an excuse about why she'd been following him, of course it wasn't for that reason, he should feel free to browse. He shook his head and she went silent, turning red. Another athlete, a tall man, was watching and walked toward them. Lewis put the shoes back and headed to the door. Halfway there, he turned around and said, "You know, I don't understand shoes anyway. You put your feet in the dark, where they get soft and sweaty and useless. If you never wear shoes, your feet work like they're supposed to. So... just don't." The woman was confused, but to Lewis' surprise, the man chuckled and waved him out.

He found himself on Burnside and trekked up to

Powell's Books. He understood why people wanted books. Even though he'd almost accidentally stolen books last time he was there, nobody followed him around. He remembered Chloe's kindness, but there was an edge to it now that made him momentarily sad.

No. Nobody was going to spoil books, no matter what.

After two hours of exploring the City of Books, Lewis had three books he couldn't live without. One was a used copy of *The Hobbit*, mostly to see why Bill Ben's parents thought it was worth naming a child after. At the register, he chose a reusable bag with the Powell's logo on it, feeling quite hip and urbane. If only he liked coffee.

The mission was between meals, but Eve made him a tray of leftovers and admired his books. As he ate, he began *The Hobbit*. Some of the language was dense, but he soon found himself sucked into the story. "Maybe *I* should have been named Bilbo," he muttered.

"Lewis! My man!" Rami called as he bounded down the stairs, his long, dark hair in wet tangles around his face, carrying a tote bag with "OPB" in big letters. "You're here early. What's up?" He motioned for Lewis to follow him into the back.

"Is that okay?" Lewis asked. The sign read "Staff and Volunteers Only."

"It is if I say it is. I think saving someone's life qualifies as 'volunteering,' man."

"I wish I knew how he was doing."

"Oh, yeah, so," Rami looked like he was choosing his words carefully. "I might know some people, and I might have asked a casual question here and there, and I might have been told in very non-specific terms that your boy Tom is fine and went home with his parents, who seemed very committed to some rehab."

Lewis felt a tension he hadn't consciously known he was holding dissipate. He let out a big breath. "How long does that take?"

"I dunno, man, it could be a while. I doubt they'll let him go back to Reed afterwards, too, because that's like giving the alcoholic a job in a bar. Maybe it'll be okay, but probably it won't."

Lewis wasn't entirely surprised. The arguments between Chloe and Tom had featured his parents' threats to take him home.

As Rami busied himself at the desk, tapping his mouse to turn on the computer, Lewis made a decision. "Rami?"

"Yeah?" Rami looked up at him.

"I don't know how to belong here."

Rami sat back and crossed his arms. "You seem to be doing alright. You have a job and someplace to stay, even if it's not all strictly legal. You have friends."

Lewis looked miserable.

"Okay. It's more than that. I get it, man, I really do. More than you imagine. Here's the secret, though. Everyone you see out there feels like an impostor most of the time. I moved here from a place like your *Canada* when I was younger. For a while, the only thing that kept me from going back is how much less I belonged there. That's your decision, though, man. Only you know."

"I did stand-up at open mic night."

Rami whistled. "And how did that go?"

"Bad. Titania and Bill Ben say I wasn't being myself, but how do I do that when I don't know who that is?"

"We're all here trying to figure that out, Lewis. You are pretty badass for getting up there at all. Next time—"

"I don't think there's going to be a next time," Lewis interrupted.

"There should be, dude. You have a privileged position to observe from."

"What?" Lewis had no idea what that meant.

Rami put his hands on the edge of the desk and leaned forward. "You are *outside*," he said dramatically. "Now, I gotta get this stuff done. Go read your books. Think about it. Get your hair trimmed back up, you look like a wildman."

Lewis left with directions to a barbershop where he could get his hair neatened up without "hipster influences," according to Rami. He was left wondering, again, what Rami knew or suspected about his origins. Through he'd never said, "Lewis, I know that's not your name and you're not human," he'd danced right up to the line.

After a haircut and trim involving a burning hot

towel he reflexively flung across the barbershop, Lewis took *The Hobbit* to an outdoor table at a restaurant and ordered a beer and burger. The server was not friendly, pointedly looking at his book and sighing. He knew from Numbknots not to camp at the table, but he didn't appreciate the passive-aggressive attitude. When he'd finished up, he decided to stay to the end of his chapter.

"Lewis!" Titania sat down across from him.

"Oh, hi," he stuttered, shutting his book without marking his page. Titania was wearing a navy sundress with thin straps and sparkling crystals. Her locs were pulled back with a light blue scarf. She looked like a goddess emerging from the night into the light of the afternoon. Lewis lost his breath for a moment, refilling his lungs not with oxygen but awkwardness. "You have the day off?" he said stupidly.

"No, I left my evil twin in charge of the bar. Bill Ben is going to be so surprised when she mixes all the drinks backwards."

Lewis gaped for a second, then saw the twinkle in her eye. He smiled. "What are you doing downtown?"

"I was kind of hoping to run into you, actually," Titania said softly. "We should talk."

CHAPTER 41

Lewis had a very human reaction to those words. First, the beer and burger in his stomach suddenly felt very heavy. Second, he wanted to do whatever he could to avoid whatever subject she was talking about.

"Well, I just paid for my food, and I think they want the table, so I should probably get moving," he stammered, getting up with his book bag.

"Great, we'll walk together," Titania said.

Lewis considered running away. He knew Titania wouldn't be able to keep up with him. He could abandon his job at Numbknots and live on fruit and dumpster food on Sauvie Island. As his muscles tensed to flee, the light caught the side of Titania's face, highlighting her pensive expression. She deserved better. He tried to exude casualness.

They strolled down to the river, walking through the park on the paved path. They stopped at the Skidmore Fountain, the sound calming. Misty droplets from an enormous bowl held aloft by two robed female figures played in the sunlight.

Lewis thought if he didn't talk, the talking part of the conversation might never start. His gambit didn't work.

"Lewis." Titania sat on the edge of the fountain, so Lewis sat facing her. "I don't understand what we're doing."

"We're sitting on the edge of a fountain getting wet."

Titania's eyes narrowed. "I'm going to assume you're being some kind of benign obtuse with that. I mean—what are we to each other? We went out a couple of times, and I really like you, but I have no idea how you feel about me. I think maybe I've been friend-zoned. I guess I want some clarity on that."

"Friend-zoned?"

"It's the place between dating and hanging out, Lewis, and I feel like maybe you decided not to date without telling me."

Lewis took a big breath, which Titania misinterpreted.

"I mean, I know I presumed there was something there, and maybe that was wishful thinking on my part, but my mom and I went to lunch the other day, and she had a lot to say about things I could be doing, and I guess some if it stuck in my head and made me start thinking about what I *am* doing, and I needed to know if you think there's something here or not." She had to take a breath. Seeing Lewis' furrowed brow, she sighed. "You talk now, I will stop."

"Good, it's making me sweaty," Lewis said,

earning a small smile. He thought for a few seconds. "First, I do like you, and I sometimes lose my breath when I look at you, and that's something I don't really know how to work with. Things don't work like that back in Canada. I was alone, but eventually, I would have been paired with a suitable mate and expected to make the best of it. Occasionally, pairings were made at the request of the couple, but I was..." Lewis trailed off. He was saying a lot and had to be careful. "I was...in the line of succession. Not first, well, not born first, I guess, but I would have been paired by my mother."

Titania was speechless.

"I know, it sounds bad, but a place without humor doesn't leave a lot of room for love, either."

"You were in the line of succession? Like a prince? And you would be given a *mate?*" She'd latched onto the details more than Lewis had intended.

"Um, yeah, I guess. I left, though, so that doesn't really apply anymore."

"What kind of fucked up place did you come from?" Titania blurted.

Lewis found himself unexpectedly defensive. "It's just different! They don't know anything else."

"But you did, somehow. I really don't understand, Lewis, but as long as you don't try to convert me or kidnap me, it's the past, right? I used to get blitzed out like your friend Tom half the time, but I don't anymore. You used to live in some weird arranged marriage cult without jokes. Wait—were you Jehovah's Witnesses?" Lewis shook his head.

"Okay, because *that* would be a deal-breaker."

Lewis laughed. The truth was so much weirder. Titania smiled, but quickly sobered. Lewis knew he needed to say more. He looked at her and stopped breathing.

Rainbows danced in the spray from the fountain. Sunlight hit small drops in her locs like glittering diamonds. The crystals on her dress captured bits of light and projected them back into the world as glittering intensity. Titania was a goddess perched on the side of the Skidmore Fountain, come from the heavens to speak with him. The phantom taste of strawberries made his mouth water and he swallowed.

Lewis reached out and touched the side of Titania's face with his hand, noticing the contrast between her delicate skin and his thick, yellow nails. He would have snatched his hand back, but she grabbed it with hers, leaning her cheek into his palm. Slowly, Lewis leaned toward Titania, expecting her to pull away, unsure what he thought he was doing. She leaned toward him, turning her face ever so slightly. Lewis closed his eyes.

The feel of her lips against his, light as feather, soft as the brush of a fern against his bare leg on a warm spring morning, was heart-stopping. The kiss lasted seconds and forever. Lewis pulled back first, searching Titania's eyes for an explanation for that magic, finding her searching him.

"They don't do that in Canada," he murmured.

Titania shook her head. "*Canada* gets more and

more terrible every time you talk about it." She took his hand. "I guess you *like* like me after all."

The semi-truck of reality ran over Lewis. In the harthoth clan, he would never just "have" a relationship. He hadn't gone through any of the rituals to prove he was capable or ready. His situation here was so unstable. It would be incredibly irresponsible to pledge himself to someone. He lived in a rhododendron bush.

"I have some issues, you know," he said, lamely understating the problem. "I'm not stable. I haven't proven myself worthy yet."

"What? You don't have to prove anything."

"I do. I have to prove that I'm ready."

"Ready for what? And what do you think you have to do?" Titania pulled her hand away and crossed her arms.

Lewis could see she was annoyed. "Ready for a relationship. Ready for responsibility. Ready to take on the mantle of my position, and I have no idea what that position is here or what responsibility even looks like. It's not like I can run down a deer and build a fire for you."

"Please don't start a fire, arson is not sexy." She considered him for a moment while he absorbed her use of "sexy" in the context of him. "You need a quest? Some Hellenic task to prove your worthiness?" He didn't know what "Hellenic" meant, but he nodded at the gist of it. "Well, that's crap."

Lewis slumped. Titania didn't understand how

ingrained this was. Things were off to a terrible start. His clan was right, he was a lazy, self-indulgent second son, and he would always take short cuts and underachieve.

Titania reached over and raised his chin. "Listen. You don't have to prove shit to me. But clearly, you have something to prove to yourself. What's the thing you have wanted to do more than anything else in your whole life?"

"Stand-up," he whispered.

"Say it louder," she insisted.

"Stand-up comedy. But—"

Titania smashed two fingers into his lips harder than she needed to, in his opinion. "Buts are for sitting," she said, then laughed. "My dad said that a lot, now here I am. Anyway, I know enough about you to want to take a chance, Lewis, and that's enough for me. YOU, on the other hand, need to prove something to yourself. So do it and I'll be here no matter what."

Lewis nodded once. Titania stood and brushed at her behind, which was damp from the fountain edge. She extended her hand, and Lewis took it. As they strolled back upstream, chatting about work, Lewis felt the shadow of all the things he didn't know how to fix, like his legal status. Even if he proved something to her, or himself, he had some real obstacles to overcome. He pushed them into the part of his mind that would worry about it later.

This time, when they parted at the bus stop, Lewis was not confused about why Titania waited to walk away. He watched her go after another soft, gentle kiss, and thought, "I will do whatever it takes to be worthy of that woman."

CHAPTER 42

Reed was quiet, almost spooky. The summer session didn't have many students, but this was unusually deserted. Lewis saw no one as he walked onto campus. He waited outside the Asylum Block for the door to open for nearly half an hour. Finally, a student dressed in Reed black came out and let him in.

Tom's door was stripped of its caution tape. It felt like a blow. The door was unlocked, and Lewis went in to sit on the stripped mattress in the empty space. It still smelled like marijuana, that wasn't going to go away until the building was razed, but all the posters had been torn from the walls, leaving bits of tape and torn corners.

The apparent anger and carelessness of Tom's parents while clearing his room made him think of Chloe and her anger at him. He was less confused now, knowing what magic she'd been hoping for. He was sad she didn't find it. He could say it was his unfamiliarity with kissing, in part, but it was also just that he didn't want to kiss *her*. It was a good thing she didn't know her failure had opened the door for his moment with Titania. He imagined a painful death at Chloe's hands.

Sitting in Tom's empty room moping wasn't going to turn the clock back on any of that, though, so he got back on the move. He took the opportunity to use the showers, but he needed clean clothes and soap to say he was "showered." He had some rain-rinsed jeans in the canyon he could put on.

Leaving the building, he finger-combed his wet hair back into a ponytail, attempting to keep his damp, copper curls from sticking to his cheeks. The door clicked shut behind him with a finality that was no less sad for being all in his own head. He wandered toward the canyon, distracted by his wet hair.

Crossing the bridge from one side of campus to the other, he felt watched. He'd been stalked by animals before on Mt. Adams, and this felt the same. He looked around and covertly sniffed the air. There was no trace of cougar or bear, not even a dog. Dogs tended to bark at him rather than stalking, anyway. He chastised himself for getting spooky about the empty campus and Tom's empty room.

It made him hurry into the canyon, even if it was ridiculous. He couldn't shake the feeling he was being followed. Trusting his instincts, he veered away from the rhododendrons and toward the spring where the creek originated. He was sweaty again, his shower wasted. His hair stuck to his face uncomfortably. He stopped near a pool of cold, clear water and listened. He didn't hear anything over the friendly babble of the creek. The evening air smelled like warm earth and the unruly plants on the stream bank.

Lewis knelt to the creek, cupping his hands. He splashed his face with cold water, rinsing off the sweat. His nerves calmed and he chastised himself for being paranoid. His senses were better than human, and he could handle almost anything he came up against, anyway. What did he think? A mountain lion was going to take him down in the middle of the college campus?

He scooped another handful of water, bringing it to his mouth to drink.

A startled sound of surprise made him whirl around, searching behind him. The sun hit a lens on eyeglasses, winking a tell-tale signal. "I know you're there, you might as well come out," he called. "You can't outrun me, so let's just have a conversation." He didn't mean to sound threatening, but he didn't mean to avoid it, either.

A rustle of branches was his only answer. "I mean it," he continued. "You've been following me, I want to know why," he guessed, assuming this was the source of his heebie-jeebies. He walked toward the rustling bushes.

"Hello, Mr. Clark!" Dr. Perkins popped out of the bushes, wearing dirt-smeared tan slacks and a few leaves in her brown hair. Lewis took an involuntary step back. "Don't drink that water, by the way, unless you want giardiasis."

Lewis shook his head. Humans were so afraid of water. "This stream is fine. The spring is only a few hundred feet away."

"So you've spent a lot of time down here?" Dr. Perkins probed, trying to reclaim her authority. She was sweaty from hurrying after him in her business casual, and Lewis could tell she was uneasy. Not frightened, but not entirely comfortable in the situation.

"Some. It's peaceful and people don't bother me. Usually."

"I've seen you head this way from campus many times. I was interested because you don't seem to have any contact information at the college. In fact, no one could find any record of you at all."

There it was. Dr. Perkins had finally convinced someone in the records office to help her snoop, and she knew Lewis Clark was not registered at Reed College.

"Yeah, my paperwork got messed up. I have wait for John to get back to fix it."

"*Jack* got back a week ago. He also doesn't know who you are. Who are you, Mr. Clark?"

Now that it was here, this moment of being found out was anticlimactic in two ways. First, they were way out in the woods in Reed Canyon, by themselves. Dr. Perkins didn't have anyone with her, no police, not even a grad student. Lewis was a much bigger threat to her than she was to him, if it came down to that. Second, he'd already lost every friend he had here. Leaving campus would create an inconvenience, a big one, but all the things that could be ruined already were.

"I am nobody," Lewis said mildly. It was true in the way she meant, after all.

"Oh, no, I don't think that," Dr. Perkins contradicted. "I think you're very interesting. Somehow, you managed to pose as a grad student when you're really a dishwasher at a bar. You had students assisting and protecting you, even bringing you to class. You claim to be from Canada, but I highly doubt that's where you're from. As an anthropologist, I am fascinated with whatever you have going on, Mr. Clark."

The woman's persistent curiosity was not going to get them anywhere good.

"Well, sorry, but I don't want to be studied right now. Things to do!" Lewis was spending more time thinking about outrunning women today than was entirely normal. Dr. Perkins moved to block the path back to the main trail. Lewis raised his eyebrows once, shook his head, and crashed into the water behind him with a tremendous splash. The professor's protests were drowned out in the commotion of Lewis crossing the creek and bushwhacking off into the brush on the other side.

He'd correctly assumed she wouldn't follow him. He had to get his things and get out of there, though. Reed Canyon was no longer his safe place. He didn't have one.

CHAPTER 43

He used his harthoth speed to get back to his things and pack them up. He would wait until full dark to leave. He would have an advantage with his night vision even if the professor hadn't given up. He had to make some decisions about what to take and what to leave. The clothes were easy to part with, but he had more books than he could carry. That hurt. At some point in the future, he was going to have to find a library and figure out how to use it.

Sitting under the rhododendron, packing done, he felt exhausted. Today was full of things. He closed his eyes and relived the moments at the fountain, smiling. There was the reason. Any questions he had about why he was here doing what he was doing were mostly answered in one breath. Dr. Perkins suspected he was something, but what? An imposter, sure, lying about his identity. That was as far as it went. She seemed more interested than accusing, though. Given all the sketchy behavior that was tolerated at Reed, he didn't expect her to do anything about it unless she saw him again.

When it was full dark, he crept out into the canyon.

"Olly olly oxen-free! Let your light shine!" The voice was loud, but not close.

All around Lewis, softly glowing lights appeared in the darkness. A chorus of voices began counting. "One...two...three!" The lights winked out.

"Alright, you bastards! Glow Tag begins NOW!" A cheer broke out and the sound of laughter and running feet made the night chaotic.

Lewis had a lump in his throat. The students would provide him ample cover to leave the canyon undetected, but one was missing. Tom should be out here running with the others. Lewis raised his face to the sky and howled, a chord of harthoth mourning that sounded something like a cross between a coyote and an elk.

"Fuck, what was that?" yelled the student closest to him. She uncovered her glow stick, using what little light it provided to search the area.

"Gotcha!" She was roughly pushed by the current It, who laughed an unhinged, inebriated giggle.

"Fuck off, Trevor, didn't you hear that?"

"Yeah, Natalie, it was probably the ghost of your thesis after Dr. Lynnhower read it."

"Shut up, loser. It was right there."

Lewis stood still, enjoying their reaction. When the students crashed through the bushes toward him, he decided not to take credit.

"Holy shit! That was big!" yelled the boy, no longer disbelieving. Lewis used his speed to get away from them, stifling a laugh that might ruin the legend of the Reed Canyon Monster.

The bus wasn't running this late, so he hiked across the river and into downtown Portland. The river smelled like algae and chemicals and mud, running swift and dark under the bridge as he crossed. Traffic was light. The few people who were out let their eyes slide over him as if he were insubstantial, a ghost. A guy carrying all his things in a few sacks on his back was not remarkable.

The doorways and benches downtown were already heavily populated. Men and women, dogs and one cat, some still awake and most sleeping heavily. He had a job and money, and still didn't have access to the same things as someone with the right kind of legal status. He couldn't say he was any different than the man resting on his duffel in a doorway on Oak Street. There was a tiny dog cradled in the man's arms, awake and watching Lewis walk by. Lewis realized the man was less alone than he was. He didn't want to sleep outside tonight, with all his things huddled around him.

The mission was closed and locked, but Eve came to the door when he rang the bell. Her long, gray hair was in a loose bun on her head. She squinted at the door light. "Lewis? Everything okay?" she asked.

"Hi, Eve, not really," he admitted. It was a relief to say it out loud. "My place to stay isn't safe anymore."

"Well, come in," she said, moving aside to let him through the door. Once they were downstairs at a table, she searched his face. "Did something happen? Are you hurt?"

"I'm fine. I just can't go back to my place, someone found out I didn't belong there."

Eve looked like she was tempted to press, but she finally shook her head. "You know you can stay here," she said, "but you had a bad reaction last time. We can't have any violence because you get scared by being underground. Is that going to be a problem?"

Lewis didn't know how to truthfully answer that, so he didn't. "I can sleep apart from the other people, can't I? Maybe in the office, or the kitchen? I can sleep on the floor."

"You really need a place to stay, don't you." It wasn't a question, and Lewis let Eve think. If she decided it was too disruptive or risky to have him down here, he didn't know where he'd go. Eve let out a long breath, her mouth set. "You can stay, Lewis, but on the condition you don't create a disturbance. I don't know what you need to do to prevent that, but do it. You can sleep where you want. I can trust you to leave our things where they belong, I think."

"Yes, you can," Lewis confirmed. "Thank you. I will try to figure something else out as soon as I can." He said that knowing "as soon as I can" might be a long time.

"Rami says you know how to wash dishes. Would you be willing to do a shift or two in the kitchen? We can't pay you, he also told me about your legal status, but you could volunteer?"

Lewis brightened. "Sure, I'd love to. It's my

superpower."

Eve's face broke into a kind smile. "I'm sure it's not your only one. Get settled. Remember, no disturbing the other folks." She got up and came back with a key to the non-public spaces. "Do not lose this," she warned. "It's a real pain getting the locks changed when one of these goes missing."

Lewis stared at the little piece of metal, running his fingers along the teeth. He had a key to a door for the first time in his life.

He woke up several times in the remaining few hours of the night in a mild panic, but nothing as bad as the first time. He'd set up a cot in the dish room, and the familiar scent of detergent and disinfectant helped him place where he was. When the breakfast volunteers came in and flipped the lights on, he was glad to stop fighting his nervous system. If they were surprised to see him sleeping there, no one said anything.

Lewis picked up his cot and other things and stored them out of the way, using the opportunity to take a shower and find some clean clothes. The terrible pine shampoo had been replaced by an equally terrible strawberry version that smelled less like strawberries than floor cleaner. He braided his hair and wiped the fog off the mirror.

He had a brief flash, thanks to his exhaustion, of non-recognition. He needed his beard and eyebrows cleaned up, but he was not the harthoth he was a few months ago. He looked and acted, mostly, like a man. A pang of sadness hit him for the life he'd left behind. It had been simpler in many ways, at least when he left it. It wouldn't have stayed that way, not with Manura's injuries (he refused to think his brother had died). He closed his eyes and reopened them, settling into the features that were still familiar. He was still himself.

Then again, was he? He wasn't using his real name, he hadn't admitted his origins to anyone, he hadn't corrected the impression he grew up in a Canadian religious cult.

Maybe it was the sleep deprivation, maybe it was the useless adrenaline from his claustrophobic dreams, maybe he was hallucinating from the artificial strawberry fumes, maybe it was an epiphany—Lewis couldn't say—but he got his notebook out and started writing.

CHAPTER 44

"I see that's going well," Bill Ben smirked. Lewis was coming back from dropping off glasses at the bar when his boss stepped out of the walk-in freezer.

"Yeah, dishes getting washed," Lewis said, trying to step around him. Bill Ben casually put an arm in front of him.

"You can pretend we are talking about the dishes, but we both know dishes don't make you walk several inches off the ground. You are also taking some very curious smoke breaks, considering you don't smoke. Let's see, who smokes around here?" Bill Ben tapped one finger on his chin, pretending to think.

Lewis blushed a little, but he was smiling. "She doesn't smoke anymore, but she's pretty amazing."

"Yes, she is. Lucky you." Bill Ben moved out of the way to let him pass.

The week had flown by. He was washing dishes at the mission, checking the brewery chemistry alongside Bill Ben, washing dishes at Numbknots, writing his new act with feverish concentration, and taking too many "smoke breaks" out back with Titania and her new nicotine patch.

They weren't out there making out, exactly, but they weren't really complying with any nun's idea of appropriate personal space, either. Laughter was losing rank on the list of greatest things humanity had over the harthoth. He wasn't surprised it was obvious to Bill Ben. They were both acting like fools. They had a day off coming up, right after the next open mic night. Lewis was looking forward to spending the day wandering around the Oregon Museum of Science and Industry, a big glass-domed building he could see across the river from Numbknots. He had no idea what was in the place and didn't care.

Sometimes he thought about how different this was from his customs. Even though Titania was going along with his quest to prove himself worthy, he knew she would still be there even if he bombed. No one had forced them together—they'd *chosen* each other. He had never considered that possibility in his entire life. It was thrilling to control his own romantic destiny.

The open mic was two days away. Every time he thought about it, his testicles shriveled and his breath caught. He had never been so scared of something in his life. Titania hadn't asked about it more than once, because that time he verbally barfed all his anxiety out in a puddle at her feet. She said, "I'm sure it will be amazing," and left it at that. He was not at all sure of that.

On the day, he washed the breakfast dishes at the mission and showered, indecisive about whether to dress like he normally did or go for something more upscale, like khakis and a button-down.

"You got a date or something, Lewis?" Rami had a pile of jeans in his arms to restock the shelves.

"Not today."

"Not *today?*"

"I have a date with my girlfriend tomorrow, but tonight I'm going to do open mic again."

Rami shook his head. "That is a lot of information in one sentence, dude. Since when do you have a girlfriend? Actually, never mind that, is this open mic thing at Numbknots again?" Lewis nodded. "What time does it start?"

"I think tonight starts at 6:30, but I'm not going to go on first this time. That was kind of bad."

Rami chuckled. "See, you are a show business pro already. I might come by and watch. Will this *girlfriend* be there? I'd love to meet her."

"Yeah, she's the bartender. You don't have to come, though, it might be terrible." Lewis imagined his friends all seeing him die a horrible stage death and felt sick.

"No, it's alright. If it's good, I can buy you a beer. If it's bad, I can buy you two." Rami clapped him on the back. "Wear what you normally wear, you'll be more comfortable if you don't look like you work at Best Buy."

A trip to the barbershop completed his

preparations. He'd taken the day off from Numbknots, so he had a few hours before the show. The weather was warm, the mid-afternoon temperature as high as it ever got at elevation on Mt. Adams. Sweat trickled down his back as he wandered downtown, muttering his routine under his breath, solidifying the words and the rhythm. His meditation was abruptly broken when he realized he wasn't sure where in the city he was. He'd wandered uptown, dwarfed by the monolithic bank buildings. The Wells Fargo Center loomed over him. Forty stories of marble and anodized aluminum, it was the tallest building in Portland, industrial and impersonal. Looking up, Lewis felt how alien this city was more keenly than he had in a long time. He wondered if he could see Mt. Adams from the top.

He turned and looked around, getting his bearings. In the heat, it was harder to tell where the river was, but he found it as he headed downhill. Feeling less lost, he went back to mumbling to himself as he walked.

When he couldn't put it off any longer, he turned down Naito Parkway toward Numbknots. He stood outside for a moment, remembering that first night on the lawn listening to the show. He wanted to create that magic tonight. He was taking a huge risk, and if it didn't pay off...well. Best not consider that.

He signed up to go in a later slot, a little before 8PM, when the crowd was warmed up but not yet exhausted. The hostess smiled brightly at him and gave him a few words of encouragement.

Titania was busy behind the bar, but she wasn't alone tonight. There was another bartender helping. It was packed. The warm weather had people heading inside for a drink and the air conditioning. It felt too cool on Lewis' sweaty skin.

"You ready for this?" Titania asked, letting the other bartender handle things for a minute.

"As ready as I'm going to be. I'm more prepared than last time, at least."

"Well, I have a good feeling about this," Titania said. She reached across the bar and squeezed his arm. "You want a beer or something? You look hot."

"Why, thank you," Lewis said, mugging, and she laughed. "I better not. I'll take a water, though." He sat at a table with easy access to the stage on the right side of the restaurant and sipped his ice water in a dissociative panic. Later, he wouldn't remember one thing from the other comedians' sets.

Sooner than he expected, the MC was introducing him.

"Back to face you all again, and what a face it is! Welcome to Numbskulls at Numbknots, our very own dishwashing prodigy, Lewiiiiissssss Clark!"

Lewis stood and walked to the stage, very conscious that all eyes were on him. He put a smile on his face and tried to ignore the urge to run or vomit or both. The crowd was warmed up, and applause buoyed his steps.

"Hey, folks, thanks." He raised his hand, quieting the room, and took one deep breath. He saw Titania sitting at a table watching and nearly choked up.

Now he understood the second bartender. Another breath.

"I came out here a few weeks ago, and I died. That's my opinion, and I see a few of you are back who might share that opinion. I bet you're not looking forward to this. I don't blame you. Me either." A few confused chuckles drifted to him.

"I'm going to be honest with you. A few weeks ago, I wasn't myself. Not in some hypothetical or metaphorical or not legally-binding sense—I mean, I was pretending to be someone else."

"See, this may come as a surprise, but my real name isn't Lewis Clark." Scattered laughter. "I'm not from Canada. I do not know shit about maple syrup or hockey. In fact—and you are going to have to use your imaginations to go somewhere you weren't expecting with me here—I'm not even human."

He let that settle for a few seconds. People were leaning in. No one was talking to their tablemates this time. They didn't know what was happening here, but it wasn't a line-up of half-lame jokes anyone could tell. Even if it turned out to be terrible, it would be interesting enough to talk about later.

"My real name is Elko. Just one name, like Bigfoot." He raised an eyebrow, but paused only a moment. "I've been studying humans my whole life, lurking in the woods and listening to the radio. Since I came to Portland, I'm realizing that passing as human thanks to my flannel and completely foolproof alias isn't the same as *being* human."

CHAPTER 45

He paused to let that sink in and saw most of the audience was focused entirely on him. He didn't dare look at Titania, though. He had no idea what she was going to think about this "act."

"You might think it's brave, coming back, but I have so much experience bombing. See, my clan doesn't have humor. Not a chuckle. So the first time I snuck over to a campground and saw kids laughing, I was totally weirded out. I didn't know English then, either, so it was all just uncivilized barking and grunting, but when they stretched their faces out, that was especially feral." He made a big grimace to mimic his first impression of a smile. The audience hooted and clapped. He resisted the urge to give them a genuine smile. Not yet.

"As a non-human, I normally have an inhuman amount of hair. I have it pretty well under control where you can see it, but where you can't see it…" He made a bursting motion with his free hand. "It's definitely on the very edge of believability, even for Portland. You should see my mom's beard.

Magnificent."

He riffed on drinking water, and his sense of smell, and how much food was in the dumpsters "for just anyone." The crowd was invested in this persona, the real Elko under a Lewis disguise pretending to be a character named Elko. Lewis had chills despite the sweat running down his back. He swiped his flannel shirt across his brow. He talked more about his hair and how he'd promised Tom he'd never have a man bun despite its camouflage effect in downtown.

"Shoes are another thing. I hate shoes. I am only wearing them tonight because I have to or something called the 'Health Department' gets mad. Shoes are the most counter-productive thing I've ever seen. You put your feet in these cages to 'protect them,' and they get all white and soft and unable to protect themselves. Go barefoot. Empower your feet. Someday they may need to stand on their own two... themselves.

"Humans are scared to walk barefoot, but they'll go under the earth without a thought. Where I'm from, we are born afraid of being under the earth. Darkness? No big deal, since we can see pretty well in low light. Our scary stories are about Moogo trapped in a cave or buried alive. Since I'm rebelling against everything that's good for me like an exceptionally large toddler, I live underground now. It's terrible. I wake up several times a night ready to punch people." He made a fist and gave a weak, loopy left hook. "Very, very punchy. So, I saw a sign for tours of the Portland Shanghai Tunnels, underground tunnels that are most certainly haunted. Sounds really scary if I went. Just a lot of people getting punched by a very hairy dude having a panic attack."

He gave the laughter time to swell and feed on itself. He felt a big, silly grin on his face, and didn't care. He glanced at Titania and saw her equally goofy smile. Relief flooded him. It was going to be okay as long as she wasn't upset.

"I really prefer being outside most of the time. I got on a bus and ended up at Sauvie Island one night. That's really pretty up there. Inspires a person to certain freedoms they might not indulge in the city. Not being from around here in a really big way, I did not know that 'U-PICK' wasn't an open invitation. Stolen fruit is sweeter, everyone knows that, but is a strawberry sweeter if you don't know you're stealing it? Anyway, long story short, the farmer's dog is named Danger, and I put my clothes back on after Danger had ceased." He paused. "Chasing me."

It was even better when it took the crowd a second to catch up.

"Believe it or not, I was next in line to be in charge back at the clan. My brother set himself on fire during the fire god ceremony rehearsal—yeah, I know, it seems a little ironic, but it was more just dumb—and so after being the spare my whole life, living down to some really low expectations, they suddenly said, 'Hey, you're going to be in charge after all, how about that?' I said—what? You don't want that. And you know what they said? Yeah, we know, but what else are we going to do? That is not the kind of faith in my abilities that was going to make me want the job.

"So, I ran away. I hid in someone's camp trailer and stepped out on Barbur Boulevard a new man. I mean, not a man, exactly, but close enough once you take a weed-whacker to the parts that show." He made the finger burst gesture again.

He was riding high, but it was time to wrap it up. He'd already been on for over ten minutes. The MC was standing at the side of the stage, poised to intro the next comic. He wasn't going to rush Lewis off when he was killing, but the slots were short and he had a show to keep rolling.

"I've spent the last few months thinking about what my clan would be like if they could bust out a big belly laugh once in a while. Maybe I could lead them if they had the imagination to laugh at themselves—because they might also have the capacity to follow me where I would want to go —to a world beyond unquestioned traditions and superstitions, outside rigid rules, and into much more complicated and twisty knots of connection. Specifically, human connection. Because you guys, you have something here, something so precious and you don't even think about it. Babies get it. People who don't even speak the same language can share it. I came here, giving up the birthright I didn't want in the first place, I admit, because I couldn't stand being the only one laughing."

He took a long two or three seconds to look at the

crowd. They were rapt.

"Thank you!" he said, waving and walking to the edge of the stage, handing the mic to the MC. The applause was loud and long, following him as he left the stage and headed to Titania's table. She stood, clapping and beaming at him. A few other scattered audience members stood, not quite an ovation, but a hell of a lot more than he'd expected. He turned and waved again, and the crowd quieted, ready to move on to the next set of jokes.

"I feel sorry for whoever has to follow you," Titania said, leaning in to speak into his ear. She kissed him lightly on the lips and squeezed his hand, heading back to the bar to help the harried second bartender. Lewis followed her, settling on an open barstool. He soon realized it was open because the view of the stage was terrible.

Titania slid a beer in front of him. "From him," she said, pointing behind Lewis.

"Killer set, man," Rami said, taking the other poorly situated stool next to Lewis.

"Thanks," Lewis said, taking a long draw on the pint of Clown Car Brown Ale he'd helped Bill Ben brew. He realized he was parched and exhausted, and he hadn't eaten anything for dinner. He decided he didn't care and took another pull. The euphoria of the performance fizzed on top of the beer.

"Seriously, though. That was bold. I don't think I could have done that." Rami tossed his hair back and drank a quarter of his much lighter Businessman IPA.

"I helped brew that," Lewis said, pointing to the pint glass.

"Wow, you are a man of many talents, Mr. Lewis Clark. And is this lovely woman the girlfriend you spoke of?"

"Yes, I am!" Titania said, winking at Lewis. "You are?"

"Rami. I met Lewis when he was new in town." Titania nodded and moved down the bar, busy.

The men watched the comedian after Lewis, a college-age kid with a mediocre act, and drank their beers. After a smattering of half-hearted applause at the end, Rami excused himself to use the restroom.

"Is this seat open?" Lewis knew that voice.

"My friend is sitting there," he replied.

"Well, I'm sure he won't mind, Mr. Clark, if I just sit down for a moment."

Dr. Perkins plopped down on the seat next to him, signaling to Titania that she'd have two of what Lewis was having. She slid one pint over to Lewis. "A little peace offering, I suppose. Your set was good, Mr. Clark. Very interesting."

"Thanks," he replied, turning back to the stage as another act started. He silently finished his first pint, feeling a gentle buzz that was altogether extremely pleasant after the stress of performing. When he set it down, Dr. Perkins quickly switched the glasses, queuing up the full one. He nodded at her, feeling generous, and drank most of it to show there were no hard feelings.

The next act was okay, but he had trouble

following the act after that. He was losing track of the jokes before the punchlines hit. Rami returned at some point and left after a whispered conversation with Dr. Perkins, clapping Lewis on the shoulder as he walked away. Lewis shook his head, feeling fuzzy. He realized he should have paced his drinking better on his empty stomach.

"Imma go outside," he slurred, struggling a little to maintain a completely sober posture.

"Here, let me help you," Dr. Perkins said, steadying his arm as they walked out together.

CHAPTER 46

The following 45 minutes were a hazy, terrifying blur. Lewis' last clear memory was sitting at the bar at Numbknots. He was in a car, a new experience he did not like, then down some stairs. The stairs seemed to go down forever, but he couldn't place where he was or where he'd started. When he was finally allowed to collapse on a narrow bed, he gratefully drifted into the dark for a while.

"He's going to wake up soon. We should take samples before he does. I don't imagine he'll cooperate."

"Dr. Perkins, you have a man tied to a bed under the Chemistry wing. How is this okay?"

"He's not a man, for starters, I don't know what he is. He's the find of the century. He's my next book."

"Even if he wasn't human, which he clearly is, he's still a being with self-awareness and agency. No anthropologist would endorse these methods! We don't even treat animals this way."

"There was no other way."

Lewis tried to open his eyes, but they were much too heavy. The conversation wasn't making a lot of sense to him yet, but he knew the voices.

"Chloe?" he rasped, too quiet for them to hear.

"He's trying to talk," Dr. Perkins said. "We can't stand here arguing. I need blood and tissue samples. I need to get them to the lab as soon as possible to verify this."

"This is unethical in every sense of the word. And illegal. Who even is this?"

"Chloe?" Lewis tried again with a little more effort.

A light came on, blazing through his closed eyelids and making him wince. He tried to move away from the glare but couldn't. Strong straps held his arms and legs to the bedframe. More straps crisscrossed his chest. One circled his neck loosely. He struggled against the bindings, but they were strong enough to thwart his harthoth strength even without drugs.

"Lewis?" Chloe's voice was incredulous. "Dr. Perkins, you kidnapped *Lewis*? He's a homeless guy from Canada."

"Not according to him. And I've been watching him, he absolutely is not just a homeless guy from Canada."

"Not according to him? What does that mean?"

Dr. Perkins moved to the bed and Lewis felt a sting in his upper arm. "There. That should knock him out for longer. He metabolized the rohypnol very quickly."

Lewis felt himself floating out to sea and was surprisingly unconcerned about it.

"I'm surprised you suddenly have ethical concerns, Chloe," Dr. Perkins' voice was soft, and he could see the words floating by in pink puffs, even with his eyes closed. "We should talk about your last three research papers in that context if you don't want to—"

Lewis let go of the thread there and went on a long, strange trip.

The next time he woke up, he needed to pee worse than he ever had before in his entire life. He managed to open his eyes, and saw Dr. Perkins sitting in the darkened room, watching him. She had a clipboard in one hand and a pen glowing with a little internal light in the other. The scratching of her pen on paper made his head pound. The smells in the room were strange and unfamiliar. His own smell was strange, the taste in his mouth foul and unpleasant.

He cleared his throat. Dr. Perkins started, nearly dropping her pen.

"Yes, Mr. Clark? Or should I call you Elko?"

He explained his issue in as few words as possible without acknowledging the question.

"That is a problem. I couldn't catheterize you. There's a floor drain right underneath you, however."

Lewis was horrified, and it cut through some of the remaining fog. "I am not peeing in my pants!" he exclaimed.

"It's a good thing I removed them, then."

Lewis took a quick inventory and was mortified to find out his clothes had been removed and replaced with a light sheet. His reaction surprised him, and he chuckled.

"What's funny?" Dr. Perkins asked.

"You wouldn't get it," he said. He was more human than he realized, if simple "nudity" was now embarrassing.

"I was surprised to see so much body hair, but that means you were telling the truth. What are you, Mr. Lewis? A different evolutionary branch? The result of inbreeding in a closed community? Chloe seems to think you lived in a cult, but clearly there's more to it than that. I have samples to process, but until then, we are going to have some very interesting talks."

"I don't think we will," Lewis replied. He wasn't going to give his kidnapper more reason to keep him here. "Where am I?"

They were interrupted by a light knock on the door. After peeking through a small slit in the black paper over the window, Dr. Perkins opened it. "Chloe, right on time. The subject just woke up."

"I am only here because you threatened me."

"Unfortunate, but you left yourself open to that. Perhaps you'll make better choices in the future."

"I have some conditions if I'm going to help you, though." Chloe wasn't looking at Lewis. Her body language radiated unexpected power. "I want credit on any publications."

"Not likely!" Dr. Perkins was taken aback.

"I don't mean co-author, but I don't want to do whatever *this* is for uncredited research hours. You can tell the administration about my improprieties, but most of the evidence conveniently disappeared last night thanks to a friend of mine. I want credit."

Lewis' heart sank. He knew Chloe was mad at him, but he'd underestimated what she would do to get back at him. He couldn't think of anything to say that wouldn't make it worse.

"If you think I didn't keep evidence of all the liberties you've taken, you're very naive."

"And if you don't think I can pull the plug on this with one phone call, you are very arrogant, Dr. Perkins. I am, after all, just a student *under duress.*" She stressed "under duress" in a way that promised dramatic implications.

The women stared at one another for a long moment. Lewis fervently wished for further disagreement. He did not get his wish.

Dr. Perkins relented. "I respect your initiative. You remind me of myself at your age. The things I had to do to be credited were positively distasteful. You provide the level of assistance I require, I will credit you on the research in a limited and appropriate way."

Chloe inclined her head in agreement and pulled her laptop out of her bag.

"Be aware, Chloe, that I will expect a lot from you. I am very likely making your career for you."

"Thank you, Dr. Perkins," Chloe said. She was smiling in a way Lewis did not like. Any small doubt he had that Chloe was also using the opportunity to get revenge evaporated.

"First, I would like to find out his cultural region. That accent isn't Canadian. Also, he mentioned a fire god, so we'll pursue religion and religious practices. Easier to tease some information out when we have a thread to pull." Chloe typed as the professor talked.

Lewis couldn't hold out anymore. Sick with embarrassment, he peed on the floor like the lab animal he guessed he was.

CHAPTER 47

For the first two days, Dr. Perkins was in the room around the clock, taking breaks only to use the restroom. She smelled so bad, Lewis asked her to stand back, giving her another unintentional insight into his physiology. He could smell himself, too, despite any efforts to clean by Chloe or his captor. He was also sore from being tied down in the same position for so long. All entreaties to untie him were met with blank refusal. He was miserable.

He wasn't giving them what they wanted, either. Sticking to his story about being Canadian and growing up in a cult wasn't convincing, but he wasn't going to give this horrible woman a clue to finding the rest of his clan. She had to be content with pulling out patches of his hair. She seemed fascinated by his answers about the religious traditions of the harthoth, all of which he made up on the spot. He thought the duck god, "Quackers," should have tipped her off, but she kept nodding and writing.

Dr. Perkins had her hair in a limp, greasy topknot.

Her clothes were stained at the armpits and smelled of unhealthy intensity and sour coffee. Chloe came in with breakfast, startling her out of a half doze. After handing another cup of coffee to the professor, soon to join the overflowing trashcan, Chloe sat down to feed him.

"If you let me go use the bathroom, I won't go anywhere," he said, hating the pleading tone in his voice. It was one thing to pee on the floor, but he needed to do more.

"Dr. Perkins, we can't continue keeping him this way for much longer. He'll get bedsores and get sick. Maybe we could use some of your pharmacy to keep him docile? Might get him to talk a little more freely as well?"

"He is very strong, Chloe, I don't think you appreciate just how much stronger he is than a human male. I had quite a struggle getting him down here."

Lewis felt cold. "Down where? Where are we?" he asked.

"Never mind," Dr. Perkins said quickly. "Forget I said anything."

"Chloe, where am I?" Lewis tried, looking directly into her eyes.

Chloe just shook her head and looked away. Lewis felt like crying, but he wasn't going to give them the opportunity to collect his tears or study his "sadness rituals." The conversations had been dry and clinically over his head. It made him feel not just harthoth and "other," but unquestionably less than

260

human. He closed his eyes and willed his body to quiet, a trick that was no longer effective after two days of overuse.

Dr. Perkins stood and stretched, yawning a big mouthful of unbrushed coffee breath into the room. Lewis winced and tried to breathe less. "Oh, man, I need to go home and shower," Dr. Perkins said through her yawn. Chloe and Lewis both nodded. She glared at them. "Chloe, let's sedate him again, and you can stay here with him while I go get some sleep. He'll be fine for a few hours as long as someone is watching him."

"I can do that," Chloe answered, moving to check his restraints. "How much do you want to give him?" She grabbed the syringe kit.

"Oh, I'll do that," Dr. Perkins said, taking the heavy canvas roll from Chloe and extracting a syringe and vial of ketamine. "Can't have you accidentally overdosing him with the wrong thing before we get the research done." Lewis frowned. Was she saying it would be fine to accidentally overdose him *after* the research was done?

The last thing he heard was Chloe asking for the keys so she wouldn't have to pee on the floor. Unfair, he thought, as he floated up and out of the room in a canoe made of newspapers.

Some time later, Lewis found himself hallucinating that all his friends had come to visit him in the room that was "under" something. He smiled broadly and tried to raise his hand, remembering too late that he was tied to the bed. His hand seemed to float up anyway, and he stared at it.

He felt some jostling at his feet and tried to look, floating up off the bed into a roughly seated position. Dream Rami was cutting through the thick webbing straps binding his feet. He took a big deep breath, the first good one in two days, and marveled at how real the air filling his lungs felt. Dream Titania grabbed his face and looked into his eyes, staring right into his soul. He drifted.

"How much did she give him?" Titania asked Chloe.

"A lot. I didn't see the exact amount, but she said his metabolism required extra dosing. She is not that kind of doctor, though, and it's entirely possible she gave him too much."

"He wouldn't have any tolerance, either." Titania turned to Rami. "I know you brought a kit from the mission, but do you have any idea what to do about ketamine?"

"Also not a doctor, unfortunately. I do know that it's unlikely to kill him, but I can't say when he'll be lucid."

"Can't we just carry him?" Chloe asked. "There's three of us, or we can get that big guy out of the car…"

Lewis was back on Mt. Adams, sitting on his favorite tree stump. He was reading a book, but he couldn't make out any of the words. It was okay. He didn't need to know what the book said for it to be good company. He leaned back, resting against another tree, breathing in the clean smells of grass and sun-warmed earth. He swatted at a fly buzzing around him, but it didn't go far. The sound was annoying and persistent.

"Can you get the seatbelt around him? He smells awful." Bill Ben was in the driver's seat of the large SUV he used for the restaurant. The Numbknots Yachtery logo on the side had been covered with blue painter's tape.

"Yeah, I've smelled worse, but not much." Rami got the seatbelt fastened with a loud click.

Lewis felt the straps tightening around his torso again and flailed in panic. His fist struck something meaty and there was swearing. Titania's voice cut through his fear, telling him it was just a seatbelt, but that didn't make any sense. The sheet was bunched under the straps now, and how that could be puzzled and distracted him. He tried to find Titania's voice again and relaxed when he did. He reached out to find her, and was filled with warmth when he felt her small, delicate hand fold into his. He followed her in her sundress, the sunlight filtering in and out around him as she led him through rows and rows of blooming roses.

"Do you think this will work? It's not like he's been drinking, this is heavy shit." Bill Ben was helping keep Lewis upright.

"It's the only thing we've got for this particular

chemical situation," Eve said. "Why he would do this after the thing with his friend—"

"He didn't do this to himself," Rami cut in. "It's a long, weird story."

Eve swore colorfully. "Well, go ahead and try this. How is it too 'complicated' for the hospital again?"

"More weird and longer story," Rami replied. "I'm sorry, Eve, if it was anyone but Lewis, I wouldn't put you in this position."

"I know." Eve patted Rami on the arm. "If it was anyone but Lewis, I wouldn't let you."

The door closed behind Eve as she left the room. Lewis was at a table in his mind with a dozen beers arranged before him, all different colors and glassware. Bill Ben sat across from him, challenging him to guess the beers. Bill Ben's bald head was painfully bright.

Icy water hit him squarely in the face and did not let up. Lewis struggled to get out of the spray, but something was keeping him directly in its path. Men had a hold of both of his arms, and they were torturing him with cold water to the face. The terrible woman must have become impatient for answers.

The shock cut through his drugged haze enough that he could tell one grip was much stronger than the other. He twisted his arm in the weaker man's grip and almost freed himself, but as the water cascaded down his front, freezing on his stomach and privates, dim reality peeked through.

He reintroduced himself to the world with a question.

"Hrrungh Buuh Buh?"

CHAPTER 48

It wasn't Bill Ben's bald head shining; it was the shower light in his eyes. Lewis got enough understandable syllables out to rate warm water. It washed off some of the despair of the last few days. The strawberry-ish shampoo was used by someone. When a washcloth started to rub his torso energetically, he roused himself and took it. He might need help standing, but he would wash his own crotch.

The process of drying off and putting on pajamas was fuzzy, but he heard Titania's voice one more time before he collapsed into a soft bed Eve had made up in the office.

"Is he going to be okay?" Titania asked.

"Yes, I think so," Eve replied. "He needs to sleep it off now."

"Can we stay?" It was Chloe, and Lewis was confused to hear her. "I would like to talk to him before I go face the college."

"Of course," Eve said gently. "And if you're in some

kind of trouble, we are here for you, too. Rami didn't tell me much, but he said you were very brave."

Lewis heard a sharp intake of breath and a little sob. "Thank you," Chloe croaked.

Lewis' dreams were convoluted and dark that night. Manura came to his bedside still aflame, calling him Elko the Coward. He relived the first time he'd seen children laughing, but they weren't playing tag. They were hitting a raccoon with a stick and laughing as if it were the most fun they'd ever had. He was still trapped under Reed College, and Chloe was cutting slices of skin off his arm and putting them in plastic bags.

When he woke up, he ran for the bathroom and spent a very long time in there. When he came out, it was dark in the mission, but Chloe and Titania were sitting in the office chairs waiting.

Titania gave him a worried once-over but didn't say anything.

"Everything come out okay?" Chloe asked.

Lewis smiled. Even he knew that one. "Eventually." He opened his arms to Titania, and she rushed into them. A long hug later, he glanced over at Chloe, wondering why she was there. He was so confused about everything. His mind was still foggy, but he was past the compulsion to sleep.

"Chloe?" he said tentatively, releasing Titania to stand next to him. "What happened to me?"

Chloe dragged a hand through her black hair, making no improvement in the mess. She'd cried through her mascara and her eyes were red and smudgy. She was making a good attempt at composure now, even though he still saw something hurt in her eyes. "Dr. Perkins kidnapped you and held you under the Chemistry Wing at Reed for the last few days. She took a lot of blood and other samples, but I destroyed what I could. No matter what your deal is, you deserve your privacy."

"But I heard you make a deal with her to get publishing credit?"

"I was good, wasn't I?" Chloe said with a genuine smile. "I had to be, or she would never give me the keys."

"I don't really understand why you didn't just call the police?" Titania asked.

Chloe bit her lip and looked at Lewis. After a pause, she said, "I don't know how much to share. It's really Lewis' story."

Lewis hesitated, but he was so exhausted and confused that any dissembling he did would be obvious and ridiculous. He opted for part of the truth. "I don't have legal ID, a friend made it for me."

"I know, you're here from Canada, though. Wouldn't they just send you back?" Titania still wasn't convinced. "I think being deported would be better than being dissected. Portland is a sanctuary city anyway, I don't think they would even do that."

"I am not from Canada," Lewis said with gravity, looking directly into her eyes. He saw shock and surprise, and she leaned away but didn't move away. He also saw curiosity. Maybe it would be okay.

"I don't think I want to know more in case they question me about how this all went down," Chloe interrupted.

"I remember her threatening you, are you really in trouble?"

Another genuine smile, bigger this time with a spark of Chloe's trouble-making gleam. "Tom is very bored at home with his parents. They sent him to rehab and then brought him home for what he's calling 'house arrest.' Dr. Perkins severely underestimated what he could do to fix any inconsistencies there might have been in my work. She also had no idea he'd taken a tiptoe through all her personal files and devices."

"She was blackmailing you?" The tone in Titania's voice had shifted. She'd been impatient and mildly accusatory before, but she was softening as she realized how much she didn't understand about the situation.

"Yeah. It's still possible she'll make it impossible to continue at Reed for me." Chloe shrugged, but her casualness was belied by the worry in her face.

Titania's face hardened. "We will see about that once I'm done with her."

The raw clan leader energy pouring off Titania in that moment made Lewis dizzy. He hadn't realized she had it in her, and it was intoxicating. He sat down heavily, causing both women to lean in. Not until he had a glass of water, a plate of cheese and crackers, an assortment of over-the-counter medications that he didn't want, a blanket, a cold compress, and several deep stares into his pupils were they ready to move on.

Lewis refocused the conversation between stuffing cheese-loaded crackers in his mouth. "What else happened? I remember some parts, but not very much." Chloe ran through more of the details, speaking in a businesslike monotone with her gaze on the floor.

The reality of his captivity finally sunk in. He'd been kept underground in the basement of the Reed College Chemistry Building. His skin prickled, and his awareness that he was currently underground became unbearable. "I have to go outside," he said, stumbling out of his chair and upsetting his plate on the floor. He knocked the water over with his elbow, hearing the glass smash on the floor as he careened around the women to the door of the office.

"Lewis!" Titania tried to grab his arm, but he shook her off.

In a matter of seconds, a red-haired harthoth in striped pajamas burst onto Burnside Avenue and took in a lungful of sort of fresh, free air.

CHAPTER 49

Footsteps pounded after him. Rami stopped and sighed in relief when he saw Lewis standing on the sidewalk.

"I thought you might be making a break for it again. C'mon, man, let's sit down." Rami gently but firmly guided Lewis to a doorstep. Trash was piled in the corner, and it smelled terrible, but Lewis sat. "It seems you are a little worse for wear, dude, and I do not blame you."

"I don't remember very much of it," Lewis confessed. "I have all these bandages, and everything hurts. My head hurts worse than anything else. I know the broad outlines, but the details just swim around and won't stay in one place. I don't know what was real."

"That sucks. You went on a bender, man, one hell of a bender, and it's so much worse because you didn't even do it to yourself. Talk about a roller coaster, you go from killing it on stage to nearly being killed in a basement."

Lewis shuddered. He closed his eyes. "That

doesn't seem real anymore, either. When I try to think about being on stage, how that felt, it doesn't seem real either. I can't remember a lot of it."

"Shit. I'm sorry, man, that blows. You're gonna have to take our word for it that it was awesome until it comes back."

"Will it?" Lewis didn't think he'd ever unravel the past few days.

"Maybe? Let's assume so."

Lewis felt a sudden flood of fury. He was free, and that was the important thing, but Dr. Perkins had stolen things he might never get back. He slammed his fist into the wall next to him, cracking the brick. Rami grabbed his arm before he could do it again.

"Whoa, man! That's not going to help anything!"

Lewis struggled to get his arm free, but Rami held him firm until he calmed down. Realization hit him almost as hard as he'd hit the wall.

"Wait. Why are you this strong?" he asked, staring at Rami's hand. Hair furred the back of his friend's knuckles. He let his arm relax and Rami let go. The effort of holding back the totality of Lewis' harthoth strength should have strained Rami beyond his limits, but he was barely tensed.

A moment passed. Lewis studied Rami's face, seeing the lines differently.

Rami caught his gaze. "I am also not from Canada."

Lewis' system was not prepared for another shock of this magnitude. The first chuckle escaped in a burbled cough, but he was soon in tears, laughing at the absurdity of this, letting go of his raw emotions in a glorious, belly-aching, soul-cleansing gale. Rami joined in at some point, helpless to resist.

The two men had a tough time getting themselves under control, creating two camps of passers-by. Some people smiled and went along with the joke, even if they didn't know the punchline. Others made a point of skirting the doorway with as wide a berth as possible. Their obvious discomfort made Lewis laugh even harder, as he was reminded how dumb he looked, laughing helplessly in his pajamas on Burnside Avenue.

"Whoooo, don't get me started again," Rami finally said, holding his stomach.

"How?" Lewis gasped. "You aren't harthoth, or I would know about it."

"No, I came up from the Klamath region as a little one. I wandered away and some hikers found me. They thought I was a feral child."

That sobered Lewis up right away. "They took you from your clan? Have you been back?"

"I have not been back, Lewis, nor will I ever go back. I am doing so much more here than I would have cloistered in the mountains, secreted away and moving constantly. I remember enough about it to know it's not what I want now. It wasn't at all like what you described, Lewis, with a family and leadership. It was just hiding and surviving. I don't know how much of what I remember is real, but most of it was brutal."

Lewis wasn't in any fit state to unpack that, so he moved on to his next question. "So...did you know the whole time?"

"Yeah, I don't think my sense of smell is as good as yours after all these years in civilization, but I suspected when I met you at the river. By the time we got back to the mission, I knew." Rami smiled. "You were a riot, dude. When you picked your name off a street sign, I knew I needed to keep tabs on you just for the entertainment value. Where'd you learn English?"

"I have a transistor radio. I used to listen to comedians at night and stole a lot of books."

"That's pretty amazing, man. You are one talented dude. Not only did you perform a solid comedy set, you did it in your second language you taught yourself." Rami shook his head. "Your clan missed out on you."

Lewis nearly burst into tears. He wiped at his cheeks as he felt his exhaustion creep back up on him. Everything was too much. He leaned back against the wall and closed his eyes.

"Hey, man, let's get you back to bed. You've had a thing." Rami helped him downstairs, shooing away the questions of Titania and Chloe with a settling hand and hushed "Later."

Lewis expected to fall back to sleep, but he spent the next two hours tossing and turning on the narrow mattress. He couldn't get the convoluted mix of dreams and memories to quiet long enough for him to sleep. The one light doze he managed was ruined by the sounds of the crew making lunch in the kitchen. A tray hit the floor with a loud, clattering bang, and Lewis bolted upright, ready to run again.

Breathing hard and drenched in sweat, he decided this was worse than being up and exhausted. He wandered back to the shower room and turned the water on very hot. His knuckles stung in the soapy water where he'd scraped them on the brick outside. He put on clean clothes and braided his hair. The mirror showed him a man who needed a shave and an exorcism for his personal demons.

He didn't see any of his friends and wondered if they'd left. He wouldn't blame them, he had no idea how long he'd been here, and they thought he was going to sleep.

"Lewis, you're up. Looking a little better." Eve came bustling out of the kitchen with a tray of fragrant, spicy rice, reminding Lewis that he was hungry.

"That smells really good."

Eve smiled. "Come and have some. We can chat while you eat."

CHAPTER 50

Eve took a minute to call Titania and let her know Lewis was up and just fine, and she could see him later. Eve sat down across from him while he shoveled rice and the main dish of veggie curry into his belly.

"How are you doing? Feeling more yourself yet?"

"Sure," Lewis replied automatically. Eve cocked one silver eyebrow. "Well, no, not really," he amended. He stopped eating, putting his utensils down. "I don't know. It's all just a jumble in there, and I don't know."

"Lewis, that's normal. I would be concerned if you really thought you were fine. We have people come through here every day with their own stories of trauma they haven't dealt with for many reasons. You won't be fine for a while, and it'll be a different version of fine. Rami says you can't get the police involved, though I wish you would. I respect it as your choice, I suppose. If you need anything, though, we have all kinds of confidential resources, and I will personally make sure you get the right ones."

"Thank you," Lewis replied, not knowing exactly what she was talking about and certain he wouldn't be able to use any of it. That she'd offered meant something, and that would have to be enough.

Eve was called away to deal with something in the kitchen, and Lewis found himself alone at his table in the busy dining room. The artificial lights bathed the space in harsh brightness and shadows. As he looked around at the other diners, people in various stages of street life and hard times, he suddenly felt very alien. In this complicated web of reasons and realities for their situation, his strands were unconnected to any other.

He pushed the rest of his food away and clumsily got up from the table. He nearly dumped his chair over and attracted a few startled glances. He went back to the office and got his radio out of his bag. KLOL wouldn't come on until later in the evening, if he could get it at all, but he tuned it to a station called KOPB where the voices were all soothing and measured. He finally slept while two women talked in muted tones about the themes in movies one of them seemed to have made herself.

When he woke up later that evening, only one of the chairs in the office was occupied. Chloe sat slumped over, looking at something on her phone screen and scrolling. Her face, illuminated by the soft screen light, looked impossibly fragile.

"Hey," he croaked.

Chloe jumped. "Oh... hey."

"Have you been here long?" he asked, sitting up and stretching his stiff muscles. It was going to take him some time to recover from being held down in one position for over two days.

"Not long. I wasn't sure when you'd wake up and didn't want you to be by yourself."

"Oh, thanks. Can you get the light?"

"Sure," she replied, sniffing and quickly wiping at her face.

Lewis stood, squinting his eyes in anticipation of the coming brightness.

When his eyes adjusted, he saw Chloe's were rimmed with red. Her skin was paler than the inch of blond roots in her messy black hair. It was a portrait of misery.

Lewis took a few steps toward Chloe and put his hands on her shoulders. "I am so sorry, Chlo. About everything."

Chloe's face crumpled and tears slid down her cheeks. "Me too," she gasped. "I was just...mad, I guess."

"Yeah, I know. You saved me, though, didn't you?"

"Part of me didn't want to. You misled us about some particularly important things."

Lewis let go of her shoulders and stepped back. "I don't think you would have believed the truth anyway. I'm a different species, I can see in the dark, I'm stronger than a human and can run faster? That seems like a lot to expect."

"Wait...you can do all that?" Lewis nodded. "Now

I'm rethinking this whole thing. I might kidnap you myself so I can get all the credit." Chloe smirked to show she was joking. Lewis was happy to see some of her attitude return.

"I wasn't really talking about that, though," Chloe murmured, looking at the floor.

Lewis didn't know what to say, but saying nothing seemed very cruel.

"I don't know what to say," he finally said. "I don't think of you that way. In fact, I didn't really know I could think of someone that way until Titania. There are a lot of customs that we don't share."

"Titania is pretty dope, I have to admit." Chloe was studying his face again. "What customs?"

Lewis was embarrassed by this turn of the conversation, but it would make Chloe feel better if he explained. "We don't kiss. I'd heard of it, of course, but that's not something I'd ever seen myself doing. We also don't choose our own mates, so it never crossed my mind that I'd be able to 'date' someone."

Chloe narrowed her eyes, thinking hard, and then a big, mischievous grin lit her face. "Was I your first kiss, Lewis?"

Lewis thought that was a stretch, considering how catastrophic it had been, but he nodded. He felt his cheeks burning.

Chloe began to laugh, covering her eyes with her hands and shaking her head. She sat and scrubbed her hands down her face. "Tom knew I was being stupid. He had no idea how stupid. Now he's never going to let me hear the end of it."

Lewis jumped on the opportunity to change the subject to Tom. Things weren't right between him and Chloe yet, but he could see a way for them to get there. They talked about Tom and let the tension between them slowly erode in the flow of smaller words.

"I can tell him, can't I?" Chloe asked. It was an afterthought.

"I think so, if he's got himself under control." Tom wasn't a risk unless he started blabbing under the influence of something.

"I'll wait until I see for myself. He's going to be back next term on very strict probation, including regular reports by me to his parents. We will have no shenanigans."

"That's good." Lewis was relieved Tom was doing well enough to return.

Chloe got up, making excuse noises about needing to head back to see if there were any new developments with Dr. Perkins. The professor had been silent and unseen since his escape.

As she reached for the office door handle, it turned and Bill Ben barged in. "Did I hear you mention the bad doctor?" Chloe nodded. "She turned up at Numbknots an hour ago with crazy eyes and crazier threats. She had a police officer with her, and her face was all bruised."

All of the skin on Lewis' body was contracting in panic, waves of tightness flowing across his scalp and up from his groin. "Her face?" was all he could breathe out.

"She says you beat her up, Lewis. She's trying to have you arrested."

CHAPTER 51

"She WHAT?" Chloe exploded. She was up and out of her chair in a flash of energized outrage.

"It looks awful. Not just convincing, real. I don't know what she did, but she's in bad shape." Bill Ben looked at Lewis critically. "You still look like shit. Did you realize your hands are shaking? You look like a junkie who's been in a fight. She thought this through."

Lewis looked at his hands, unable to keep them still. As he watched, they trembled at a higher frequency. He didn't know how to respond to this new threat. He just wanted to go back to before, when he was peacefully washing dishes and stealing kisses with Titania behind Numbknots.

Chloe had a lot to say, most of it laced with expletives and threats of further bodily harm. "How can she do that? Does she think I won't say anything? And he's been here the whole time! What kind of fucking checkmate does she think that is?"

Bill Ben looked grim. "We can't prove any of what she did, Chloe, because we kidnapped Lewis back out from under her. Meanwhile, she has all kinds of evidence on her face."

"I need to make a call." Chloe left the room with her phone in her hand.

"I would not want to be on the wrong side of that woman," Bill Ben murmured.

"It's not fun," Lewis answered. "This will all settle down, won't it? I just need to stay out of the way for a little while? I don't have to stay here, I can go up in the hills."

"I don't know. I would like to think that, but the level of obsession this woman has doesn't just fizzle out overnight. You are really under her skin. Chloe said she believed everything in your act, too, so she has some crazy ideas about making her name professionally."

Lewis almost corrected him. He didn't know what stopped him, but he held his truth for just a moment. Chloe burst back into the room with a satisfied and not altogether pleasant look on her face. She did not explain.

Bill Ben sighed, running a hand over his bald head. "I have to get back to the bar, Lewis, but you can't come in until we get this straightened out. Titania is on her way. I just couldn't risk you showing up for work because you didn't know. Hang in there, buddy. This'll get settled and we'll get you an immigration lawyer or something. Get you legal."

Lewis felt a rush of guilt and sadness. He had no right to expect all of this help from his friends, and he was keeping the truth from some of them.

Including Titania, an outstanding issue he needed to fix as soon as he could.

Bill Ben left to go back to the bar. Chloe followed right after him, mumbling something about giving Lewis and Titania some privacy and furiously texting at the same time.

Lewis sat down, overwhelmed. Bill Ben was talking about something like Rami had, legal status, but Lewis wasn't a child. It wouldn't be the same. A lot of uncomfortable questions would have to be answered convincingly. That was assuming he could get out from under the scrutiny of Dr. Perkins and the police department. It all seemed like too much. For the first time, he really considered what would happen if he wasn't successful at humanity.

Titania walked in on this mood and stopped in the doorway. "Lewis? You okay?"

He shook his head, tears spilling down his cheeks into his beard. Titania sat down next to him and took his hand, holding it softly and silently while he cried.

When he had himself under control, Lewis grabbed a wad of tissues from the box on the desk and blew his nose. He looked into Titania's eyes and saw worry, but he also saw caution, and he nearly lost it again. Her trust was bruised.

"Lewis, I need you to tell me what's going on," she said softly. "I don't know what to think right now."

"I'm sorry," he replied. He scooted his chair to face her, gripping the arms and looking at the floor between them. "I would have told you eventually, after the open mic night, but I didn't get the chance."

"Now is your chance." There was steel underneath her words, and he realized "now" was his only chance.

"I am not human. I am something called 'harthoth,' a related species living undiscovered in the mountains. Much of what I told you was true, things like a lack of humor, and my mate would be chosen for me. I just…left out a lot. People seemed to fill in the blanks with guesses, and I let them. That's why you all thought I grew up in a Canadian cult."

Titania let out a big breath. "I don't know whether I believe any of this. Maybe you're just delusional, like really mentally ill, and you believe all this? That doesn't make it real."

This curve in the conversation derailed Lewis completely. He thought of his double-life digitally, either she would believe he was telling the truth or lying. This was a weird stop in-between. "What? You think I'm crazy?"

CHAPTER 52

"It makes more sense than all that stuff you told me before. You can see in the dark? You're stronger than humans? I watched you on stage thinking you were brilliant—you found a way to express how new everything is here for you and entertain people—but now you want me to take it as the literal truth."

Lewis studied her face. Her eyes pleaded with him to explain, to give her something to hang onto in the face of this insanity.

"Okay. You're right. I'm asking you to believe something you have no reason to believe. I don't know how to prove it. The professor probably had convincing evidence before Chloe ruined it."

"Yeah, that's one of the reasons I'm here rather than just writing you off as another bad chapter in the Book of Titania's Terrible Choices. I don't understand why she wanted to capture and test you if you're living in a fantasy land in your head. The odds you're both bonkers in such a specific way are not good."

Lewis thought for a second. He could lift the desk,

but that was probably within the realm of human ability.

"Turn off the light," he said.

Titania hesitated and it broke his heart a little.

"I am not going to move from this chair, I promise. I am going to show you something I can do that humans can't, but I can stay right here."

Titania flipped the light off, creating near perfect darkness in the space. There was a tiny amount of light from the crack under the door, enough for Lewis to see but barely. Titania wouldn't be able to see anything.

"Is it completely dark to you?" he asked her.

"Yeah, I can't see my hand in front of my face," she said, waving her hand.

"Hold up any number of fingers."

She narrowed her eyes, but she held up both hands, one with two fingers and the other with four.

"Your left hand has two fingers up, and your right has four. You made a face at me when I asked you to do it, and now you're biting your lip." He hesitated, but the rest of the words spilled out. "Even in this pitch blackness, you're the most beautiful thing I've ever seen in my life." He held his breath. His gut immediately screamed it was the wrong thing to say by balling into knots.

Titania flipped the light back on, and they blinked at each other. She gave him a small considering smile. "Say I have room in my philosophy for more things than I've dreamt of," she said, "where do we go from here?"

Lewis felt like a condemned man reprieved. She wasn't walking away, at least not yet. He unclenched his insides. "I didn't expect that," he confessed. "I know I don't deserve it."

"I'm not saying I'm convinced," she backtracked. "I might just be indulging a morbid curiosity. I really like you, though, and I feel like the person I know is the real you, even if your story is a little murky. Lord knows mine has a few blanks, even to me. No more half-truths and omissions, though, Lewis. I can't deal with even one more."

"That's fair. I promise." Lewis took the risk of reaching for her hand. To his relief, she took his hand in both of hers. "My name was Elko."

He spent the next thirty minutes talking, answering a few questions as they came up. Titania was curious, listening intently to each new aspect of his life before and after he'd run away from his clan. She wasn't completely over the deception. She did understand why he'd done it, though.

"This is so unbelievable, Lewis. I mean—there are all these legends about creatures in the woods, but we've made them all into monsters. You're describing a more, I don't know, 'primitive' living situation? But you're also in line for the throne? Sort of? It's all so different than the campfire stories." She stopped. "Wait—should I call you Elko?"

"No," he blurted, looking up from the floor where he'd let his eyes rest, afraid to see what might be in the depths of hers. Her eyes weren't filled with disgust or pity or unbelief. They just were. "I like the way you say Lewis. That's who I am now."

Titania smiled and cupped her hand on his cheek. He closed his eyes and leaned into her hand. "I cannot imagine the bravery required to leave absolutely everything you ever knew to come here chasing a dream." She leaned forward and kissed him lightly. He dared not protest or even breathe, afraid he'd ruin the moment.

The door crashed open and ruined the moment for him. He and Titania both jumped and stumbled out of their chairs.

"Oh, sorry," Rami said cheerfully. "Didn't realize I'd be interrupting something!" He winked at Lewis, who was turning the same color as his copper hair. Rami's face sobered. "We probably should have a conversation, though, my friend."

"Can we do it outside?" Lewis pleaded. "I am starting to feel panicky down here."

"You guys go ahead," Titania said. "I need some time to process some of what I just heard."

Rami's eyebrows shot up and he looked at Lewis. "You told her?"

"Yeah. I told her. No more secrets." Titania gave him a light kiss on the cheek and left, promising to be back in the morning.

"That was bold, dude. How'd she take it? Wait, never mind, I saw how she took it." Rami laughed.

Lewis headed to the door, feeling his anxiety mount now that he'd admitted it was there, but Rami held an arm in front of him. "You gotta wait a minute, that's what we need to talk about."

Lewis almost pushed past Rami anyway. When he didn't actively think about being underground, it was still just barely okay, and mentioning it had him thinking about it. Rami shook his head, closing the door behind him. Lewis relented, sitting in his chair. His leg bounced a manic drumbeat.

"You remember my friends, Officer Sweeley and Officer Ramirez? I ran into them on my way here this morning. They had some extremely specific questions about my 'friend who ran through town barefoot.' I guess there's a description being circulated with some pictures, saying you assaulted someone?"

"Yeah, the professor beat herself up and accused me. The police were over at the bar earlier."

"If they knock on the door here, Eve will let them in, Lewis. She's already uncomfortable with all this, and she has bigger considerations than one weird dude with a likable personality. You can't stay here."

CHAPTER 53

The Stumptown Ethical Atheists Mission wasn't even Lewis' favorite place to be, underground, but having it torn away as his refuge was a blow he hadn't expected. He sat back down. The exhilaration of Titania's conditional acceptance was replaced by an acute sense of helplessness.

"But where do I go?" he asked.

"If it seemed like something that would blow over, I'd take you to my place, but this is big and weird, man. It's not going to go away in a couple of days, and my wife doesn't like having people over for more than—"

"Your what?" Lewis wasn't sure he'd heard correctly.

"My wife. I don't talk about her around here because there are good reasons to keep my work and personal life separate, but I'm married and she doesn't like strangers around the kids."

Lewis felt betrayed for no reason he could articulate, so he tried to smooth his features over. Rami saw enough of the emotion to guess.

"Look, she doesn't know about my origins, either. It didn't need to come up. The kids are adopted, because I told her I wanted to do for someone else, and that was true. I tell her I don't remember much of my childhood before, and that's true as well. I'm used to keeping things in their proper places. You're out here mixing everything about you up in a big stew pot and the smell is not appetizing."

Lewis was hurt. "So this is all my fault? I shouldn't have told anyone? I shouldn't have done my stand-up?"

"Hell, maybe especially the stand-up, Lewis. It seemed okay at the time, because no one would believe it literally, but then the crazed up academic came along. Chloe knows enough, and now you're telling Titania—what's next? A billboard?" Rami was agitated, a stark contrast from his mild, even demeanor.

"Why are you so upset about this, Rami?" Lewis was upset about his own situation, but this seemed different.

"Because I'm at risk, too. Some secrets—they need to stay secret, you dig?"

Lewis had a flash of Rami separated from his family by force and studied by scientists, hounded out of his comfortable anonymity into a spotlight he absolutely didn't want. It was different. Lewis wasn't responsible for anyone but himself, and he was doing a poor job on that front if he was honest.

"Bill Ben thinks he's going to get me a lawyer," Lewis murmured.

Rami eyes were full of sadness. "Believe me, man, if there was a way, I would let him use my phone."

"I have to think."

"I'll help you pack up."

It didn't take long to pack Lewis' few things. Rami grabbed him a couple of fresh outfits from the clothes closet and tucked a bottle of the fake strawberry shampoo under them. He put a ball cap on Lewis' head, pulling it down low.

"You could shave. That would make a big difference. Cut off your hair, too. All that red hair is distinctive."

"Yeah, maybe." Lewis had no intention of doing either. He tucked his braid up into the hat, creating a weird, uncomfortable lump. He left it there to prove he had things under control.

Finding Eve in the kitchen, he tried to make a decent job of thank you and good-bye, but the mishmash of words that came out sounded like he was dying and she was responsible for his death in some way he was very grateful about.

"Lewis? Are you telling me you're leaving?" she asked.

"Yes. I am leaving, and I wanted to say thank you for everything."

Eve pulled him into a hug. "You are always welcome here, Lewis Clark. I hope we'll see you again really soon."

He didn't have the heart to say anything contrary, so he just nodded.

As he walked up the stairs, Rami behind him, he had an unexpected pang of regret. He hadn't given his mother the same consideration. It might have been because he knew she wouldn't accept his decision or support him, but he'd disappeared without a word. How did this near stranger merit so much more?

On the street, it was early evening and most of the people on Burnside were lined up for meals and shelters. He stood for just a moment, taking in all the humanity with its noise and smells. Rami put a hand on his shoulder, bringing him back to the moment.

"If I go somewhere else, this is what I'll be, isn't it?" Lewis asked.

"Wherever you go, Lewis, I suspect you will be something special, but yeah. This is probably what you should expect, unless you can figure out some way to get legal." Lewis shook his head. Rami patted his shoulder and let go. "Yeah. It's complicated with the police involved."

"I guess I'll just start walking." Lewis looked at Rami's face and could tell this wasn't adequate. "I mean, I'll see you around, right?"

"Before you do anything permanent, brother, you come back here and talk to me, okay? I may not be able to help you as much as I want to, but that doesn't mean I can't help at all." Rami grabbed Lewis in a tight hug, slapping him soundly on the back three times before letting go. Lewis nodded, pulled his cap lower, and started walking.

He stayed on smaller streets and cut through alleys to avoid being spotted by the infrequent patrol cars on Portland's streets. An officer on horseback was busy talking to some tourists and posing for pictures. Lewis turned down another street and kept his head down. Eventually, he found himself back on the bank of the Willamette River, instinct turning him toward the water once again.

CHAPTER 54

As he sat on the bank, watching the water roll by, the sun moved behind the buildings and mountains at his back, stretching his shadow to the river's edge. He raised both hands over his head, imagining the water flowing over and through his fingers. It was an illusion. All of this had been a kind of illusion.

The existence of Rami's family had thrown him more than he could explain. The life he thought he was mastering, with his job at the bar, Titania, and his spot in the woods at Reed, was so much smaller than he realized. It was pretending to be human. He couldn't see a path to what Rami had. He would start thinking about his relationship with Titania, imagine it getting more serious, and then it just blanked out, a white, unmarked canvas with no indication of where he should start. He didn't even know if he had it right side up.

He was near the River View Natural Area. The trees would give him a place to sleep for the night. He was exhausted. Every possible decision from here on out seemed catastrophic in some way. He needed to talk to Titania, but that would have to wait. Realizing he could have a cell phone and hadn't ever considered it left another mark on his bruised psyche.

Crossing the busy road with considerably less style this time, he walked into the nature preserve in the glooming dark. He felt a shiver of unfamiliar unease. The dark didn't bother him, except now it did, because there were people hunting him. This danger was not the clean need of animals or the earth. It was devious, and evil, and the darkness of that soul-corrupting intent made the night press against him, hinting at all the things he couldn't see.

The dawn rubbed its sandpapery tongue across the inside of Lewis' eyelids after a terrible night of nightmares and startled awakenings. He awoke groggy and disoriented. He'd slept using his bag as a pillow, and his neck hurt when he looked to the side. The morning dew soaked everything. He took off his hat and let his hair free, feeling the skin on his scalp relax. His damp clothes stuck to him, and he considered taking them off as well but decided against it. He had to keep moving.

After a quick few minutes of straightening things and peeing behind a tree, he headed toward the other side of the preserve. The extent of his plan for the day was to find somewhere to hole up less frequented by dogs and runners. Then he would find a map of North America and poke a finger at it with his eyes closed.

"Hey!"

The shout came from behind him. Lewis didn't look back, he just ran.

"HEY!" The voice was louder, but not keeping up with him. He veered into the brush, intending to cut across the treed area to get away.

"DAMMIT, LEWIS! SLOW DOWN!"

The voice gave him pause. He knew it. That didn't mean he should trust it, though.

He ran for another thirty seconds and quickly hid his bags in a clump of blackberry bushes, scratching his arms through his shirt and staining his hands with blackberry juice. The smell of the crushed berries made him salivate. His stomach gave an angry rumble. No time for that. A large oak tree had excellent climbing limbs, and he easily ascended to the upper branches. He had an unobstructed view of the forest almost to the path he'd abandoned.

While his other senses were better than human, his hearing was not. That didn't matter, however, as his pursuer came flailing and swearing through the brush as fast as she could.

"When I find him, I am going to chop pieces off him just for fun," she grumbled, disentangling from a thorny vine.

"Chloe?" Lewis peered down at the sweaty, annoyed young woman.

"Yeah, Lewis, it's me." She brushed her black hair back from her face and scowled at him.

"How did you find me?"

"The perpetrator always goes back to the scene of

the crime," she replied. "Come down."

"Huh?"

"COME. DOWN."

Lewis scrambled down and retrieved his bags. Chloe was already making her way back to the pathway, still swearing under her breath.

Lewis caught up to her and lightly touched her elbow. "Chlo?"

"You're just lucky I'm a genius and you're a predictable oaf. Let's get to a place we can sit down," she said. "I've been wandering all over Portland since I found out Rami kicked you out of the mission, and I'm exhausted." She did look it. Her eyes were rimmed with black circles and her purple t-shirt was rumpled and stained under the armpits. He let her set the pace until they found a picnic table under the shade of enormous pine trees.

"Rami didn't exactly kick me out," he ventured.

"Oh, sure he did, he just had a good reason. Dr. Perkins is being a crazy bitch. I got called into the administration office and asked what I knew about the situation in front of campus security yesterday. It was strongly implied that any information I withheld would be used as grounds for disciplinary action."

"That's not fair!" Lewis protested.

"Yeah, well, Tom and I have had a little project brewing that will take care of that, should the need arise." She smiled in a way that wasn't at all reassuring.

Lewis decided not to ask. He wasn't sure he would understand it anyway. "Why were you looking for me?" he asked.

Chloe picked apart a cluster of pine needles on the table while she talked. "Well, I didn't think cutting you loose in the world without a plan or any resources or contact information was really a great idea. I don't know what Rami was thinking. Anyway, we need to plan your next move. Where are you going to go? Tom can FedEx me some new items with a different name, new address, but we need to make it work for what you're going to ... what?"

She looked at Lewis and realized he was beyond overwhelmed by this conversation. She waited for him to say something.

He had to be honest. "I don't have a clue what I'm going to do next. I didn't have a plan when I came here." He was painfully aware of how naive that had been now. "I'm not a guy with 'plans.'"

Chloe was silent for a few long seconds, appraising him anew. "You can't just hide up trees and hope no one finds you."

Lewis shrugged. "I was going to poke a map with my finger." Chloe shook her head in disgust.

"Come on, then, we need to get you something to eat, and we need to get you in touch with Titania. Maybe she knows a place you can hide out until you have an actual plan."

"I don't want to put her in danger."

"She's a grown woman, idiot, she can make up her own mind. Give her that choice. Nobody needs you to be some kind of noble homeless hero right now, especially not Titania. You didn't see her last night when she showed up and you weren't there."

Lewis felt his gut roll over. "But I didn't think she was going to come back...I was going to find her at work later...I mean..." He stopped stammering and felt the blood rush to his face.

"Yeah, because she was just going to go on with life as normal while you're out here running around in danger. Fucking hell." Chloe wiped a hand across her tired eyes and sighed. She reached into her small crossbody pack and handed him a pair of sunglasses. "You break these, I will be very unhappy, Lewis, but we need every advantage we can get here."

CHAPTER 55

It was still early when they caught the bus to Raleigh Hills. Lewis slumped into his seat with his head down and sunglasses on. Chloe sat next to him taking up as much space as a slightly emo, obviously hassled young woman could. It was a surprisingly large amount. The seats around them stayed empty. It didn't hurt that they were going against the morning commute.

Chloe was watching the stops carefully. She had Titania's address from a hurried text exchange on the walk to the bus line, but she hadn't been there before. "I think it's the next stop," she said, looking at her phone and the marquee at the front of the bus. Lewis shook off the sleepiness of the rumbling bus motor.

The neighborhood where Titania lived was mostly older, brick apartment buildings with small houses on big lots in between. It was very hilly, and the warming temperatures and effort made Lewis sweat immediately. He wished again that humans weren't so attached to clothes and shoes.

Chloe consulted her phone again and texted Titania to let her know they were close. The building was less well-maintained than the others around it, a three-story post-war box with a mix of new and elderly asphalt shingles. A man in pajama pants and a stretched-out t-shirt sat outside the breezeway in a lawn chair, smoking. He stared at Chloe without smiling as they approached. Chloe gave him a casual middle finger, making him laugh and shake his head.

Titania's apartment was on the second floor. Chloe raised her hand to knock, but the door flew open before her fist hit the faded red paint. She put her hand down and stepped back. Titania stood in the shadow of her dark apartment, studying Lewis in his hat, sunglasses, and sweaty clothes.

"Are you okay?" she finally asked.

"No," he admitted. His face crumpled into ugly tears. Titania reached out her hand and took his, leading him inside to the couch where he struggled to regain his composure and she lost hers. Chloe followed, shutting the door. The inside of Titania's apartment was full of mismatched furniture and art, all of it in passable condition but none of it new. A beaded batik curtain with a swirling rainbow pattern separated the living room from the small kitchen. The light curtains on the small windows were overlaid with macramé panels in tan and brown.

"Nice, very boho," Chloe said in the awkward, hitching conversational lapse.

"Thanks," Titania gulped. "I like to thrift."

The mundanity of the compliment calmed the roiling emotional tide in the room. Chloe tossed them a box of tissues off the table and gave them a moment to mop themselves up.

"You scared me," Titania said to Lewis. "I didn't know if I would ever see you again."

"I scared me, too. I'm sorry. I thought I would come to Numbknots later, but I kind of didn't think any of it through. That's my style."

Titania laughed softly. "Yeah, I'm getting that. Well, let's get a better plan in place this time." She turned to Chloe. "Thank you. I mean that. I had no idea where to even start."

"Riverview was a desperation move, honestly. When I found out he wasn't in his little den at Reed, I thought maybe I'd lost him."

"You knew about that?" Lewis asked.

Chloe raised her eyebrows and smirked.

"Oh. Sure you did," Lewis mumbled. He wondered if he would ever realize the depths to which he'd underestimated this young woman.

She stood then, tugging at her wrinkled shirt and sighing. "I am very tired, and you two need to talk about whatever people talk about in this very unique situation. I'm going to go grab a shower and I'll text you later after I nap." She spoke directly to Titania then. "If *anything at all weird* happens, you call me. Call Bill Ben. Call everyone." Titania nodded.

After Chloe left, Titania gently said, "Lewis, you

smell terrible."

Lewis laughed. "Yes, I know. I've had a rough couple of days." He made a show of sniffing an armpit and gagging, and Titania laughed with him.

"I'm not really ready for you to be out of my sight, though." Titania grabbed his hand and held it in her lap.

Lewis looked at her in the dim room and saw what she'd been through in the last few days on her tired face. Her eyes were red and sunken, her locs were in disarray. Her dress, a brown one with embroidered flowers around the neck, had several spots that looked like food on it. There was a large crease up the front of the skirt where she'd slept in it. Her vulnerability on his behalf broke his heart.

He reached up and touched her face, leaning in to kiss her gently. She was holding her breath. A tear traced the tracks of its predecessors. He brushed it off with his thumb, smearing dirt across her cheek.

"I really have to take a shower," he said.

"I know," she replied.

Titania's shower was clean and stocked with spicy soaps and cleansers that were a huge improvement over the cheap stuff at the mission. Lewis felt awkward being naked in her apartment, so he engaged the flimsy, symbolic lock on the door. He toweled off with her fringed cotton towels and looked in the full-length mirror on the back of the door.

Without clothing, his human facade was less

successful. His body was an uncultivated meadow of thick hair with a marginally maintained garden on top. He was overdue for a shave and a trim, and that didn't help. He dressed, avoiding looking in the mirror again.

Titania had changed into a blue peasant top and faded jeans with her locs pulled back in a paisley bandanna. Lewis smelled coffee. He refused the cup that was offered.

"Coffee is terrible," he said. "Why you drink it will forever remain a mystery to me."

"To mysteries," Titania said, lifting her cup in a toast.

The muted light in the room backlit her in a glowing aura, and Lewis felt an electric shiver ripple through his skin.

"I have something else I need to tell you," he blurted. He couldn't see her expression, but she shifted slightly, tilting her head in an "I'm listening" posture.

He almost chickened out then. She waited him out.

"Titania, I'm not sure what this means, but I think I love you."

Titania dropped her coffee cup on the floor. It bounced on the thick carpet, spraying hot coffee in a physics-defying arc that reached halfway across the room.

Lewis closed the distance and felt his foot squelch in the warm, soggy carpet. He put his arms around Titania and kissed her deeply, tasting the coffee and not caring. She put her arms around his neck, holding his mouth to hers as she responded. Lewis had never hated clothing more. He pressed her body into his, wanting to become intertwined at the molecular level. She grabbed a handful of his hair, and he moaned softly.

Lewis was keenly interested in seeing where this was going. Passion wasn't something he'd seen much of other than an occasional flash of harthoth anger. He was realizing there was an entire emotional universe lacking in the clan. Universes. Galaxies in universes in metaverses.

Titania's hand migrated to the front of his shirt, unbuttoning the buttons in the random order of need. As her fingers found his skin, Lewis gasped. She brushed her fingertips through his thick hair, each light fingertip leaving a comet tail of sparks.

He was overwhelmed by the sensations of his body responding to hers. He let her go and pulled back slightly, looking into her eyes.

"I think you're right," Titania announced, grinning. Lewis smiled back.

"And how do you feel about that?" he asked.

Titania continued to smile. "I think—"

Pounding on the front door drowned out whatever she said next.

CHAPTER 56

Titania sprung away from Lewis as if they'd been caught setting a fire, which was true enough, and he scrabbled at his buttons.

BANG! BANG! BANG!

Titania peeked out the window curtains and swore. "Shit, it's Dr. Perkins and one of my neighbors," she hissed. "You have to hide!"

BANG! BANG! BANG!

Lewis scrambled into the bathroom and closed the door. The flimsy door didn't stop any of the sound from reaching him.

"Go away!" Titania yelled.

"I know you are hiding him in there! He's a violent monster, you don't know what he's capable of!" Dr. Perkins was laying it on thick.

Lewis checked the small window in the bathroom, realizing that even if he did fit through it, he'd have a two-story drop. He could probably deal with that, there were taller trees he'd fallen out of, but it would leave Titania dealing with Dr. Perkins on her own.

"I am calling the police right now! You are not appreciating the danger of this situation!" Dr. Perkins yelled.

"Oh, I think I have a great handle on this situation," Titania replied. "You are crazy. Go away."

"I. AM. NOT. CRAZY!" More pounding on the door with both fists and possibly a foot belied her claim.

Titania risked leaving the door to talk to Lewis about this new development. "I don't know how she knows you're here. Do you think Chloe…?" she hissed.

Lewis shook his head vigorously. "No. Definitely not." He thought for a moment. "I mean, I don't think so. I know she was threatening Chloe?" He shrugged, feeling dejected. "I can't say she didn't say something." The possibility of Chloe betraying him for real made him a little sick. Even if it were under duress, it was an elaborate trap she'd lured him into.

Dr. Perkins was talking to the police dispatcher on her phone. "Yes, he's here right now and I just don't know what he'll do. Yes, I'm afraid he might attack me again! Send officers. Yes, I will get to a safe place."

Titania peeked through the window and saw her neighbor, the guy in the t-shirt and pajama pants, holding out his hand to the professor. She gave him a small stack of bills from her wallet, and he nodded and left.

"That asshole!" Titania exclaimed. Turning to Lewis, she said, "It wasn't Chloe. She just paid off my neighbor."

"The smoking man?" Lewis asked.

"Probably, he sits down there in a ratty lawn chair all day."

BANG! BANG! BANG!

"The police are on their way, Elko! It's only a matter of time!"

Facing this situation here, in Titania's apartment, made Lewis realize he had to stop hiding behind all the other people in his life. He strode from the tiny bathroom to the front door, pulling hard on the knob. The locked doorknob flew off in his hand, causing him to stumble back. The other half fell on the concrete walkway outside.

"Lewis, what are you doing?" Titania whispered.

"I need to take care of this," he said, grabbing the hole where the knob had been and yanking the door open. The deadbolt tore the door framing into sharp splinters. Dr. Perkins flinched away from the crack of the wood giving way. Lewis stood framed in the dim doorway, breathing hard and looking at the woman who'd taken his whole new life away.

Dr. Perkins pasted on a false smile. "If you come with me right now, I will drop the charges, *Elko*." The emphasis she put on his harthoth name was both violatingly intimate and threatening. "We can try again. It'll be different this time! I'll let you give interviews. You can be famous. People will want to watch your little act just because of what you are, don't you see?"

Titania grabbed his arm. "If there's anything I know, it's never different this time," she said seriously.

Lewis was stuck on something else in that offer. "My 'little act'?" he said incredulously. Of all the things he could and should be mad about in her presumptions, the insult to his one crowning moment, the moment she'd mostly stolen with her mind-wiping drugs, was the thing he could least forgive. The patronizing way Dr. Perkins referred to his ambition told him everything he needed to know about her intentions.

He squared his shoulders and looked into her wild eyes. "I came here because I was underestimated and shoved aside every minute of my life. I was never going to be more than a shabby backup plan. Why would I agree to be some kind of zoo animal? Will you give me a little machine to get my food from so I don't get bored? Maybe I would like a barrel to roll around in my cage?"

"No, no, you're taking it all wrong." Dr. Perkins tried to look sane and in-control, straightening her blouse. "We can help each other! I get the credit for the scientific part, and you get to be..." She trailed off, not sure what she could offer him. Lewis kept his silence, not wanting to participate in her fiction.

Titania did not keep her silence. "You horrible bitch," she said evenly. "You kidnapped him, drugged him, and treated him like a lab rat, and now you expect him to trust you? Why would he do that?"

"I can see how you might take that and make it into something it isn't, but you don't know how hard it is to make it as a female academic.

You're what, *a bartender?* You wouldn't understand. Flinging drinks and collecting dollar bills all night," she sneered. Turning back to Lewis, she said, "I can even give you a share of the money. There will be publishing, speaking engagements, maybe even television. I'll give you five percent." Dr. Perkins tried to give him an encouraging smile, but it was too hungry to be comforting.

Sirens approached from a distance, and Lewis knew it was only a matter of moments before the police arrived. Looking at the railing, an image of Dr. Perkins flying off the second story flitted through his mind. He was horrified.

"I'm not going to cooperate with you, Dr. Perkins. Never." Lewis stepped closer and growled the rest at her in his first language. "Meg al bar nino agan."

It was a mistake. At the sound of his native harthoth, Dr. Perkins' interest flamed higher. "Is that your language? Say more," she demanded, grabbing Lewis by the arm. He shook her off, but she wasn't deterred.

The sirens were getting louder, and Titania looked worriedly out at the street and parking lot. "Lewis, you have to go," she pleaded.

Dr. Perkins rounded on her. "You stay out of this!" she screamed. "I have done more and been more and worked harder all my life, and it's never enough! Every time I think I'm going to break through, the goalposts move! FINALLY, I have the chance to get the recognition I deserve, and no one is going to take that from me! NO ONE!"

Lewis used her momentary preoccupation with Titania to grab his bags just inside the broken door. Dr. Perkins whirled to see what he was doing and lunged toward him, screaming again. Apartment doors were opening a crack as people heard the professor's ranting.

Titania was between them in an instant. "GO, LEWIS, NOW!" she yelled. The sirens were very close, and he thought he saw the flash of red and blue lights a street over.

There was so much left undone, and unsaid, he nearly faltered, but his fear of being in the hands of human authorities won out. Lewis bolted for the stairs as the incoherent professor pushed at Titania, trying to get to him.

"Oh, no, that's not how this is going to go," Titania muttered, and she hauled back and punched Dr. Perkins in the face as hard as she could.

CHAPTER 57

Lewis glanced back at the sound of fist hitting flesh and saw the professor stagger back, clutching her face and yelping. Titania waved her bloody hand at him, encouraging him on. She winced at the movement, likely because of the finger jutting at a wrong angle, but she grinned and bobbed her eyebrows. There were so many things about her Lewis had not yet learned.

Dr. Perkins recovered enough to lunge at Titania again, blood streaming from her nose. Her howl of rage forced Lewis to take an involuntary step toward the women, but Titania matched the professor's battle cry, screaming, "GET OUT OF HERE! I HAVE THIS!" The sirens were loud and present. Lewis ran.

Putting on full speed, he flashed through the older homes and yards, leaping over low chain-link fences and through sprinklers. The police officers had a K-9 unit with them, and Lewis could hear the dog whining and yipping, ready to go. A police officer yelled, "Zelda, reveiren!" The dog stopped barking and started working. She had little chance of catching up at this pace, but he knew he could lose his head start to a dead end.

His heart pounded in his chest and his lungs burned. He realized he'd gotten a little out of shape. He slowed very slightly to give his body a chance to recover, but the sirens switched on his panic mode. The police cars were pacing him on the edge of the neighborhood, trying to use the K-9 to draw him into a funnel where they could cut him off.

It was a good strategy for most fugitives, but most fugitives hadn't grown up playing hunting games with Fliggo on Mt. Adams. Lewis stopped in the space between two fences for a moment and thought. If he went straight back toward Titania's place, the dog would be on him with its handler not far behind. If he cut up and across, forming a kind of V-shape, he might be spotted, but it was unlikely. He decided to take a serious risk and backtrack half a block before cutting over. As he veered to the right down a jogging path, he saw a flash of brown fur coming at him down the hill at full speed.

Lewis felt like he was running for his life. The confrontation with Dr. Perkins and his heightened emotions surrounding Titania created a chemical maelstrom he turned into anger and motive power. A small part of him knew he'd pay later, but right now, he used every bit of that whirling emotion to power his tired legs a little faster.

Zelda the K-9, seeing a fleeing figure, knew exactly who she was chasing and tried to catch up. Only Lewis' harthoth speed saved him. The dog was a swift and determined pursuer, and there weren't enough barriers for him to lose her by jumping fences or ducking through underpasses. She barked once, more like a signal for her handler than excitement. Lewis and Zelda had outrun the officers on foot, and it was now just pursuer and pursued. Lewis was dashing across the residential streets without looking.

He could fight off the dog if it came to that, but he didn't want to hurt her for doing her job. He couldn't afford the delay, either. He looked desperately around him, trying to will an escape into existence. He heard the traffic noise of a major highway. He couldn't keep track of his direction anymore, he was blindly running away from the K-9. There were still sirens, now coming from several directions and confusing him, but farther away than they'd been a few minutes before. Reinforcements were headed in his general direction but not straight for him.

He entered a mixed business area with a small strip mall. Mexican and Thai restaurants sat next to a hair salon and shipping specialist. As he ran through the alley past some especially pungent dumpsters, he realized what he was going to have to do. If the dog couldn't see him, that meant it was following his scent.

He lifted the lid of a dumpster behind a Mexican restaurant. The smells of rotting food were spicy and permeating, including a piquant onion salsa, rancid refried beans, carnitas that were no doubt delicious three days prior. It was a raccoon's paradise. It hadn't been emptied in a while.

Leaving his own bags on the ground, Lewis climbed into the dumpster, frantically spilling the contents of several clear plastic garbage bags in a mound on top of the other trash. The stench made his eyes water. Every individual smell demanded his attention. His olfactory virtuosity broke the different odors into their individual notes and brought them crashing back together in a discordant disaster. Without giving himself time to think about it, Lewis threw himself into the pile of garbage, rolling around and rubbing it into his hair, all over his clothes, and on the bottoms of his shoes.

He flung himself back out of the dumpster and grabbed his bags. He wanted to vomit, but it was a toss-up whether it was the smell or the exertion. A yip from Zelda a block over told him he'd lost more time than he wanted. He went back over his trail for a few feet to a narrow walkway between the Mexican restaurant and a laundromat. The overwhelming scent of laundry soap and fabric softeners made him gag again.

The strip mall faced SW Canyon Road, a major four-lane artery with fast traffic and huge overhanging trees. He sprinted down the sidewalk, desperately dodging uneven pavement slabs pushed up by massive tree roots. The few people he sped past might have reacted to his smell or his flight, but he was going too fast to see.

Uncomfortable with the busy traffic and possible police presence on the larger street, he dashed across the road and turned left on Camelot Court. He'd had a copy of *The Mists of Avalon* that was his favorite book for a season. Camelot seemed like a good omen, if you didn't think too hard about the fate of the Round Table.

It turned out to be a good move. The road crossed over Highway 26, the main route out of Portland to the west. The noise of the traffic on the highway meant he wouldn't be able to hear Zelda if she were still behind him, but he hoped she was too confused by his eau de refried beans to follow.

He ran across the overpass, slowing down a little as he wound onto the street beyond. It descended into a park with wide open spaces and several wide paved lanes. On the right, he could see and hear a large fountain with a circular surrounding pond. It was peaceful and deserted, but there was little cover and no obvious place to hide.

He slowed to a fast walk, feeling his heart and lungs protesting at the prolonged flight. He turned and looked behind him, searching the overpass for any sign of a pursuing police dog. His dip in the discarded salsa seemed to have worked. The bridge remained empty.

Even so, it wouldn't be good to hang out next to the highway in plain sight. There were a few trees, but they were all trimmed up the trunks too far to climb. He kept going, hitting a jog. As he scanned the park, he realized why it was so open and deserted. He froze.

Row after row of headstones arced around the

lawns in shades from alabaster to brick red to onyx. There were areas of upright markers, some with artificial flowers in attached vases, and sweeping acres of inset gravestones. A shiver crawled down Lewis' sweat-soaked spine. This was an enormous field of underground corpses. It was the beginning of a harthoth horror story.

He nearly bolted back the way he'd come. Only the realization that he would put himself directly in the path of the searching police stopped him. The only solution was another exit from the cemetery. That meant going through it. He balled his fists and girded his loins.

Camelot Court ended in a choice, left or right? Lewis chose the right-hand lane, toward the large fountain. The field to his right was mowed, but not yet in use by the funeral home. The absence of grave markers soothed him a little. He focused on that side of the road, walking quickly but no longer running. He smelled himself with every step. The gagging stench of the Mexican dumpster and his panic sweat were thick in the air around him. He could imagine a cloud following him.

The water in the fountain grew louder as he approached. The central jet shot straight up in the air for fifteen feet, crashing back down into the pond in a circular cascade. Smaller jets ringed the center, adding a tinkling counterpoint and creating ripples that joined and flowed across the pond. Plantings of shrubs and trees circled a walkway around the water, providing some shade and privacy.

Given his current state, it looked irresistibly refreshing. Lewis looked around the memorial garden, seeing no one. Putting his bags on a bench, he quickly stripped off his clothes to his underwear. Briefly considering the sweat soaking his tighty-whities, he shimmied out of those, too. He stuffed his ruined clothes under a bench and waded into the fountain. The water was cool and not especially pristine, but it was cleaner than he was.

While the pond only came up to mid-calf, the outer ring of jets shot chilly water as high as his testicles. He jumped, letting out a little squeak as his body registered the shock. Deciding that living dangerously was the theme of the day, he plunged into the curtain of water in the center, letting the drops fall from the sky onto his entire body. It took his breath away.

He sluiced water into his hair and beard, dislodging any remaining ground beef and tortilla fragments. Busily scrubbing through all the hair on his body, he felt better. He would put on some clean clothes, head somewhere he could sleep tonight, and figure out how to contact one of his friends in the morning. He shook his head, letting the cool water fan out into new ripples in the pond, shaking off fear and adrenaline.

Once he'd rinsed off every inch of his body, he slogged through the water toward the bench where he'd left his bags. A sound from the bushes behind him caused him to whirl around, ineffectively covering his privates with his hands, but a bird hopped from branch to branch, unconcerned with his lack of modesty.

It was a reminder that he wasn't in the forest under a secluded waterfall, however, and he rifled through his pack, looking for the clean change of clothes he'd stuffed in there during his exit from the Stumptown Mission.

Words came to him from outside the sheltering vegetation, moving away toward the larger buildings to his right. The woman's voice was hushed, but her whisper carried.

"Yes, Finley Sunset Hills. There's a man here, I don't know if he's dangerous or not, but he was taking a naked shower in the fountain. That's really not allowed."

CHAPTER 58

The fear and adrenaline hit again. Someone was here, and they'd seen him in the water, and now they were on the phone with what had to be the police. Lewis didn't think he had time to get dressed now. Yanking his bags closed, he bolted out of the serenity garden surrounding the fountain to the road through the cemetery.

"Hey! Hey! You can't run through here naked!" yelled the woman on the phone, a short brunette in a somber navy suit.

I already am, Lewis thought, putting on a little more speed. He was quickly out of sight of the woman and in a copse of trees, but again, there were none that would provide a good hiding place. He resisted the urge to go off the paved drive, loathe to run across rows of graves stepping on Beloved Grandmother's remains.

He found out his decision to follow the road out of the cemetery was not a good one. The road turned back on itself, returning to the center of the park. He stopped and looked around, but there was a tall fence topped with wire coils at the edges of the cemetery. Why anyone would need to be kept in or out, he had no idea, but he was not going to be climbing over sharp wire naked.

Hoping helplessly for a fork in the road or exit in front of him, he took off again at about three-quarter speed. As he came back into the populated cemetery grounds, the path ended in another left/right choice. He went right again, past buildings constructed of granite and marble with names inscribed up and across the walls in large rectangles. Horrified, he realized there must be more bodies in those buildings, shelved like loaves of bread at the store. He shuddered and kept moving. No place to hide in those halls, anyway.

He was so distracted by the thought of a cabinet of corpses, he didn't see the flashing lights of the police cruiser until he was nearly to the next split in the road. The black and white had its lights going, but no siren. They must not have put together the manhunt and his impromptu shower yet. He bolted behind a tree, watching the car slowly glide into the cemetery from what had to be the exit.

There was an equal chance they would turn right, and he quickly sent a wish to the old harthoth gods he didn't believe in for it to manifest. His gods laughed and waved the officers left.

Lewis saw nothing he could hide behind, no trees that would provide cover, and no buildings that weren't completely open to scrutiny. If he tried to run for the entrance by the fountain, no doubt he'd find another cruiser waiting to pick him up there.

His eye finally caught on something out of place, something besides ranks of gravestones. A dark green tarp was laid out on the ground with several large cement blocks holding down each corner. Next to the tarp was a large mound covered with a bright green blanket of artificial grass. It was directly behind him through the trees, and he thought he could make it over there without being spotted if he were quick.

He nearly didn't do it. He almost walked out of the trees with his hands up. He probably would have if he'd been in something besides a thick layer of hair. He took a fortifying breath. Scrambling back from the trees, he reached the tarp in just a few steps, lifting the chunk of concrete on the corner to the side without trouble. Peering into the darkness of the freshly dug grave, he had a panicky impulse to run anyway. Another deep breath, and he threw his bags down into the hole. Pushing his fear down, he followed them.

The earth around him smelled like clay and minerals, mold and decay. The dark was not absolute. Some faint greenish light shone through the tarp. That was fortunate, as every cell in his being screamed at him to get up out of there, NOW. The hole wasn't deep enough for him to stand, it was about four feet, so he knelt and arranged the tarp back over the hole as well as he could. Claustrophobia buzzed down his spine like a swarm of bees. He closed his eyes and tried to breathe like

Titania had shown him on the train.

It worked enough to keep him from bolting out of the grave, but just barely. He sat down, trying not to imagine the soil sinking and pulling him under. The feel of damp earth and pebbles on his naked rear was startling after so long in clothes. Not that many months ago, it would have been normal. Now it felt too intimate, but there was no way he could find his clothes and dress in the shallow hole without making noise or bumping the tarp like a trapped spirit.

He tried to think of something else to avoid fixating on the fact that he was in a grave. He thought about Titania, kissing her in her apartment, the feel of her hands on his skin. The resulting arousal made him even more aware of the absurdity of his situation. He didn't know when he would see her again. In a flash of clarity, he realized he didn't know *if* he would see her again. His rosy daydreams deflated quickly. Panic finished the job when he heard voices a few feet away.

"I don't see anything."

"Yeah, me either. I guess he probably lit out of there when he realized someone had spotted him."

The two men were on the road through the cemetery, but Lewis heard them clearly. A radio burst on with an update from the other side of the cemetery. "Hey, Mike, I found his clothes over here by the fountain. It looks like he was rolling in garbage, the poor bastard. I see why he was in the shower. What I do not see is any sign of him."

"Yeah, us either. I'm gonna ask the lady in the office if she wants to file a report and call it. The mausoleums are all open, nothing in any of them either."

"Okay. I'm going to clear, then."

"Yeah, thanks for the hand. Have a good one."

The voices moved away from Lewis, and he sighed. If the police were going to take a report, he would have to stay put for a while longer. In fact, he needed to stay put until dark so he could get dressed without causing another manhunt. The idea of being in a grave in the cemetery at dark made his body go cold, but there was no other option.

He moved his bags to the head of the grave and used them as a pillow, carefully lowering his body to the earth. He'd still been a little damp when he slid under the tarp, and he felt slick mud coating his body hair. His shower hadn't been worth the attention in any way.

As he stared up at the bottom of the tarp in the gloom, his situation overcame him. Tears leaked from the corners of his eyes, making more mud beneath him. He was in more trouble than he'd ever conceived of in his life. He was one thin piece of plastic away from being exposed in every sense of the word. He'd found so many things in Portland he wanted to hold onto with all his might. He was good at things here. He was an excellent dishwasher. He was funny. He had a lovely, kind, complicated woman who (maybe) loved him back.

He was also entirely out of his depth navigating

a world he barely understood. Listening to hours of stand-up comedy had given him the impression of a world that was observable from an arms-length distance. The real world had engulfed him in a wave of consequences set in motion by other people without his consent. Now he was washed away in the tide to a place he didn't want to be.

He was angry, too. He didn't deserve any of this. He was different. He wasn't human, he acknowledged that. It didn't make him any less deserving of basic respect and autonomy. If he was clumsy about how he lived his life, it was likely no clumsier than a lot of "real" humans. Dr. Perkins could have asked him some questions. He could even see a scenario, unlikely but possible, where they had collaborated. Instead, she treated him as an object she had every right to study and possess. Being odd or different didn't negate him, even if it went all the way down to the DNA.

He realized his fists were tightly bunched and his muscles were taut. He was close to punching something, maybe the side of his grave. A brief flash of the walls caving in on him stopped that thought dead. He worked to control his breathing again.

It was untenable. It was all becoming impossible in ways he never could have anticipated. He realized what he had to do in a moment of terrible, inescapable clarity. The tears came faster.

CHAPTER 59

The hours of waiting under the stifling tarp were miserable. Lewis sweated out whatever water remained in his body, so he didn't have to pee, but he was feeling light-headed from dehydration and hunger. His nerves wouldn't let him sleep. His imagination made up scenarios that terrified him too much to nap.

It was possible the funeral would be today, wasn't it? They would remove the tarp to lower the coffin into the grave and find a very hairy, naked man already in residence. That kind of comedy gold was a lot funnier in later retellings. Imagining the moment, his balls shriveled up again.

If they connected the dots between the fleeing suspect at Titania's and the free-spirited fountain frolicker, Zelda the K-9 would easily track him to his hiding place. He didn't want to roughhouse with a police dog naked, either.

He was trying very hard not to relive his captivity in the Reed College basement by Dr. Perkins, but the trap of trying not to think about something had him obsessing on it. So much of that ordeal blurred into a drug haze. He wasn't sure how much of what he remembered was real and how much was his brain filling in the blanks. He tried to walk back in his memory from escape to captivity to abduction to performance, hoping to recapture some of the events of the night. He was still most bitter about the memory gaps.

His near delirium made the exercise akin to an out of body experience. He remembered the sensations of Numbknots first, the hot lights and the nerves in his stomach. The room smelled of beer and bar food, with a comforting tang of industrial dish sanitizer. As he breathed the air of the night in, he saw Titania watching the stage, and in his imagination, he smiled broadly at her. She returned the smile and waved, giving him a thumbs-up.

He saw himself stepping to the mic and introducing himself. He heard the words he knew he'd intended to say, but he couldn't swear it was really what came out of his mouth. The audience laughed and cheered and clapped. He might never recapture the events of that night, but inside himself, he found the feeling again. The triumph of being on stage and not just telling jokes, but connecting with people at the human level. He chuckled despite his situation. If they knew he wasn't human, wouldn't they be surprised? If they knew it was all true?

Another wave of sadness hit, a sneaker wave out of the past. The harthoth were missing so much.

It wasn't just sad, it was tragic. It was like living without one of your senses. Humans were ruled by their passions, but at least they had passions. He thought about his mother, living with the grief of losing her oldest son to the flames and her younger son to the world, and the tears started again. Her road walked through the shadows, always, and never came out of them. She might not feel her grief as deeply as a human, but it wasn't fair for him to judge that. Maybe she did, and wasn't able to express it. Maybe it was all a matter of degrees—even though her pain was different, it was still the worst thing she could imagine.

He sobbed silently for a few minutes for his mother, and his brother, and his clan's missing humanity. When he finally mastered himself, the light was beginning to change as evening pulled the sun's rays toward the west. Soon they would lose their reach, and the already dark pit would grow pitch black. He'd been lucky that no one needed that particular grave while he occupied it, but he was anxious to get out as soon as he possibly could.

He sat up, smearing at his damp cheeks and feeling weak and wrung out. He needed water, he needed to get dressed, and he needed to find one of his friends as quickly as possible. Fishing around in his bag in the murky dimness, he found his underwear and wrestled it on under the tarp. Managing that without too much disturbance, he slipped on a shirt. Pants were going to have to wait, though. Wearing pants for a few months did not make him an expert on getting into them, and the mechanics of putting them on while sitting down escaped him. It was just like underwear, but it wasn't, and he was too exhausted to try to figure it out.

The temperature in the hole didn't go down very quickly, and the shirt he'd put on was sweaty and uncomfortable almost immediately. Just before the blackness took hold, he grabbed a pair of pants and stuck his head out of the tarp. The cemetery was deserted, with a few security lights he could easily avoid.

Quickly slipping his jeans onto his filthy legs, he threw his bags out of the hole and climbed up after them. It was already after 9PM, darkness came late in the Oregon summer. He wasn't bothered that he'd left his shoes at the fountain. He doubted he would ever wear shoes again. He put the cement block back on the tarp and silently apologized to the deceased. He didn't understand why someone would want to be buried, but he was certain they didn't anticipate getting a used grave.

Using his night vision, he was able to move through the hills and neighborhoods without detection. The active manhunt would have ended hours ago. He wondered what had happened between Titania and Dr. Perkins after he left. A frisson of worry sparked across his skin. She had put herself in harm's way for him, and he was helpless to help her.

In less than an hour, he came to Hoyt Arboretum,

around 200 acres of trees and paths preserved as a natural park a few miles from downtown Portland. He realized he was right next to the Oregon Zoo. He could smell the hay and dung funk of the elephants and the sharper smells of the big cats. There was a note of fish oil from the penguins. He wondered if the zoo had security and decided it probably did. There was some beautiful irony in evading capture in a zoo, but it wouldn't be worth the trouble of breaking in to appreciate it.

He moved through the Arboretum more slowly, comforted by the cover of the trees around him. These trees were massive firs and hardwoods, as big as any on Mt. Adams. The smell of the green space was polluted by the car exhaust and city smells around it, but this was close. If you ignored the viewpoints and groomed trails, it could almost pass as a forest.

On the other side of the Arboretum, Lewis walked in the gardens. The Japanese garden was sedate and orderly, a place meant for peace and tranquility. That wasn't at all his current frame of mind.

Beyond that was the Rose Garden. The smell of the roses was still lush but less overwhelming, as many had passed their peak bloom by now. The smell made him think of Titania, and what he suddenly realized was their second date, even if he'd been too stupid to know it at the time. He forced himself not to think about it. He couldn't sit here all night weeping in the roses like a lovelorn maiden.

When he left the Rose Garden, the city swelled up

before him. He'd heard about cities that were bigger, that were vast stretches of concrete and skyscrapers. He had trouble imagining that, but he no longer felt crushed by the magnitude of Portland. It was a large city, but he had been part of it. He wasn't invisible, even if being seen had been traumatic and dangerous. Portland was weird, and so was he, and they could have made it work in different circumstances.

He walked into the city to wait for Bill Ben to open the brewery in a few hours. Lewis sat on a bench watching the Willamette flow by until the sun rose.

CHAPTER 60

"AHH!" Bill Ben screamed as Lewis put one hand on his shoulder.

Lewis yanked his hand away as the big man whirled, fumbling with his keys and dropping them. "Bill Ben, it's me," Lewis hissed.

"Jesus, Lewis, what the fuck." Bill Ben looked at Lewis in the early morning light, clearly worried. "What's going on, man? This seems to have gotten away from you. You were on the news. Well, Titania was on the news, they had her picture, but they did an artist's rendering of you that was fucking hilarious."

Lewis did not want to have this conversation outside the back door. He motioned to the brewery entrance. Bill Ben got the hint. Scooping his keyring off the ground, he let them both in.

Bill Ben started a pot of coffee and let Lewis do nothing for a minute. Stirring cream into his steaming mug, he came back over and sat across from Lewis. "You look like shit, man. What is going on?"

Lewis explained as much as he could without bringing Bill Ben into his origins. He liked Bill Ben and was grateful to him for a lot of things, but he didn't think he needed to know about the harthoth. It felt like maybe too many people already did. Something Rami had been right about after all, he thought.

"Well, that is crazy, chaotic bullshit. You know Titania got arrested for punching that professor in the face?"

Lewis felt sick to his stomach. "Is she okay?" was all he could manage.

"Yes and no. That is another weird story. She called me and said she wouldn't be in because she was in jail, but by the time I got down there after work, she was already gone. They wouldn't tell me anything, because why would they, and she's not answering her phone this morning."

Lewis stuffed the panicky fear he had for Titania down as far as he could. She wasn't in jail, that was the important thing, and she was probably just asleep. He would talk to her later. Right now, he had to make plans.

"I need to talk to Rami," he said.

Bill Ben shook his head. "I don't have his number. We could try the mission later, but I don't know if Eve'll give out his number if he's not there."

Eve definitely would not give out his number, Lewis was sure of that. If he tried to send a note, it could be intercepted or lost, and that would take more time than he felt he had. He closed his eyes and thought. He and Bill Ben had a realization at the same time.

"Chloe!" they said in unison, both grinning. The solution to any of his problems, no matter how small, felt like a win.

Bill Ben woke Chloe up. She answered on the third try.

Her voice was fuzzy over the speaker on his cell phone. "Fuck off," she said in greeting. "Wait...Bill Ben? Do you know where Lewis is?"

"He has some idea," Lewis said.

Chloe squeaked. "Dammit, Lewis, do you have any idea how worried we all were?"

"Yeah, I probably do. I spent the day hiding in a grave yesterday."

"What? You what? Never mind. Are you at Numbknots?" Lewis confirmed. "Okay, I will be over there as soon as I can get an Uber. STAY PUT." The line went dead.

"Oh." Lewis said.

Bill Ben laughed. "You got more Chloe than you bargained for, didn't you?" Lewis shrugged.

The two men fell into the routine of caring for the beer brewing in the vats. The mood was subdued but companionable.

"I'm going to miss beer," Lewis said, mostly to himself, but Bill Ben overheard.

"Miss beer? Beer is everywhere, man, it's a universal human language." Lewis laughed. "What?" Bill Ben asked. "Am I wrong?"

"No, that's right." Lewis didn't explain.

Loud banging on the door interrupted their work. Bill Ben went to see who it was while Lewis hid ineffectively behind a vat.

"Where is he?" Chloe demanded. She barged past Bill Ben and cupped her hands around her mouth. "Lewis, get your furry ass out here right now!" she yelled.

Lewis stepped out from behind the vat, and Chloe flew at him. Her hug was unexpected and fierce. He'd expected violence. Her hair was still wet from a hasty shower, and he smelled her understated shampoo, something floral and natural. He returned the hug, feeling the racing of her heart as he did.

When she finally let go of him, there was a damp patch where her hair had been and another where her face had been. She swiped at her eyes and looked him over. "You look like shit, Lewis."

"Thank you?" he replied. "I've been having a shitty time."

Chloe chuckled. There were dark circles under her eyes and her all-ebony clothes were rumpled. Her hair was a drastic study in contrast between several inches of shining golden roots and black ends. "You are not the only one, but I think some of it might cheer you up."

Bill Ben grabbed chairs and plopped them down in a triangle. Making a show of looking at a watch he wasn't wearing, he nodded and walked into the bar, propping the door between the two spaces open. He came back with three pints of an amber bock beer called Bock-a-Doodle-Doo. When Chloe raised an eyebrow, he said, "This is like a breakfast beer. It's fine." She accepted a pint.

Lewis' first sip was malty and delicious. He wanted that flavor, the first sip, to last forever. He took another sip and resolved to drink this beer as slowly as he'd ever drank anything, just to make it last. His empty stomach growled at him to hurry it up.

"Geez, Lewis, when was the last time you ate?" Chloe asked. Lewis shrugged. Bill Ben frowned and shook his head. Without a word, he got up and walked into the restaurant.

"Okay, so he doesn't know about *things*?" Chloe asked in a low voice.

"No, he has not been informed about *things*."

"So, while he's doing that, let me tell you a couple of other *things*. I had a friend in the biochem program run some tests for me, I told them it was a bet I had with Tom that we could make people believe we were aliens."

"Testing what?"

"You, and all the things Dr. Perkins had."

Lewis was aghast. "Why would you do that? Won't they find out about—"

"Shut up. No, give me some credit. Anyway, the biochem guy came back and said, 'I don't know what you did to these, but I never want to see anything like that again. That's like, top secret government experiment level shit. Keep me out of it.' So—that's bad, Lewis. Like, if anyone did get their hands on you, it wouldn't take much to confirm that you're not human."

Lewis nodded. "I think that was probably a risk I wouldn't have taken," he chided.

"I know," Chloe said, "and I know I said I didn't want to know, but then I thought maybe all her tests would just show you were human after all, and we could get to her that way."

Lewis shrugged. It was done now.

"I did get all the samples back and I told my friend it was a practical joke. He's stoned most of the time anyway, so I don't know what he'll remember."

Bill Ben walked back in with a tray of food and Chloe sat back, the confidential part of her presentation complete. Lewis ate the burger and crunchy potato chips on his plate while Chloe launched into the public portion of the program.

"I know why Titania was released," she announced, stilling the crunching sounds immediately.

"Why?" asked Bill Ben. "She said she punched Dr. Perkins."

"Yes, she sure did. What you boys don't know is that Tom and I have been working on a plan to take down Dr. Perkins for weeks." She smiled her smug canary cat smile, the one with more than a little evil in it. "I told you she was threatening me and had pulled the university into it. Reed was pretty close to expelling me, and that takes a lot, let me tell you. Ever since she kidnapped you, though, Tom has been in all her accounts and devices from his computer at his mom and dad's place.

"At first, it was just a search and destroy, where he was looking for anything about you, Lewis, so we could delete it. Then she accused you of assaulting her and me of cheating, so we decided to be a little more proactive." Chloe paused and looked at Bill Ben. "How much of this do you want to know, dude?"

"Pretty sure I know enough to be in trouble already, so I have to know how the story ends now. Go on," he said, rolling a finger at her.

"We planted a lot of interesting correspondence on her computer and in her email accounts on the servers, things about kidnapping homeless people and selling them to foreign agents for illegal human experiments. We used some of the pictures she had of you, Lewis. I'm sorry, but it made the whole thing very believable. When I saw the news story that Titania had been arrested, I called and gave some anonymous info that flipped the script. Dr. Perkins is being treated like the villain, which she is, just maybe the evidence leaves you out of it. Tom was able to make some wacky financial things look like they'd happened to back it up. They let Titania go, and the last call Dr. Perkins made on her cell phone was to a law firm on Morrison."

"Wow," Bill Ben breathed. "Remind me to stay on your good side."

Chloe smiled. "You are. This was all done *in extremis*."

"You used pictures of me? From when I was naked and tied up?" Lewis was happy enough to have Dr. Perkins in trouble, but he hadn't really followed much except the part where the police were looking at him in all his glory.

"Yes, but all unidentifiable. Close-ups, you know." There was a wickedness dancing behind her eyes that Lewis really didn't want to understand.

Titania was free. That was the thing that mattered more than his new modesty. Thinking about Titania not answering her phone, he remembered why they'd called Chloe in the first place.

"Do you have Rami's number?" he asked.

"Yeah, I have everyone's numbers. What do you need to call him for?"

"I need a ride out of Portland. A long one."

CHAPTER 61

Bill Ben and Chloe looked shocked. Lewis didn't think that was quite fair. After all, leaving town had been suggested multiple times. Now that he was working toward that, no one should be surprised.

Chloe recovered first, coming to much the same conclusion. "Where are you going?" she asked, confident in her right to know.

"I can't tell you."

"What do you mean you can't tell me? Like—you don't know?"

"No, I mean it's not something I'm going to tell people."

Chloe opened her mouth to protest and then realized why he wouldn't tell her. "You're going home?" she blurted. "Why would you do that?"

"I didn't say that. I just said I'm not telling you." Again, he'd forgotten how much smarter she was than him. He closed his mouth before he gave her another little clue that solved the mystery completely.

Bill Ben looked befuddled. "Are you going back to

the cult?" he asked. "That seems like a terrible idea."

Lewis crossed his arms and stared straight in front of him. He pretended he was at some very traditional harthoth ceremony, required to be bored and keep his mouth shut. It occurred to him that his future very likely included doing just that.

Lewis was going home. Nothing else felt safe, not just for him, but for the friends he'd made or any future friends he would make. Calling it "home" was inaccurate, but Portland wasn't "home" either. Fleeing to safety was probably closer to the truth. Moving from city to city wasn't going to work. In his naivete, he'd come into Portland and lucked into a group of people who helped and protected him. The professor had taught him exactly how naive this was. She'd turned out to be an excellent teacher in her horrible way.

"I won't make it here," he said quietly. "I can't stay in Portland, and I can't count on finding people to help me in another city."

Chloe was out of her seat. "What about a smaller city? I don't think you've thought about—"

"I have thought about a lot of things for a very long time," Lewis interrupted. He gave her a sympathetic look. Her eyes were wet, and he felt his own mist up. "I'm sorry, Chlo. I really am. I need to stop expecting everyone else to save me."

She looked down at her feet, breathing slowly.

Bill Ben picked up on the subtext in the conversation, but he had the grace not to ask. Lewis was grateful for all the things Bill Ben had never asked. After running his hands over his face and bald head, Bill Ben stood and said, "You needed to call Rami, right?"

"Yeah, I need to call Rami."

Chloe raised her head and searched his face for any cracks, any places she could pry into and change his mind. There weren't any. She sniffed and wiped her nose on her sleeve. "Okay." She pulled out her phone and dialed.

The conversation with Rami was brief. Lewis told him he needed a ride home. Rami said he needed to make a couple of calls. Lewis said he was safely at Numbknots for the moment. Rami asked if he'd told anyone where he was going. Lewis said no, he hadn't shared specifics. Rami said that was good. He ended the call.

"He's going to take you then? Today?" Chloe asked, slipping her phone back into her pocket.

"Yeah, he'll probably be here pretty soon," Lewis replied. Bill Ben got up and hurried into the restaurant.

"Have you told Titania about this wonderful sacrificial decision you've made that affects her in ways she might not agree with?" Chloe had moved past shock and sadness to anger already.

"Not yet," Lewis admitted. He'd been trying hard not to think about it, actually, and he knew he was being a coward. It was sneaking out of the clan grounds all over again. Returning to face one act of cowardice by committing another would burn away another piece of his soul.

Chloe fished her phone back out of her pocket and tapped the screen a few times. Lewis shook his head and flailed his hands in a panicky "wait" gesture, but she ignored him.

"Hi, Titania? You okay?" Chloe paused for the response. "Yeah, I know where he is, and he's fine. Stupid, but physically okay. Can you come over to Numbknots? He wants to talk to you." She nodded a few times. "We're in the brewery, just knock on the door. Yup. Come on over right now. Glad you're okay." She put her phone away and gave Lewis a challenging look.

"What?"

"You are not running away from this," she said.

Lewis sighed. "No. I'm not."

Chloe waited with him for Titania to get there. Lewis couldn't sit still. He paced back and forth. He washed all the tools and containers in the brewery sink. He felt claustrophobic inside. He wanted to be on a mountainside under tall trees, the breeze on his bare skin. He wanted to dive into a frigid river and hold his breath. He'd rather be sweating on a Tri-Met bus next to a man smoking unfiltered cigarettes. It was 45 minutes, but it seemed like a countdown to a midnight execution.

The banging on the door wasn't hard or angry, but it was firm. Chloe looked at Lewis, raising an eyebrow. He took a deep breath and nodded. She let Titania in, quickly stepping out of the way as the woman flew to the harthoth. Lewis took Titania in his arms and squeezed. He let time stop for a moment, feeling her solid body, the pressure of her arms around him, her quick breath in his beard.

Titania pulled away first, searching him with her eyes and taking in his dusty, rumpled state. Lewis could see a red mark on her arm and a bruise on her jaw. Two of her fingers were taped together. He reached up and gently brushed the purple skin.

"How did that happen?" he asked.

"Dr. Perkins has a nasty right hook," Titania said, shrugging. Lewis winced. "I gave worse than I got, Lewis. I'm okay. Not my first rodeo with a crazy heifer."

"Hey, so Lewis has some news," Chloe interrupted with some bitterness. "I think I probably don't need to be here for that part. Also, Rami is going to be here pretty soon. Lewis will tell you why when he explains his stupid plan." Chloe checked around for her stuff, more a stalling tactic than organization.

Lewis let go of Titania and took the few steps to Chloe. She was looking under the chair. When he touched her shoulder, she turned to reveal the tears on her cheeks. Lewis pulled her up and into another hug. In her ear, he murmured, "You saved me more than once, Chlo. I will never, ever forget that.'"

"You better not. I am a lot of things, Lewis Clark, but forgettable will never be one of them. You be safe, or I will come and kick your ass myself." She pushed him away gently.

"I absolutely believe that," he replied, smiling.

Chloe gave him a shaky smile back, and not trusting herself to more words, waved a hand at Titania and left.

Titania was standing with both fists bunched. She was not a fool.

"Where are you going?" she asked, preempting his lame opener.

"Home." It was so much more than one word. He saw it hit Titania like a blow.

"Were you going to leave without telling me? Is that why Chloe called me?"

"No, no, I just didn't know how to do it," he said, reaching for her hand and finding a chasm between them instead.

"When are you leaving? Is that why Rami is coming?"

"Yes. He knows a lot about me, about what I am, and I can trust that he won't tell anyone where I'm going."

"But you can't trust me?" Titania looked at the floor, tears filling her eyes.

Seeing her there, knowing how he felt, Lewis made a decision. He had to know how she felt first, though.

"Titania?"

"Yes?"

"What would you have said, if Dr. Perkins hadn't come to the door?"

"What?"

"When I said I loved you, what were you going to say back?"

"Oh." Titania swallowed. "Well, the moment has passed, hasn't it?"

CHAPTER 62

Lewis felt his stomach drop. The next words died on his lips. She didn't feel the same way.

"Wait," she said, realizing how he'd taken her hesitation and trying to salvage things. "Lewis, don't assume things, but this is all a little awkward, isn't it? You're *leaving*. Do you just want to know because of some academic interest? Things like that should happen spontaneously, not just...I don't know. Be a thing?"

Lewis looked at the ceiling for a moment. Even if this was the worst idea in the world, he had to take a chance.

"Titania, come with me."

"What?" she exclaimed.

"Come with me." Lewis took advantage of her shock to pull her closer. He put his hands on her shoulders. "Come with me to my clan. I mean...I did win you fair and square by defeating the open mic. I completed my quest. Come be my mate. It's not safe for me here, but I can make it safe for you there."

Titania searched his eyes, not sure if he was

serious. "First, you did not win me, you merely proved you were worthy. Second, that's a really crazy idea. You want me to simply walk away from everything? Today?"

"I know. I know how it sounds."

"Do you? Because it sounds like something a child would propose. Magical thinking." Titania was angry, but more than that, she was confused. "How do you think that's going to work out?"

Lewis admitted he hadn't worked out all the details. Working out the details wasn't really his special talent. He did know he loved her, and he knew that leaving her would rip away a part of his soul. He could also feel the answer coming, and he didn't want to let it be born into the world to harden into reality.

"Okay, wait, just wait," he stammered. "Don't say anything."

Titania stared at him in silence for 30 seconds. Then she whispered, "Why aren't we talking? Is someone here? Do we need to hide?"

Lewis surprised them both by laughing. "I just want to say something and then you can tell me what you think. Okay?" Titania nodded.

Lewis waited a few beats for comedic effect. Titania gave him an annoyed look, but there was a glint of humor in her eyes.

"I love you, Titania. I love you more than I've loved anyone or anything on earth. I know *we* are very complicated. I'm wanted by the police. I have to leave, and I have to leave now, before it gets worse.

I'm not even human. I'm offering you a place beside me in a place where I'm not even sure they're going to welcome me back." He was making a mess of this, he knew. He ran a hand over his face. "I'm an idiot, Chloe is right. I mean it, though. I will do whatever I have to do to make you happy there. Please, come with me?"

Titania's sad face already gave him his answer, but he waited for her to say it. "I am the first to admit that I'm not great at living with humanity," she said, "but I can't walk away from it all on a moment's notice, Lewis."

Lewis felt the tears spill down his cheeks. He couldn't blame her. It was a ridiculous offer, at best, and an impossible dream in reality.

Titania came to him then and kissed him tenderly. He breathed in the smell of her, of her locs and soap and a cigarette she must have smoked hours before. Both of them were crying now.

"I can tell you one thing, though," she said, wiping his cheek with her fingertips. "I love you, too, Lewis Clark."

They stood like that as their hearts crumbled in unison for a beat, two, and then Lewis kissed her fiercely. He could feel the longing in her kiss, her arms clinging to him, but it could only last for the moment they had left. When he pulled back, the distance between them was fathoms. He felt like throwing up.

"Okay." He knew it wasn't okay, but he said it for

her anyway.

"Okay." She stepped back and sniffed loudly. "If it's okay with you, I'm not going to wait for Rami and the big waving good-bye thing?"

He nodded. He'd give his right arm for another half hour with her, but he understood a public scene wasn't how she did things.

She walked to the door, making her way around him with enough safe space to resist touching him. At the door, she turned and looked at him one last time.

"Be safe, Lewis. Knowing you're out there, it will make things a little more magical, even if I hate it every minute."

"You too, Titania." He had more he wanted to say, but it felt like his feelings were sharp, like they would hurt her if he unleashed them. He spared her.

The click of the door felt like death. It was the end of the last thing that could have kept him in Portland. He sat down, leaning back in the chair. He tried to let his mind go blank. It was easier than he expected. He was exhausted.

"Was that Chloe leaving?" Bill Ben asked, startling him back to reality.

"No, it was Titania."

Bill Ben's eyes widened, but he didn't say anything. He was carrying an armload of brown bottles with swing caps. Each one was labeled with masking tape and black pen. He set them down on the counter.

"I don't know where you're going, and I get why I don't know, but I want you to take these with you. You helped make several of these brews."

Lewis was touched by the gesture. He was going to miss beer. "That is really nice, but—"

"No, I'm not taking no for an answer. I may have to go back to dealing with Jaxopher and Vinnie, but I would never forgive myself if you didn't take these." Bill Ben grabbed a divided box and loaded the dozen bottles in.

Lewis gave in and thanked him. He could carry a box easily.

Rami knocked on the wrong door, but Bill Ben heard him from the kitchen and let him in. Lewis was dozing upright in the brewery. Startled again, he nearly fell out of the chair.

"Dude, this is some serious shit you have going on." Rami looked tired. He was wearing his black hair in a ponytail threaded through a ball cap, topping off a rumpled t-shirt and pajama pants. He plopped down noisily in the chair across from Lewis. "So, you need a ride home, eh? You sure that's where you want to go? I gotta hear it one last time before we set out on this road trip."

"It's the only way," Lewis replied. "I have some things I should have done there, anyway."

The men stared at each other for a moment, then Rami nodded. "Yeah, man, maybe someday when all this blows over, you can visit under the radar. Right now, though, this is all too hot. You have everything you need?"

Lewis did not have everything he needed. He had everything he was going to get. He had one last, desperate idea.

"Give me a minute," he said, running through to the restaurant to find a pen.

CHAPTER 63

Bill Ben saw them off, waving and holding Lewis' last-minute note. Lewis wanted to just look at Numbknots for a minute, but Rami was parked with flagrant illegality right in front of the bar on Naito Parkway. Turning off the flashers on his Subaru, he eased into traffic. He punched the touchscreen on the dash, bringing up some music just loud enough to discourage any conversation. Lewis hadn't ridden in a car sober, and he found it disconcerting. All these other cars were traveling around them, and the perspective from the low Subaru was like being in a herd of unpredictable animals. He preferred the height of the bus.

Rami turned left into downtown and circled to hit Naito south for I-5. Lewis looked at the Willamette as they drove over the ugly Marquam Bridge for the last time.

"I never did drink it," he said. "Not that I couldn't. I just didn't need to."

"Drink what?" Rami asked, lowering the music.

"The water. I didn't drink out of the river."

Rami chuckled. "Yeah, well, you should have seen yourself. You were dressed like a middle-aged quilter. Not the weirdest thing I've ever seen, but you made an impression."

"Thanks for helping me. Not just this trip, but everything. You did a lot for me."

"No problem, dude. Sorry it didn't work out for you."

The music went back up.

Other than a stop for gas and snacks in Hood River, the trip was shorter than Lewis expected. The Columbia River Gorge funneled them past waterfalls and thickly treed hillsides. Lewis saw bald eagles and osprey nesting on poles right by the highway. In Hood River, fluttering windsurfers skated across the water like huge dragonflies. The wind gusting to the west felt like it was urging him back to Portland.

He ate his Snickers bar in such a melancholy mood that Rami turned the music down again.

"What's up?" Rami asked.

"Nothing."

"No way. Not nothing. What's up? You just sad, or is there something else?"

Lewis didn't want to talk about Titania or Portland, or what leaving his human life meant. He didn't want to talk about the likely reception he was going to get returning as the disappointing second son, either. "Just sad, I guess."

"Yeah, okay. If it helps at all, I think you're probably making the best choice out of a lot of bad choices. I can hide in plain sight, but you didn't exactly hide. I should have discouraged that, maybe. I got caught up in the dream, too."

"You weren't responsible," Lewis said softly.

"Maybe not. Maybe I could have been more involved," Rami murmured.

They traveled in silence until they got to the campground at Takhlakh Lake. Lewis could smell the mountain air and the familiar scents of Mt. Adams. It overwhelmed him for a moment. He'd missed this place more than he'd realized. The campground had its "Campground Full" sign out, and people were busily biking and hiking all over.

Rami looked at all the activity and let the car roll to a stop in the middle of the camping loop. "Where am I gonna let you out?" he asked, peering around at the families crowding every possible trail.

Lewis thought it was not that big of a deal to just wander through the campsite, but he was content to let Rami stall. On the way to Mt. Adams, he'd been able to zone into the timelessness of the highway. That was over, but he wasn't really ready to face the next step.

"There's a parking lot for day use over by the lake," he said. "Maybe I can get out there and not be in the middle of all these people."

Rami drove to the day use parking lot and found it overrun with the annual Skamania County Sheriff's Department picnic. Official vehicles crowded the parking lot alongside personal rides. Families of law enforcers and future deputies were playing games and grilling various meats. Sidearms had not been left at home.

"Damn, Lewis, your luck is not good today," Rami muttered.

"Do you think they would know? All that stuff happened in Portland."

"I'm sure they get notices from Portland and Seattle." Rami turned and rummaged in the backseat. He held out a pair of sunglasses and a black hoody. "Put these on."

Lewis complied, tucking his copper hair back into the hood. "Better?" he asked.

"Hell no, now you look like a ginger Kaczynski. I gotta throw away those sunglasses now." Rami stared at the off-duty deputation. He whacked the steering wheel with one hand and swore. "Alright. I have one idea and I don't like it, but it's all I have." Without explaining, he backed out of the space and went as far away from the picnic area as he could. He parked next to a trailhead sign.

"Take off the glasses but keep your head down and don't look at the cops, okay?" Lewis nodded. "We're going to get out and start hiking up this trail with all your stuff like we have a plan and we're executing the plan and it's going to be a real blast. Lots of laughing and good times? Can you pretend we are having a good time?"

Lewis was not having a good time, but he thought he could fake it well enough. He grabbed his bags, and Rami grabbed the carton of beer bottles. They tossed a few nonsense remarks back and forth and pretended to laugh together, a sound that made Lewis die inside. Fake laughter was worse than no laughter at all. Rami, in his pajama pants and a pair of flip-flops, hiked up the trail and Lewis followed.

"They aren't expecting two dudes, just you," Rami explained after ten minutes of fast-paced hiking. "I'll go with you for as long as you need to stay on the trail."

"Thanks. I owe you."

"Yeah, you do. If you ever come back to Portland, get in touch and I'll have you mow my lawn or something," Rami groused. "I was not planning to scale Mt. Adams today in my pajamas."

They gained elevation. Lewis felt the air thinning out and realized he'd have to get used to it again. Portland was close to sea level, and his clan lived almost two miles up. At least Rami was huffing as well.

Feeling that change in the air made him realize it was time to send Rami home. He trusted him to know he lived on Mt. Adams. He didn't trust him with the clan's location. Besides, he didn't really want his friend to see how his clan treated him, if he was honest with himself. He'd been able to be someone else without all of the baggage of his birth, and he didn't want to spoil that.

"This is where we part ways," he said, pointing off the trail. They'd met hikers, mostly coming down this late in the day, but they were coming less frequently now.

"Thank god," Rami said, unceremoniously

thrusting the box of bottles into Lewis' arms. "I just decided I definitely do not hike, man."

They stood awkwardly for a moment. Lewis was too burdened to hug or even shake hands. Rami finally clapped him on the shoulder, patting three times. "Freygge," he said.

Lewis smiled. "The same for you." Hearing the word for "peace" in a language close to his native harthoth was surprising and touching. Rami gave him a half-hearted salute and turned back down the trail, his black ponytail swaying and surfing on the breeze.

Lewis stared after him for a moment, feeling very alone. He had a moment of panic and almost ran after him, but he mastered himself. Commanding his uneasy stomach to settle, he stepped off the trail and into the wilderness.

Traversing the undergrowth in the middle of summer carrying a dozen glass bottles of beer and numerous bags was a chore. His stamina was not what it had been, and he frequently stopped to rest. He was really thirsty. Realizing he had the solution right in his arms, he pulled out a beer and opened it.

As he put the bottle to his lips, he imagined facing his mother for the first time with a little buzz going. He flipped the swing cap closed. He needed all the inhibitions he could muster.

After an hour, the main heat of the day was passing, and he knew he would hit a creek soon. It wouldn't be more than a trickle this time of year, but it would be enough to splash his face and get a drink. He sat down on a log and considered how he wanted to present himself to the clan. He had to have a good story, but it had to be the truth, mostly. No more sneaking around and wishing things were different. He'd be open and honest and get himself banished if that's what his people decided.

He rose and rearranged his bags across his back. He bent over to hoist the carton of beer to one shoulder, trying a new hold to relieve his arms, and fumbled it. He barely caught it with some ungraceful, grabby dancing.

"What is in there, Elko?"

Lewis nearly dropped it again at the sound of a harthoth right behind him. He should have been able to smell the approach, but he'd lost more than his lung capacity. Ten feet away, gaping with childlike fascination, stood Fliggo.

"What do you have on your body? Why do you smell like strawberries, but not like strawberries? Where have you been?"

"My name is Lewis now, Fliggo, and it's a very long story."

"I have time," Fliggo said simply.

CHAPTER 64

Lewis knew Fliggo wouldn't understand a lot of what he was talking about, so he kept to the main story. He'd gone to the human civilization, found a job and friends, been hunted by a human with bad intentions, and fled back to the safety of the mountains. He stumbled a little with his harthoth language at first, but quickly regained the rhythm of it. It hadn't been that long since he'd spoken it.

Fliggo listened to this simplified version of a lifetime of experience with his face scrunched in a confused frown. "Elko, are you a human now?" he asked when Lewis finished.

"It's Lewis, please, and no. I am harthoth. I'm just...different. I always have been."

Fliggo nodded. "Okay." He tried out his friend's new name a few times, getting close enough. "I should go tell them you are back."

Lewis brightened. He hadn't considered the possibility of an intermediary breaking the news. He knew he was giving in to weakness. He should march into the clan grounds and announce himself.

He'd left a coward and he didn't want to reinforce that, but...Fliggo was offering. In fact, while Lewis wrestled with questions of integrity and dignity, Fliggo took off and answered the questions for him.

Slowly, he picked up his box and trudged after him. He'd arrive when the timing was best if he dawdled, in his opinion. He was a professional on timing, after all. Kind of.

As the air cooled and the sun dove toward the sea, he felt himself coming back into some version of Elko. Old insecurities reared up, telling him he was nothing, would never be anything. He wondered if they would still expect him to lead after his mother. They couldn't, could they?

He stopped in a clearing, breathing raggedly from the elevation and emotion. Surely he'd slammed the door shut on that possibility. He tried to breathe like Titania had taught him, and thinking of her didn't help. A few rogue tears streaked his dusty cheeks. He swiped them off with his shirtsleeve.

He stared at his arm for a second. Should he take his clothes off? No, he decided. He would make a more convincing case he'd changed if he didn't. Assuming they didn't just throw rocks at him and chase him away.

"Stop," he murmured to himself. He kept going forward.

As he approached the clan grounds, he smelled something cooking and sped up. He was starving and tired after the hike up the mountain. It was twilight, which didn't affect what he could see, but it did make things colder. He hoped to sit by a fire, eat something, and be mostly ignored. Even two out of three would be great.

It was not in his future to be ignored. "ELKO!" roared Yongo, and running footsteps came to the edge of the dwellings. It looked like the entire clan was there from the oldest to the youngest. Fliggo stood on the periphery, looking proud of his work.

Lewis put his box down and set his bags on top of it. Leaving it behind, he straightened his spine and walked to meet the crowd. The harthoth parted to allow his mother, Maura Clan Leader, to approach him.

"Elko," she said.

"I am called Lewis now," he said gently.

"Is that so," she said, looking him up and down with a tight expression.

"Yes. It is. I am changed."

"You left in our hour of great distress." She said this to encompass the entire clan, but it was clear she meant herself.

"I did. That was cowardly."

Maura breathed in sharply. Lewis couldn't tell if she surprised at his admission or hurt by the bluntness of it. He took two steps toward her.

"I owe you a great apology." Elaboration was the enemy of sincerity, so he left it there.

Maura turned and yelled into the crowd. "Manura, where are you?" A harthoth pushed through the rest, putting an arm around Maura. He was badly scarred.

Bare patches of red, angry-looking skin surrounded his chest and ran down his legs like he'd melted.

Lewis stood dumbstuck. His brother was alive. He'd not dared hold out hope Manura had survived.

"Hello, Lupus," Manura said.

"Lewis," Lewis corrected, but he was touched that his brother had attempted his new name. He closed the distance between them and hugged Manura gently. Confused, the older harthoth stood still for a moment and then closed his own arms around Lewis. His fingers brushed over the unfamiliar feel of fabric on Lewis' back.

"I am glad you survived," Lewis said.

"I am glad you came back," Manura answered. Their mother was watching with a neutral expression.

Lewis stepped back and addressed her. "Am I welcome?"

Maura nodded once.

There was no cheer, no congratulatory back-slapping, and Lewis felt the tiniest disappointment along with the relief. This was the harthoth clan, though. He needed to temper his expectations. He was welcome, he was safe. It was more than he deserved.

They did have a bigger than normal meal waiting for him. It wasn't a feast, but someone had made an effort. He was seated on the left hand of his mother. He kept his clothes on, not yet willing to let go of his humanity entirely.

"We were not sure what to expect when we saw you," his mother said during a pause in the eating. Lewis was surprised to find the simple harthoth food comforting. It wasn't as varied or bold as human food, but it wasn't bad.

"Huh?" he said around a mouthful of venison.

"Fliggo came back with some very confusing stories. Well, you know how he is. We thought maybe he'd found a lost human and given in to some wishful thinking."

Lewis chuckled. His mother widened her eyes and pounded on his back twice.

"I'm not choking, but if you keep doing that, I might be," he said. "I'll be right back." Lewis scurried out of the main hall and to his little dwelling, which they'd kept empty. He grabbed two bottles out of his box and ran back to the hall.

"Mother, I have something for you to try." He glanced at the masking tape, finding one was the relatively laidback "Pirates of Pennance" hefeweizen he'd helped brew. The label at Numbknots had nuns with eyepatches on it. He undid the swing latch on the bomber and handed it to her.

Maura sniffed the top of the bottle, a very long inhale that seemed impolitely suspicious, but she was satisfied it wouldn't kill her. She tipped it up to get a small taste and smacked her lips. Then she upended the large bottle and guzzled the entire thing.

"No, wait!" Lewis tried to stop her, but it was too late. His mother, the revered leader, let out a large, loud belch.

"What do you call that?" she asked.

"It's beer, Mother."

"I like the flavor. Is this something you learned about?"

"Yes, I can make that with the right equipment and ingredients." She looked pleased, so he stopped there. She was going to learn about it, too, very soon.

The big meal slowed the effect of the alcohol, but in 15 minutes, it was obvious Maura was on her way past a good buzz. Lewis watched her closely. He'd put his own bottle back after a few sips, wanting to be fully present for whatever happened next.

"Well, it is warmer tonight than I exshpected," she said, fanning herself.

"Let's get away from the fire," Lewis suggested, helping her up. He led her a little way way into the forest and sat her securely on the ground. No one followed, probably thinking they had things to talk about privately.

"My thoughts are running around strangely," Maura said.

"Yes, Mother, you are…" Lewis stopped. There was no word in harthoth for "drunk." He shrugged and said, "You're *drunk*," using the English word.

"Durounk," Maura repeated. "I don't think I care for it." She laid down on the grass, looking up at the stars. "Come over here," she said, patting the grass next to her. Lewis laid down next to her, looking into the Milky Way with the clarity of a mountain sky.

"You ran around strangely, too, Elko," Maura said. "You were always looking for something I didn't understand."

You don't know the half of it, he thought, but didn't say.

"I just wanted you to be like your brother, be easy, be content to be a second son and a harthoth. You never were, though. You were always sneaking off to spy on those humans and now look!" She waved her hands in the air. "You are wearing clothes and talking like them and bringing beer to make me durounk!"

Lewis had never seen his mother this talkative. He was both amused and terrified by it.

"So, Elko, do you know what I thought while you were out playing human? I thought—if Elko ever comes back, I will try to understand him. I might not be able to, but I will try. Because it turns out, I missed you. I can't explain it, but I did. I even missed all those stupid things you say." She grabbed Lewis by the hand and squeezed, hard. "It turns out, there is more than one way to be a good son. So if you cannot exist without being strange, you be strange."

Lewis wondered if she would remember saying all of this in the morning. He guessed not, but that didn't prevent a few tears from tracking their way into his beard.

"Mother?"

"Yes?"

"It's Lewis."

"Okay, Loowhiz." She said it again. "Lewhis. Looshiiiis. *LooWHis.*"

Something in her tone made all of the hairs on Lewis' body stand up. He sat up and peered at her as she experimented with his name again and again, mangling it differently each time. "Mother?" he asked.

"Yes, LEEEWEES," she said louder than necessary. Definitely tipsy, but there was another sound he'd never heard before. A little burble of something came from her. Her lips trembled and curved the slightest amount.

His mother was giggling. AT him and his name, but he didn't care. It was a tiny sprout in the concrete of her facade, and he would nurture it to life if it was the last thing he ever did.

CHAPTER 65

Manura came to his home after noon the following day and beat on the door twice with the long staff he used to walk with less pain. Lewis had a momentary panic because he was unclothed. As he snatched his pants off the floor, he realized he didn't need them. It was a relief, even if it felt strange.

"Come in, brother," Lewis responded. It was hard to imagine the strength Manura must possess to survive an injury like the fire and recover so quickly.

"Good morning, Lewis." Manura raised a questioning eyebrow.

"You have it right. Thank you. What do you want to talk about?"

"You have changed in more than just your name. I will say it plainly, then. You will not be Clan Leader, even though I am injured and must often rest."

Lewis was surprised. "I don't want to be Clan Leader. I never did. That's why I left." One of the reasons, he mentally added.

"Good, because it has been decided that you are no longer in the line as the consequence for leaving.

That will be the entire punishment."

Lewis nearly laughed, but he managed to murmur his understanding with a straight face.

"Our mother could have told you last night, but she was distracted by your human beverage and now has decided to sleep late." Lewis did smile at that, causing Manura to frown. Lewis thought he saw some curiosity there, though, a new trait for Manura.

"Also, I want to tell you I will not lead the clan the same way as our mother. I am still sure in all I do, but I find I tire quickly. I will have others acting as my arms and legs and ears and eyes."

"You will have the support of the Elders, I am sure."

"Oh, them." Manura practically rolled his eyes, and Lewis was shocked. "They are so stuck in the old traditions, they are like scared children. They are interested only in what they have always seen, always done, always been too frightened to do. But look at you! You went into the human world and came back alive! You can speak their language and make their beverage that our mother praises. I wonder what else they have that is good? I will be the one to bring those things to my people."

"I am not the only one who has changed," Lewis said to his brother.

Manura nodded. "Before, I could be happy banging sticks together and strutting around with my chest puffed out, imitating the old ones. Now I must also use my brain to think. Your journey made me see how foolish it is to follow blindly down a narrow path." Lewis opened his mouth to protest, but Manura held up a hand. "No, I will finish. I want you to help me, Lewis. The Elders cannot forbid it, and you will be one of several. I would like you to tell me about the humans and spy on them as you always have." Even Manura knew about that. Lewis hadn't had any secrets, really. "I would like you to share things you think will help us or we might enjoy. There is no reason why we shouldn't benefit from your knowledge, even if those old ones cower before change."

"I...I would be honored to do this, but I am very surprised. As you said, mostly I know the Manura who bangs sticks on things, including me."

"I had a lot of time away from my sticks."

This was the closest thing to a joke Lewis had ever heard a harthoth utter. It wasn't intentional, exactly, but it was enough to feed his smudge of hope into a tiny flame. "I have one request."

"What is it?"

"I would like my full ceremonial name to be 'Lewis Clark.'"

"Clark. Lewis the Clark. Done."

After Manura left, clearly exhausted by the effort of the conversation, Lewis wandered through the clan grounds. His mother wasn't terribly hungover, but Lewis did suggest she drink some extra water. Her attitude toward Lewis was as close to fondness as he'd ever seen, though, so she must have remembered some of the conversation from the night before. The pressure was off both of them now. He didn't have to pretend he could lead the harthoth, and his mother didn't have to turn him into that leader. He was not a disappointment; he was different.

All of his visions of his homecoming in his imagination had been disastrous and difficult. This reality was surreal. Lewis walked into the forest to spend some time just being there, absorbing everything he'd been told.

He was not going to be banished. He was not expected to lead the clan. Both of those possibilities were bad scenarios well avoided. He was not just tolerated, but welcome, at least as far as his family was concerned. The other harthoth would take their cues from Maura and Manura.

This was better than he could have hoped for and much better than he probably deserved. He knew he should be ecstatic. As he walked through the trees, finding the familiar creeks and clearings he'd known all his life, what he felt most was melancholy.

This future was objectively good. It would be enough, in time, but right now he felt his world shrinking back into its place. It was a loss. He would not lose all of it, he resolved. He turned and hiked down the hill to the edge of the campground, to listen and watch the humans living their ordinary, extraordinary lives.

CHAPTER 66

As the summer burned through August and into fall, Lewis made his pilgrimage to the campground every afternoon. He told Manura it was part of his new advisory role, and no one questioned him.

He hoarded the bottles of beer, doling out a few sips here and there, wishing he'd brought equipment and supplies to make more. He had a stack of money from his job at Numbknots, but how to buy what he needed was a challenge. He realized he could also buy more beer at the little market serving the hikers and campers, but his money wouldn't last forever. More than once, he wished he'd bothered to figure out phones.

Every day, he sat and spied. Whenever he could, he snuck in and traded one of the books he'd read for a new one. If he could, he waited to hear the reaction of the camper. "What the hell?" was the most common. One woman was delighted by the random chaos of it, and she laughed. He let the sound soothe his soul even as it broke his heart a little.

He tried listening to his radio a few times, but

it made him too sad. Maybe someday he could hear Penny Coyne sign off KLOL without thinking of the broad horizon of hope he'd had before his departure for Portland. "There's a fine line between tragedy and comedy, don't stop until you find it." He'd found the line and tripped on it.

As the summer waned, the Forest Service prepared the campground for closure. It was too cold and remote for year-round camping. A few hardy souls persisted, eking out some frigid, solitary moments on the beautiful lake before the snow came.

Lewis watched the campsites empty and thought morose thoughts. His clan life was better than it had been before. He had to admit that. He felt like he was being listened to and understood more than any other point in his life. He was getting along well with almost everyone, and the harthoth youngsters pestered him with enthusiastic questions as much as he allowed.

There were even a couple of females making excuses to talk to him now, bringing him special food. He'd stopped wearing clothes in order to save the ones he had, but they would ask to touch his flannel shirts and marvel at the roughness of his jeans when he let them see his folded laundry. He didn't want either of them, but he expected to be asked to mate with one of them in the spring, and he thought he probably would. Being able to be himself had emphasized how very different he was. It was lonely.

Three days before the last possible moment to camp miserably on Mt. Adams, Lewis made his way to the campground with a copy of *The Goldfinch* to trade out or possibly just throw in Takhlakh Lake. The story was too long and heavy for him, and he didn't finish it. It made him think of Tom, but a version of Tom who was sadder and even more self-destructive. He wanted to find something lighter, which wasn't a high bar. A truck repair manual would be hilariously funny in comparison. A pamphlet about childhood diseases. A religious tract about Hell.

He realized he was unlikely to find any books at all when he saw there was only one campsite occupied. The tent hadn't been there the day before, and he wondered who would come all the way up here for a couple of days of freezing nights in a flimsy nylon shell.

Peering around the campground, he saw the Campground Hosts packing and stowing things in their RV. Their little dog was wearing a sweater, which was one piece of clothing more than he was. The little mutt started yapping at the other side of the RV as the lone intrepid camper rounded the corner.

The sunlight shone on a red bandana holding back a tangle of locs. Her skirt was teased by a chill breeze, and she kept her arms tightly folded in her puffy, hip-length jacket. Large sunglasses covered her eyes. Lewis' heart stopped.

As he ran toward Titania, Lewis remembered he had no clothing on. The commotion in the underbrush had the little dog yapping again, and all three people in the campground were looking to see what kind of wildlife was crashing toward them. Said wildlife abruptly stopped and crouched low.

Remembering there was a canoe stowed down by the lake, Lewis ran at full harthoth speed. He ripped the tarp off the canoe and wrapped it around himself, wincing as the cold, scratchy plastic touched him. He shambled back to the campground, sounding like a bag of fall leaves falling down a staircase. No sneaking was going to happen in this outfit.

Approaching the lone tent, he whistled from behind a large pine. The front flap unzipped, and Titania popped out, looking wildly into the trees.

"Over here," he hissed, and she saw him as he stepped out, a tangle of ginger hair over the bright blue plastic tarp.

"Lewis?"

He smiled, and Titania ran to him, but she stopped a few feet away, suddenly shy.

"You came," he murmured.

"So did you. I thought maybe I was too late."

"I would have checked every day for the rest of my life."

They stepped to each other then, the crunch and crackle of the tarp adding a cozy fireplace effect to their chilly, long-imagined kiss. Lewis didn't notice. He lost himself in the feel of her in his arms.

She broke the embrace first, holding his arms and looking into his face. Most of his facial hair had grown back in, and he was self-conscious. Remembering they were different raised all the questions he didn't want to think about.

"So, how long will you..." Lewis couldn't bring himself to finish the question, now that it was halfway out. He should have just been happy with the present.

"What are my options?" Titania said, searching his face. "Civilization isn't working out that well for me." She looked thinner, and her face was pale with a few angry red spots on her cheeks.

"You're not okay." Lewis felt guilt punch him in the stomach. He'd left her behind with all the fallout, assuming she'd be fine. It was selfish and clueless.

"I wasn't. I'm better now, away from it, but I had a rough patch."

"Where was Bill Ben? Did it get bad? Like Tom?"

"He tried, Lewis, he really did. It's not his fault. And no, it didn't get that bad." She tugged her sleeves down nervously and looked away from him.

Lewis wasn't sure he forgave Bill Ben quite so easily. When she avoided his gaze, he could guess it had gotten as bad as Tom, or close enough. She'd needed a soft place to land, and Numbknots had failed her.

"Well, you could live here in the pit toilet, but I wouldn't recommend it."

Titania burst into a genuine, delighted laugh, and

Lewis felt his heart mending in places he'd tried not to look at in while.

"Slightly more appealing, but only slightly, you can come home with me and meet my mother."

Titania reached up and smoothed his rumpled hair back. "Do I have to grow a beard?"

Lewis smiled now. "We'll tell them you can't. Play the pity card. I almost made my mother laugh once, she may have feelings in there besides disapproval we can unearth."

"I would love to try. I do have experience with difficult mothers."

"We should probably get her drunk first."

Titania laughed again. That sound. Lewis closed his eyes and drank it in. He might never get a crowd going again in his lifetime, but if he had Titania, it would be enough. More than enough.

"Are you going to be King or whatever?"

"Oh, no, my brother, Manura, survived after all. He has a new perspective that involves asking questions instead of hitting me with sticks. He's decided I should advise him when he ascends due to my 'expertise in outside world matters.'"

"Manura? Like…manure? Horseshit?"

"EXACTLY like that."

Lewis took a minute to secure the tarp around his waist. Titania retrieved what she needed, which fit in two large bags. Hand in hand, they noisily hiked up Mt. Adams to sorely try his mother's fledgling indulgence.

THE END

AFTERWORD

I wrote this book as a serial fiction project spanning March 2022-December 2023. During that time, my family moved across the country, from the Portland, Oregon far suburbs to Northern Virginia. While it's ultimately been good for us, I do miss Oregon. Case in point, it's drizzling on the other side of my window right now, and I can feel my shoulders unbunch just a little.

It feels important to mention this because writing serial fiction is different in practice than writing a novel. Serials are a high wire act where each step commits the writer to forward motion on that path. For example, in my first serial, *Hansel and Grendel*, I realized I'd put the action on the wrong coast for what needed to happen next--dozens of released episodes in. Fortunately, that was a very silly project, and I could lean into the mistake.

I did not paint myself into any similar corners here. I mention it, though, because I've made the decision to print the book as it was first presented, only correcting a handful of small errors and clarifying a few word choices. If I'd written it as a regular novel, would it be different? Maybe. We'll never know. And I'm okay with that.

ACKNOWLEDGEMENTS

This being my seventh book to hit print, you'd think I would know how to write acknowledgements, but they always come out of my head as awkwardedgements. As a one-woman shop, mostly I would be thanking myself for completing all the many tasks of writing, revising, editing, and proofreading. So...that's weird. I think I'll pass on thanking myself for sometimes believing in me.

My artwork for the serial version and the cover of this book was masterfully done by Steve Ogden, my favorite partner in creative crime. Steve always makes my stuff look not just good, but fantastic, no matter what I ask for. You're the best, man. Thank you.

The soundtrack to this project was the entire catalog of AWOLNATION. I don't know why, but that was my jam. I appreciate that it was there for me.

A handful of very enthusiastic readers kept me going through some jammed up personal times. I can't emphasize enough how much it means to a writer when someone is out there asking for the next book/episode/article. Tell your writers you dig what they do. My sincerest appreciation goes out to Jill, Katie, Sophia, and Kayla, for every time you offered encouraging words or pestered me for the next episode. If you ever liked a post or shared it--thank you. It may not seem like much to you, but it makes hollering into the void a lot friendlier when it hollers back.

My family, Jeff and my kids, S and V--as always, I appreciate the space you give me to be your weird writer person. Jeff reads everything I write, even that one story about teeth that he hated, and being married to my biggest fan is a privilege and a joy.

Last, but not least--Portland, you crazy, wonderful, weird city. When I was a kid, a trip to Portland was a big adventure. My first professional job was in a highrise close to the Willamette in downtown. I've been to all of the places in the book that really exist, and I would go again in a heartbeat.

BOOKS BY THIS AUTHOR

Treefall

Fathers take on many burdens for their children, but none is so heavy as the burden of losing your child. Ned Morrow worked in the woods until the day everything changed. This powerful novelette by author Rebecka Ratcliffe (The Tiny Giant, The Only One Laughing) explores an intimate portrait of personal loss in the Oregon logging community during the 1970s.

Growing up in Oregon during the clash of environmental and economic concerns in the 1970s and 1980s, Rebecka Ratcliffe saw dozens of communities lose their main source of income as sawmills and logging outfits closed down. With her own father in the Forest Service, the woods were a constant presence in her life, whether they were camping, driving logging roads calling owls, or talking about protestors chained to the office doors. This story is set in a time and place where economic insecurity and loss would soon follow, and inspired by the idea that our foundations (literal and figurative) can be both hallowed and cursed.

The Tiny Giant

When sixth grader Dan impulsively planted a bean in his garden, he didn't expect much. Then Zeeble, a tiny giant, appears carrying the baggage of a troubled past, and Dan finds out that the wooded nature trail behind his subdivision is full of hidden magic and danger. Will Dan and Zeeble find a path through the trouble that lies ahead, or will their adventures be cut short by a creature who shouldn't be in the woods at all?

This suburban fantasy adventure for middle graders (and up) is a fast-paced introduction to the magic outside your door. Readers will meet Dan and Zeeble, and their friends Norman and Marisol, finding new ways to look at nature and the hidden potential of the world around them. Adults can enjoy an escape to the lush green setting of the Pacific Northwest, a wonderful place to explore in real life!

www.ingramcontent.com/pod-product-compliance
Lightning Source LLC
Chambersburg PA
CBHW030805260626
47169CB00001B/204